SHADOW OF THE LONE WOLF

Book 1 in the Carthaginian Series

By

Griff Hosker

Shadow of the Lone Wolf

Published by Sword Books 2025
Copyright ©Griff Hosker

For more information on all of the books then please visit the author's website at www.griffhosker.com where there is a link to contact him or visit his Facebook page: GriffHosker at Sword Books or follow him on Twitter: @HoskerGriff or Sword Books (@swordbooksltd)
If you wish to be on the mailing list then contact the author through his website.

About the Author

Griff Hosker was born in St Helens, Lancashire in 1950. A former teacher, an avid historian and a passionate writer, Griff has penned around 200 novels, which span over 2000 years of history and almost 20 million words, all meticulously researched. Walk with legendary kings, queens and generals across battlefields; picture kingdoms as they rise and fall and experience history as it comes alive. Welcome to an adventure through time with Griff.

For more information, please head over to Griff's website and sign up for his mailing list. Griff loves to engage with his readers and welcomes you to get in touch.

www.griffhosker.com

X: @HoskerGriff

Facebook: Griff Hosker at Sword Books

Thank you for reading, we hope you enjoy the journey.

Dedication
To my son, Dave, who inspired me to write this book.

Contents

The Clan of the Lone Wolf

Bruneus son of Brennus	Aed
Serpus	Green Eye
War Axe	Cestrus
Alerix	Hostus
Bellerix	Sercix
Galm	Wal
Tadgh	

Prologue

The village of Barcenis, nestled on the coast not far from the mountains to the north which protected it from the colder weather that sometimes wiped out whole clans, was prosperous. Some of the men were fishermen, others were farmers, but when the need arose every man was a warrior. The balance worked well and gave them a happier life than many other clans. They were affluent enough to own horses although they generally made war on foot. Some of those in the village even sported fine weapons. The headman, Brennus, had a helmet and a mail shirt, as well as a long sword. He had defeated and killed two enemy chiefs since he had become headman after the death of his father. The prosperity of the clan meant that there were many rivals who sought to rule the three hundred or so people who lived there. Constant vigilance was needed to ensure that they were not raided and every young man was trained in the ways of war. Because they were careful their lives in the wooden walled village were happy. They had food. Their roundhouses were comfortable and well made. The ditch and palisade that surrounded their homes afforded protection from enemies. They lived a good life.

When Brennus' son, Bruneus, passed his rite of initiation and became, along with the other young men of his age, a warrior, Brennus' brother, Barcas, suggested, during the drunken celebration of the event, that perhaps the young men ought to be given the chance to raid and to be blooded. Brennus was in a good mood and he agreed. The clan needed young men who could fight. In that way they could live in peace; a predator did not attack those with teeth. It was decided that Barcas would take the young warriors and raid the villagers who lived north of the mountains in the lands that bred fine horses. Horses were always needed. If the clan could increase the number of horses then there was a larger part of the surrounding land that they could control. Brennus and his oathsworn would guard the village in the absence of the twenty men who would ride north.

As the brother and the son of the headman, Barcas and Bruneus had the best horses. Barcas had a helmet as well as a short mail shirt. The warband headed north. They had fourteen days of travelling ahead of them for, as Barcas pointed out, it did not do to raid men who lived too close. Therein lay the danger of a blood feud and vengeance. The son of the chief learned much about leadership on the road north. Flanked by his two close companions, Serpus and Big Nose, he listened to all the knowledge that was imparted. His uncle was a good warrior and loyal to the chief. His wife and son had been taken by the pestilence which sometimes ravaged the land and, thus far, he had not chosen another. He was philosophical about it and seemed happy to be training his nephew. Barcas had made Bruneus a sort of surrogate for his own dead son.

When they left the village they rode in an easy and open formation. It was determined by friendship. Barcas and War Hammer rode at the fore, followed by the other older warriors, then came the younger men who would become warriors on this raid. Serpus was Bruneus' closest friend. Their other close friend was Big Nose. The biggest man in the village was named for his large nose and he was a huge hulking brute. He was not as clever as either Serpus or Bruneus but he was not a nasty man. He was just not a thinker like the other two. He was, however, loyal and the two friends felt sorry for him. His father had died when the village had been raided not long after Big Nose's birth It was one reason why his nickname was used. His father had died with his back to the raiders and his clan name was considered to be unlucky. Big Nose's poor horse was dwarfed by the

8

huge warrior and his feet almost touched the ground. Unlike Bruneus and Serpus, he had no sword but just a spear and a round shield. He hoped to reap the reward of the raid.

Barcas used the ride to teach his nephew as much as he could about warfare and leading men in battle. When they camped and while food was prepared the older warrior took the time to talk to his nephew. "Your father is a great war chief. We have never lost under his leadership."

"Then why does he not lead?"

Barcas smiled at his nephew, "You are clever. Work it out for yourself."

Bruneus frowned as he put his mind to the question, "He tires of it?"

Barcas laughed, "A warrior who tired of war was not meant to be a warrior. He would love to lead."

"Then he wanted you to lead."

"Ah, you are getting warm but no, that is not the reason."

It came to the son of the chief like a flash of light, "He wishes me to learn what it is to be a leader and have the glory."

"You are right but it is not about the glory. It is about being a leader. We are the Clan of the Eagle." Bruneus nodded. "That name was chosen by our ancestors for they lived closer to the mountains and felt an affinity with the bird. Since the clan was begun we have moved further south to lands that make us richer but we do not forget the bird that hunts. Your father and I were different. We are both like wolves, you know that?"

"I thought we feared them."

"Of course we do but we admire them too. A wolf pack has strong wolves at the rear guarding the old, the weak and the young. The leader is the lone wolf who leads from the front and has his lieutenants close by. Your father wishes you to become the lone wolf that leads the pack." He gestured with his thumb at Serpus and Big Nose, "You have friends who might become those lieutenants."

Bruneus nodded his understanding and in that moment his life began to change as he thought about the clan in a different way.

His uncle said, "The other thing you must learn to do is to trust yourself." He tapped his own head, "Lisen to the voices that come from here for you come from an ancient line of war chiefs. You have good instincts. Trust them."

The days were long and they rode while there was daylight. They did not cross the mountains. Instead they skirted them where the land met the sea. The sea was their friend and Icaunis was worshipped by many of the clan. Once they neared the village they were to raid then they would travel at night. Barcas knew the route. Bruneus was learning from his uncle and the other older warriors as they rode and he noted the path that they took. He had decided to impress his uncle on the homeward journey by pointing out their direction of travel. He identified landmarks that he would use to guide them back. He would make his father proud and show that he could be a leader. Twelve days after setting off Barcas told them that they were within two days of the village and they would now travel at night. That day they rested, trapped animals and sharpened weapons in a land which was foreign to the younger warriors. They had not brought the throwing spears that they practised with in the village of Barcenis. Instead they had their longer thrusting spears. Only Barcas, Serpus, Bruneus and two others were able to fight mounted. They were the only ones with saddles that had four pommels. The other twenty or so would fight on foot. They rode horses without saddles. It was impossible to fight mounted without a four horned saddle.

The warband moved, the next night, to be closer to the village. The smell of woodsmoke and the sound of the tethered horses told them that they were close. These people cared for their animals and protected them as well as the people of the villages. These were horse breeders. The herd was more than fifty strong and would be penned. Barcas and War Hammer were well travelled and they knew the way these Gauls lived and worked. Leaving the rest of the warband out of sight and downwind of the village, Barcas took Bruneus to scout out the horses. They did so on foot and just used hand signals. Bruneus was desperate not to make a sound. They reached the last piece of covered ground before the village and just watched. They saw two men on horses guarding the horse pen. The fifty or so horses milled around. The two sentries were armed with bows. Moving along to the village they saw that the gate was closed and two men watched from the towers that flanked the gate. Barcas waved for his nephew to return with him.

When they reached the camp he spoke, "We can attack at night. There are just two sentries we need to take care of. The rest of the village, when they are awoken, will pursue us." He pointed to his friend, War Hammer. He was named for the mighty war hammer with a vicious spike and hammer head that he wielded two handed in war. "War Hammer, you and the others will wait in ambush." He gestured to the trail we had taken, "We will bring the horses in this direction. You will fall upon them."

Everyone nodded but Bruneus asked, "And what if the horses are hobbled?"

Barcas liked the question for it showed him that his nephew was thoughtful, "They were moving around the pen too freely for that and there were fifty of them."

"Can we take all fifty?"

"No, that would be too risky. We take as many as we can but we open the gates to the pen and they will run free. In that way we delay any pursuit. To catch us they will have to first recapture their horses."

"And how do we take the two sentries out? We did not bring javelins."

Barcas smiled, "I believe that you and Serpus can bring down a bird in flight with your slings. Let us see if your skill can bring us the reward we seek. You will silently strike the sentries with your slings."

It was clear to all that the five mounted men would be the ones to move the herd.

"If there are no more questions then rest and War Hammer will make the noose of the ambush hard to break."

Bruneus sat and sharpened his sword. It was his most precious possession. His father had given it to him on the day he became a warrior. Serpus also had one but it was not as good. Barcas came over and sat with his nephew. Bruneus looked up, "Is there honour in stealing horses at night and slaying men without giving warning?"

Barcas chewed thoughtfully on the piece of dried pig's meat and nodded, "A good question. This raid is not for honour but for horses. It is why we have travelled so far from our home. Your father has fought others in single combat. That was for honour. We do this for the clan. Mounted men have an advantage over those on foot. Some men are destined to fight on foot," He nodded at Big Nose who was dragging a sharpened stake to the ambush site. "You and I are not. Your father is a chief. His father and mine was a chief. One day you will be the chief and you will ride your horse to battle. You will probably fight on foot too until the clan is well mounted but the horse is the symbol that marks you as a noble."

"When we have these horses then we will have a clan who is all mounted."

"No, nephew, we will not for the horses will not have the saddles that allow us to fight from their backs.

12

Eventually, we will." He ruffled the young warrior's long hair, "When your father and I are in our graves and you lead the clan then that day might be closer but until then that will just be a dream. The clan has grown and changed since your father led it and you will continue to make the clan stronger. Now get some rest."

Bruneus shook his head, "First, Serpus and I will see that we have enough round stones for the task in hand."

Barcas nodded his approval. His nephew had the makings of a good warrior. The two young men looked through their bag of stones. There were five that were as close to perfect as one could get without casting them in lead. The clan did not do that. If they found an enemy who had made their own then it was treasure to be celebrated, for a cast lead ball was harder and flew straighter. The two young Celts had just river stones.

When they woke they saddled their horses. It was only then that they ate and drank. The wine that they drank was well watered. Back in their village they would enjoy the stronger wine that would make them lose their heads. This was a raid and moderation was all. Barcas, dressed in his mail shirt and with a helmet on his head, led the other four towards the sleeping village. They did not ride their horses. Their horses were to be mounted when they had killed the sentries, opened the gate and were driving their treasure towards the ambush. Bruneus stroked the head of his horse, Stormbringer, "This night we both become warriors." The horse seemed to nod his agreement.

Bruneus, his shield strapped around his back, followed his uncle. His spear was attached to the saddle. Serpus insinuated himself behind in the same manner. The other older warriors brought up the rear. Serpus knew that their families were not as high in the village as his and status was all. That they had horses at all was down to luck. Serpus' father had been one of Brennus' oathsworn and died in battle. His horse was a horse that had carried his father to war.

There was a slight breeze and the night was a warm one. The smell of night scented flowers and herbs drifted up to them. It was mixed with the dying smell of woodsmoke and the food that had been cooked in the village. The danger was that their horses would alert the animals they intended to raid. Barcas led them so that their smell would not carry to the herd. There was a grove of wild, untended olive trees and Barcas tied the reins of his horse to it. The others chose their own trees. Serpus and Bruneus took out their slings and the best stones that they had each chosen. They knew that if they had to use a second stone then they had failed but Bruneus was a youth who planned as much as he could. His father had taught him that. He was on this raid to learn all he could from his uncle. As they followed Barcas towards the horse pen filled with the milling animals, Bruneus felt the sweat running down his back. It was not hot and the young Celt knew that it had to be nerves. He was angry with himself. A warrior should not have nerves. This was his duty and his role. He served the clan.

They could hear voices and Barcas held up his hand. They stopped and the leader of the warband waved forward the two young warriors with the slings. The two sentries were atop their horses but, obligingly, were close together and just thirty paces from them. The words they had heard were the sentries. Their language was slightly different and because they were not speaking loudly neither Bruneus nor Serpus fully understood what they were saying. It did not matter. The two guards were close enough to be hit. He noticed that they both had the four horned saddles that he had. Bruneus pointed to the sentry on the left and tapped his own chest. Serpus nodded. Neither warrior had ever killed a man. They had slain animals but this would be the first time that they had taken the life of a man. Bruneus was also aware that they had to be quick. They would only have the luxury of one whirr of the sling for the noise would alert the sentries. Bruneus knew that there were two sentries in the tower. The two friends looked at each other and Bruneus mouthed, 'One, two, three!' On three they both whirled and then released their stones. The buzz from the slings made the two sentries turn but that merely ensured that they died for the stones smacked into the centres of their foreheads. They fell from their horses and the herd moved away from the two dead men.

Barcas' wolf like grin was reward enough for Bruneus. He waved for them to bring their horses and he alone entered the pen. By the time the other men returned with the horses Barcas had dragged the two bodies away from the herd. He nodded to the bodies. Bruneus went to the man he had slain. Around his neck he had an amulet made of bronze. It was in the shape of a horse. He took it. The only other thing of value that he had was a long dagger. That too was taken. Serpus took a dagger and a short sword from the other. Barcas mounted his horse and the others emulated him. He had told them what to do the previous night and no one was going to let down their leader. They moved into position behind the herd as Barcas reached down to open the pen. The dead men, the strange horses and the smell of strangers made the horses nervous and noisy. It was as the pen gate was opened that the noise drew the attention of one of the sentries on the tower. A voice shouted in the night. When there was no reply from the dead sentries then the voice became strident. Even Big Nose would have known that the words were shouting an alarm. They slapped the rumps of the horses before them and the animals galloped from the pen towards the waiting ambush.

Barcas led them and the warriors urged the horses up
the trail. The horses did not cooperate. The large number
made it impossible to control them all and some split off
from the herd and did not follow the trail to the ambush.
As the herd milled they did not move as swiftly as
Barcas had planned. Had it all gone to plan then the herd
would have been spirited away before the men on foot
could react. Bruneus learned many lessons that night but
this was the first one. Plans could be made but the fates
and luck could alter them. As the older riders went to
drive back the handful of horses that had headed right
Barcas yelled, "Leave them!"

The command came too late for one of the men who
was plucked from the back of his horse by an arrow. The
other then made the cardinal error of looking down at the
dead man. That proved fatal and two arrows slammed
into him. Bruneus and Serpus had obeyed Barcas and the
horses before them, urged on by the flat of Bruneus' and
Serpus' swords, raced after Barcas. Other horses had
fled left. Their leader was a warrior and he knew his
duty. He wheeled his horse so that he no longer led the
herd but he joined the two young warriors who were
now left behind the herd. The ambush was up the small
slope and as the horses were funnelled into the trail so
the three warriors found themselves closer to their
enemies. Barcas did not have his shield around his back
but he held it in his left hand and his spear in his right. It
was the shields on their backs that saved the lives of the
two young warriors. The arrows sent by the enraged
warriors who were chasing them slammed into the wood
of their shields. One penetrated Bruneus' shield and
pricked his back.

The delay, as the track narrowed and the herd slowed,
helped the men who were chasing them and they sought
to slay the three men who had stolen their horses with
spears and javelins as well as their bows. Barcas wore a
mail shirt but two more arrows hit him and he was

wounded. Bruneus did not see them strike. It was only later he realised what had happened. He looked up the trail and knew where the ambush lay. They would soon be there. Indeed, some of the stolen horses were already past Big Nose and War Hammer who were at the fore of the ambush. Bruneus' second lesson came when he found himself smiling. They had succeeded. As he turned to look at his uncle he knew that he had been premature. There were twenty men from the village who were close behind Barcas. He was slashing with his spear and two men lay writhing on the ground. The third lesson was that hesitation was fatal and instead of turning to go to the aid of Barcas, Bruneus watched and as the spear was thrust into his uncle's side he belatedly rode back to attack the men who followed. He swung his sword in an arc and was rewarded when it took the top of the head of the bearded, naked warrior wielding a war axe.

Barcas was almost slumped over his horse. He managed to say, "You should have fled."

Bruneus said nothing but, after sheathing his sword, grabbed the reins of his uncle's horse as the warriors recovered from the bloody death of the naked leader. Serpus looked around and Bruneus gave his first order, "Follow the plan!"

Barcas was clinging to his pommels but Bruneus could see the blood flowing. The plan was in tatters. The first two men they had lost were supposed to stay with the captured herd while the other three joined in the ambush. That would not happen now. When they passed the last man in the ambush Bruneus let go of the reins of his uncle's horse and threw himself from his saddle. He swung around his shield and took his spear. Barcas rolled from the back of his horse and fell to the ground. Bruneus saw the blood oozing from his wounds. His uncle smiled, a tendril of blood seeping from the corner of his mouth, "Now you are a warrior. Tell my brother…" He said no more for he was dead.

The clash of arms from behind him told him that any mourning would have to wait. War Hammer was now the leader of the warband and he needed help. With Serpus at his side Bruneus raced back down the trail. The ambush had worked and there were dead men littering it but the man Bruneus had killed was the leader and the warriors wanted vengeance. It was a bloody battle with quarter neither sought nor given. War Hammer was swinging his mighty weapon in a wide arc. As Bruneus stabbed the nearest half naked man in the stomach with his spear, he saw that Big Nose had managed to get hold of a war axe and he was fighting like a wild man. He seemed not to care that he might be wounded. He screamed and roared a challenge. Along with War Hammer they were driving the enemy down the slope.

Bruneus roared, "For Barcas!" He and Serpus, with shields before them, ran down the path. It was at that moment that three arrows struck War Hammer. Two were in his body and such was his strength that he could have shrugged them off but the one that drove into his screaming open mouth was fatal. He fell and in that moment all sense of order and planning went. The four older men were now dead. Bruneus was the leader and what he should have done was take the ones who survived and head home but he was angry and the blood filled his head. He and Serpus chased the bowmen and the other survivors back to the village. The rest of the warband were also angry and as they caught up with the fleeing men the last of the village warriors were slaughtered. When Big Nose caught up with the archer who had slain War Hammer he swung his axe so hard across the man's back that he shattered his spine. It was a wild and reckless charge by young warriors but they had slain the older warriors and as the men they fought wore no mail and had no helmets then the wild anger of the raiders prevailed.

The women and children, along with the old, fled. When Bruneus led the young survivors into the village it was empty. Once it had been established that it was empty the men cheered at the victory. For Bruneus it was a hollow one. His uncle was dead. War Hammer, the mighty warrior, had joined him. Bruneus saw that every eye looked to him. He was the leader now and it was up to him to take charge. "Serpus, take two men and bring the horses and our dead here." Serpus nodded. "Big Nose, have the rest of the men secure the gates." They had lost half of the men that they had brought. They had more horses but it had come at a high price. How would Bruneus' father view the deaths?

Big Nose grinned and raised his war axe, "Aye, Bruneus! You are our leader now but I am no longer Big Nose. This day I have earned another name. I avenged War Hammer and I now become War Axe!"

Figure 1 The Blue Sea

Bruneus

Chapter 1

I looked around the village. Everything had happened so quickly that I had not had time to think and I knew that as the new leader it was my responsibility to get the twelve survivors from the raid back to Barcenis. We had taken everything that could be taken: food, horses, saddles, treasure and weapons. We had even taken waterskins and wineskins. I now wore my uncle's mail shirt and helmet. It honoured him. The mail might be old and need a few minor repairs but it was better than nothing. The bodies of our dead lay in the chief's roundhouse and kindling lay around it. Serpus and the newly named War Axe watched me expectantly as I stood with the burning brand in my hand. I nodded and shouted, "Barcas, son of Bastrus, you were a great war leader and you led us well. Now lead the dead in the journey to the Otherworld. I will tell the village of your deeds."

I threw the burning brand into the kindling and stepped back as it whooshed into life. The wind took the smoke and the smell north and west. The roundhouse burned well and when the roof fell in then the bodies began to burn. We knew that the survivors of our raid would have fled to neighbouring clans and retribution would follow. That was why we had burned and not buried them. We did not want our dead despoiled. Once the roundhouse was a pile of ash we mounted our horses. Every warrior now had a horse and a saddle. We had spare horses with the treasure we had gained. Many of the horses had fled to the wild. We had not recaptured all fifty. In truth I did not know how we would have got all the horses back. We all led one horse and a couple of the better riders had two. The raid had achieved what Barcas had intended but it had come at a high price. I pointed Barcas' spear and led my depleted warband south to ride back to our home. War Axe rode the largest horse. It had been War Hammer's, Cariosus. His feet did not quite touch the ground but they were close to doing so. The one he had ridden north had not been as big and War Axe's feet had scraped the earth as he rode. He was our rock at the rear. Serpus and I kept our horses. We knew them and, most importantly, they knew us. Stormbringer had been a colt when he had been given to me. We had learned to be as one together. Serpus rode his jet black Crow and the two of us rode at the fore.

My friend turned to me when we were well clear of the village. Without horses the survivors would find it hard to pursue us. "You now look like a warrior, Bruneus."

I was not sure if he was looking for positives to take from what, for me, was a disaster. I shook my head, "I do not feel like one. If I had gone to my uncle's aid sooner he might have lived."

Serpus shook his head, "The two arrows that pierced the mail shirt did for him. The spear thrust merely accelerated his end. You could have done nothing."

I knew that he was right but I hated that I had hesitated. I might not have been able to save him but I would feel better if I had. It was another lesson. The next time I was in such a position I would not hesitate. I hoped the other lessons I might learn would not be as costly.

Serpus and I had been friends since we had been barely able to walk. I think he knew me better than any, even Barcas and my father. He seemed to read my thoughts. "Bruneus, you think too much, that has always been your trouble. Barcas, War Hammer and the others

22

are dead. We all knew that death was a possibility on this raid. It was why your father sent so few older warriors. It was to blood the young ones. We lost but a handful of the young warriors and the others now see you as the leader. Surely that is a good thing. You are the son of the chief and you did what you had to, you led. The village will be safe for your father and the older warriors are guarding it and we have been blooded. The clan has lost warriors but we have shown that we are ready to take their place."

Serpus' words were a comfort and as we rode I let them sink in and modify my melancholy. We rode in silence. Everyone was now better armed and mounted. Our horses were laden. We had taken the weapons from the enemy dead as well as their waterskins and blankets. They could be used back in the village. We wasted nothing. We had more horses than when we had left and when we reached our village then more men would become horsemen and we could range further afield. He was right. There had been losses but we were now stronger than we had been. Three days after leaving the raided village we passed the mountains to our right. We paddled through the sea and that seemed symbolic. This was the sea that also lapped on the shore near to Barcenis. We were connected and in another five days we would be home. I began to speculate about the welcome we might receive. War Hammer had no family but the two other older warriors who had fallen had and they would mourn. The parents of the young warriors who had been killed would also mourn but there were enough survivors for there to be a celebration. Perhaps there would be an offering to the gods. Would I be given another name?

Before we neared our home we groomed our horses and combed our hair. I shaved my chin. My helmet hung from one of the pommels of my saddle. My mail shirt was polished. I knew that the two holes made by the arrows would need to be mended but the damage would not be noticed. We all now had spears as well as swords and the spear heads gleamed in the afternoon sunlight. I felt like a conquering hero as I led the warband along the beach to the village. It was easier on the horses. I was already anticipating the accolades as I led the survivors of the raid with the horses we had taken through the village. My father would be sad that his brother had died but pleased, I knew, that his son had taken the reins and led the warband and the treasure that was the horses back to the village. We left the beach to head to the road that ran down the coast. It was just a hunting trail that was so well used it had become packed earth but we called it a road. It swung around to pass the gatehouse of the village. The first sign of trouble we saw were the boats drawn up on the beach. They should have been out fishing. The next sight that jarred were the barred gates. Serpus saw that something was not right, too. We both looked around but there was no sign of an enemy. Even so a leader was cautious. "Swing your shields around and be prepared to let loose the horses." I donned my helmet and we moved down the packed earth of the road to the palisade that surrounded the village.

It was old Gerontius, the fisherman, who rose from the wall above the gatehouse at the sound of our approach. He looked like a skeleton. When we had left he was hale and hearty for someone who had seen fifty summers. "Bruneus, it is good that you have come but you cannot enter."

"Why not? Where is my father?"

"Your father, mother and the rest of your family are dead. A plague struck the village the day after you left. The gods abandoned us. I was with the ships and we were fishing and a storm kept us at sea longer than normal. By the time we returned, half of the village was already grievously sick and some were dying. The rest were ready to follow. We should have stayed outside of the walls but men wanted to see their families. We caught the plague too. We are doomed to die. Each day more die and now there are just four of us left. I was waiting for the raiders to return. I hoped to see Barcas leading you but…This is fate and you are now the leader of the clan!"

"What clan? These are all that survive!"

He shrugged. The movement made him cough and splutter. Blood and phlegm came from his mouth. "Then you start again. Bring the boats next to the wall. I will return when I can. If I do not come for one whole day then burn the boats and the village. Let this plague die with us. Farewell!"

"How did the plague come?"

He shook his head, "All I know is that a merchant was seen riding from the south. Neither his horse nor he were in the village when we returned." He shook his head, "The gods…" He descended the ladder and was lost to sight.

Some of the younger warriors wanted to enter but Gerontius' words had struck home. I was the leader of the clan. I was not ready but I had to step up and take the responsibility. "We do as Gerontius said. Keep one boat so that we can fish while we wait and pile the rest outside the gatehouse. Hobble the horses and make a camp by the beach." I spoke as the leader. I had always known that one day I would lead the clan but my father had not been a weak man. I had expected to wait for years for such a momentous change in my life. The raid had been part of my preparation for leadership. Now all that was undone. The gods had toyed with me. Perhaps my father had not sacrificed enough to satisfy the gods but it was hard to see what sacrifice would have prevented this disaster. I had made another important decision and already I was changing. The clan was destroyed. It had not been our doing and perhaps our raid was meant to save the blood of the clans. I did not think of that at the time, I was just wondering what I should do.

The men I led had obeyed me. That was not a surprise. Serpus, War Axe and I were the eldest. Serpus and I had been horsemen and I was seen as a noble. It was natural that the others did as I had told them. The problem was that I did not know what to do next. A leader did not consult. He made decisions. We still had food from the raid and as the men dragged the boats next to the wall I said, "We need food. The men must eat." We had lived off cold rations on the road but now we needed a hot meal.

One of the younger warriors, Alerix, said, "I watched my mother cook. I will make us something to eat."

I barely knew the youth. He was slightly tubbier than the others and perhaps that was because his mother was such a good baker. He had seemed too gentle to be a warrior and yet had acquitted himself well on the raid. I had not bothered about such things when I had been living the life of the son of the chief. As the warriors placed the boats where Gerontius had said I looked at the others. Outside of War Axe and Serpus I did not know them well. Now they were all that was left. I had to learn more about them. Glaucus and Trismus had been closer to me but they had died back on the raid. I would use my eyes.

Although I knew Serpus the best he still surprised me for he took charge of the horses and ordered the men take the horses to graze. I suppose I should have given the order. I realised that I should not have been surprised by Serpus' command. The two of us were the best riders and knew horses better than the rest. What did come as a revelation to me was that while I sat outside the walls worrying about what to do, Serpus just got on with it. War Axe, in contrast, was still the same man he had been before he took up the axe. He did not think overmuch and the new war axe had elevated him. He had a whetstone and was sharpening the blade. I would have to make sure that he was well employed. He would need to be ordered to do everything. As night fell and the smell of Alerix's food drifted over to me I decided that when we had eaten I would speak to them all. My father had used a council of older warriors to help him make decisions. War Hammer and my uncle had been two of the councillors. There was nothing wrong with consulting but a leader led. A leader made decisions. I was the leader. We ate and the food was tasty but I had no appetite. In the space of less than a month I had lost everyone that was dear to me and I was left to lead a dozen warriors. What were we to do?

When we had eaten I felt every eye upon me. I sighed and stood, "I know that you all want answers. There are so many questions that I fear that is impossible. You want to know what we will do and, to be honest, those questions race around inside my head too." I waved a hand at the walls behind me. "This was not expected. The deaths of warriors in battle could be understood but this…this is something I cannot comprehend."

It was Bellerix who spoke first in the silence that followed, "Perhaps some may live. Gerontius is a fisherman. What does he know of disease?"

Serpus shook his head, "He knows more of disease than we do. Did you not hear how he tried to keep the men from entering the village but they did not heed his words? It doomed him and the others."

I nodded and sat, "And the other is how quickly this plague spread. We have not been away for a long time and yet the disease has taken hold. I am not sure what we do in the future but I know one thing, when there are none left alive we burn the village and none shall enter." I glared at them all, especially Bellerix, "None!"

War Axe and Serpus nodded and that decided the matter. My word would be upheld because I had two men backing me.

War Axe was still stroking the new weapon, almost as though it was a child. He said, "I do not want to be a fisherman or a farmer." He left unsaid what he wanted to be but we all knew.

Serpus put the unspoken thoughts into words, "You would have us become warriors?"

War Axe smiled and held up the axe, "This shows we are warriors. We defeated a village and we had but a handful of veterans. They died well but we took the animals and burned the village. Had we so chosen we could have taken the women as prizes too."

I stood again, "If you would be a bandit then do so, but not I."

There was silence and then Serpus said, "One night when I was on watch War Hammer spoke to me. He said he was thinking of leaving the clan." We all looked in surprise at Serpus. No one ever left the clan. "He was my uncle and I think he was warning me. His own family were dead. His son, my cousin, did not live beyond his sixth summer and his wife died giving birth to another son. I was like the son he never had. I think the raid was his chance to show me how to be a warrior. He said that he heard the Carthaginians were hiring warriors such as him to fight in their wars against the Romans. There is a general called Hamilcar Barca. He fights in Sicily and my uncle said the Carthaginians pay well. It was a chance to do something he knew he was good at, being a warrior. I think he hoped I would go with him."

Silence followed. Serpus was honest and War Hammer had been a well-respected warrior. If he thought it was a good idea then it might just be.

I could see that War Axe liked the idea but he said nothing. He looked at me. I was the leader. Whatever I decided he would do. I asked, "Where is this Sicily?"

"Across the seas to the east and close to the land of the Romans."

It was a chance to say no for how would we get to Sicily?

Serpus added, "But they are recruiting here, on the mainland. My uncle said they were at Gades."

We did not know how far away that was but we knew that Gades was at the southwestern tip of the mainland. We lived closer to the north and east. I knew that if I said we would go it would defer a decision. Much could happen between our village and Gades.

I measured my words carefully, "If you wish to go to fight for the Carthaginians then I will lead you. Barcas put that responsibility on my shoulders. If you wish to stay here and build a new village then I will do that too."

I knew it was the coward's way out. I was not leading but letting them make the decision. I did not like what I was doing but I was afraid.

War Axe just grinned, "That is an easy one. I would find the Carthaginians and become a warrior."

Serpus smiled at our friend's enthusiasm and he nodded, "It seems to me that we went to get horses to become mounted warriors. We now have those horses. I think we travel to Gades and become better horsemen on that journey."

I looked at Bellerix, "And you, Bellerix, what do you say?"

He shook his head, "I think that my words will not change the opinion of any and the silence and the smiles around this fire tell me that everyone wishes to go to Gades. What I say is that I would have things the way that they were. I would have my mother, father, brother and two sisters alive and in our home. I would seek to court Alesia, Alerix's sister and marry her but the gods have taken that from me. I am not sure that I wish to be a warrior but I do not wish to be alone. I will come."

I waited for any dissension and there was none, "Then until we leave we become better horsemen and warriors." I patted War Axe on the head, "My friend here seems to be in love with his weapon. Perhaps we should all become as attached."

That brought a smile to everyone until Bellerix said, "And that means we leave when all are dead and we burn our past." It was not said with any malice. He was stating a fact and it ended the smiles. The funeral pyre of Barcenis was not something to smile about.

I spoke, that night, about my uncle and the conversation we had about the name of the clan. "The Clan of the Eagle is no more."

Sercix said, "But we are the Clan of the Eagle."

"And when was the last time you saw an eagle?" My question silenced him. "My uncle and father liked wolves. Barcas told me how the wolf leader protects the clan. A wolf is a warrior but he fights with his brothers as a pack. I think we become the Clan of the Lone Wolf for we will be alone in a sea of enemies. We will all be the best warrior that we can be but like any pack, our strength will come from fighting alongside our brothers. What say you? Will you be my brothers?" Everyone looked to Serpus and War Axe. When they smiled and nodded, the others all did so. I stood and put my hand out, "Swear an oath to me and we shall become the Clan of the Lone Wolf." They all put their hands on mine. I took out my dagger and cut into the palm. The blood oozed from the wound, "I would make it a blood oath."

Hostus said, "But that is an oath until death."

I said, solemnly, "I know."

Starting with Serpus and War Axe the others all copied me. We put our hands together and the blood mingled and then dropped to the sand. It would be part of the land long after we were dead. We were leaving but part of us would remain.

"I swear that the Clan of the Lone Wolf will never leave a wolf behind and we will be faithful unto death."

They all chorused, "I swear that the Clan of the Lone Wolf will never leave a wolf behind and we will be faithful unto death."

It was done and the clan was born even as the last of the old clan lay dying inside the wooden walls of Barcenis.

When Gerontius appeared on the walls, the next day, we heard him before we saw him. The sounds were those of his feet dragging wearily up the ladder and his coughing. We heard his retching as he neared the fighting platform. When he peered over the top I thought I was seeing a freshly dug up corpse. I approached until he held up his hand, "No further. I am the last. My brother died last night. I have dragged all the bodies into the chief's hall. I have laid a trail of kindling from the gate to the hall. I will say goodbye." He looked at the sky, "I do not think there will be rain. Light your fire when you are ready, Bruneus, Chief of the Clan of the Eagle."

"But what of you?"

"If I live to reach the hall I will be surprised. Farewell." As if to confirm his words he began to cough and retch. I saw blood come from his mouth and he stumbled away. We heard his footsteps and then we heard a fall as if he had been tripped.

I shouted, "Gerontius! Gerontius!" There was silence. I turned and saw the others, open mouthed, and their eyes filled with the horror of what we had seen. Men had died on the raid but their end had been far better than the end of Gerontius and our people.

That was the time for a leader to make a decision. "Fetch kindling to the boats by the gate. Serpus and War Axe, fetch three brands from the fire."

We heard the noise of a body falling to the ground. It cracked as it struck dried kindling. The silence was almost painful. Gerontius had died. He had been right and not even made the hall. I realised what courage and

strength lay in that old fisherman. It took time to gather
kindling. The gods were favouring us for the breeze
came from the sea. That would not only take the fire to
the hall it would also keep the stink of burning flesh
from our camp.

I raised my brand, "Farewell, Clan of the Eagle." I
threw the brand into the kindling. It was bone dry and it
whooshed into life as flames raced up the wooden walls
to consume the place that Gerontius had occupied just a
few moments earlier. My two friends did the same and
then, one by one, the rest of the warriors each threw a
brand. We would share the burden and I was heartened.
The fishing boats flared into life and the flames seemed
to roar up to the heavens. When we saw the flames
suddenly rise from the middle of the village we knew
that the hall was on fire. Gerontius had done his part.
The pall of smoke that rose also took our families into
the sky. It was good.

I turned and drew my sword, "The Clan of the Eagle
is no more. We hunt together and we fear no man. Now
we are the Clan of the Lone Wolf." I raised my sword.
Every one of the men took out his weapon and raised it
in the air, copying my words.

Despite the breeze taking the stink to the west we
could still smell the burning flesh. The gate and wall
burned first and when they crumbled we were able to
look and see the village that had nurtured us for so many
years. Through the swirling smoke and flames we saw
the huts flaring in the air and each man looked at the
place that they had called home. No one spoke but no
one could take their eyes from it. The last building to
crumble into a pile of ash was the hall. The intricately
carved doorposts were no more. The drinking horns, the
tables, the sleeping furs, everything was consumed along
with the bodies. All that I could think of was Gerontius
as he had dragged the dead to the hall. Once the last of
his comrades had died he did it alone. He had slept in a

cemetery. Gerontius became a hero to me. He had not been a warrior. I do not think he even owned a sword but he had died with more honour than any man I knew, Barcas included. He had died saving the clan.

I waited until just smoke and ash remained before I gave my next order. "I want the boat taken out to sea. We need fish for our journey south. We need as much game hunted as we can. We will dry the fish and salt the meat. It will take us many days to travel the length of this land and we need to avoid settlements."

War Axe frowned, "Why?"

I smiled, "If you were in a village and saw thirteen armed warriors coming down the road would your first thought be, *'how do we make them welcome'?*" I saw him understand and nod. "We will not behave as bandits but we need to avoid people until we reach Gades."

After a week of hunting, fishing and foraging, I deemed we had enough to keep us alive for the journey south. Serpus said, "What do we do with the boat?"

I had thought about this in the days since the village had been burned. "We make a sacrifice to the gods." I took War Hammer's war hammer. No one had wanted to wield the weapon for its owner had been a mighty warrior but we had brought it back to give to my father. Even his nephew feared using it. I laid it in the boat and covered it with Barcas' shield. There was nothing wrong with the shield but my uncle had marked it with his design and it did not do to bring bad luck to a warband. "Hold the boat with the wind astern. Lower the sail. Serpus, fetch me a brand."

While I climbed aboard and tied the steering board so that it would head out to sea, the others did as I asked. It was not easy for the wind had changed in the week since the burning of the village and now came from the east. The fishing boat was eager to be gone. I stood and waited for Serpus. He handed me the brand and I said, "Great God Icaunis, take this our last boat as a sacrifice so that the last men from this village might enjoy a good life. Take the mighty war hammer and the shield of Barcas for they were both great warriors." I raised the sail and, keeping the brand aloft, slipped over the side. "Release the boat." As they let go I hurled the burning brand into the boat. It landed close to the forward thwart. The wind made the ghost ship race across the water and she was five hundred paces from the shore before the sail and mast flared, like a candle in the night and then the boat began to settle in the water. I waded ashore and found that I was smiling.

Serpus said, "Why the smile?"

I shrugged, "I just felt that it was the right thing to do and did you see that the boat leapt to its death as though it was happy to leave this land? It is good."

We left the next morning. Thanks to our raid we each had a horse to ride and we had some remounts that we were using as pack animals. I aimed to make forty miles a day and to camp as far from people as we could. I had rarely been south of our home but my father and uncle had said that much of the land, the coast apart, was empty. That decided our route.

We had one mail shirt with us and that was the one my uncle had worn when he had died. There were two arrow holes in it and it would need to be repaired. My father had a better one but it was now in the ashes of our village. The shirt was placed on one of the spare horses along with the extra weapons we had taken as well as food and supplies. Those of us with helmets hung them from the pommels of our horses. We carried our shields across our backs. In the case of Serpus and I it was almost a superstition. We had worn them thus when we had fled the village and they had saved our lives. Barcas had mail but he had died. There was a lesson there.

I found myself studying my new clan as we rode and when we camped. I had only known two of them well. Alerix was quiet and was a good cook. We quickly utilised his skill and he seemed to enjoy the responsibility. His best friend was Bellerix and perhaps that was no surprise as Bellerix courted his sister. Bellerix was a doubter and that was a good thing. I was learning that a good leader needed more than men who just said, 'yes'. He needed men to question him. Galm, Tadgh and Aed were friends. Apart they lacked confidence but together they were different men. They were skilled warriors and Galm could hurl a javelin even further than War Axe, showing that it was skill rather than brute strength that counted. They fought well together. On the raid they had been a solid wall that fought for each other. I would use that.

Green Eye was named for his remarkably green eyes. The girls in the village had found him attractive because of it. He could have had his pick of any of them. It made him acutely aware of his looks and he always spent a long time on his hair and his moustache.

Cestrus and Hostus were friends and they fought well together too but while Cestrus preferred a spear Hostus liked the sword his father had given him when we left on the raid. It was a short one and his father had said it was Roman, a gladius.

Sercix and Wal were also friends but different too. Sercix was almost as reckless as War Axe but given that he was much smaller did not seem to enjoy luck. He was one of those who hurt himself falling from a horse. Wal was something of a healer and it was he who bound the wrist that Sercix hurt. He and Hostus got on well. Wal's sister had married Hostus' brother.

These were the warriors I led but I had never really led them in battle. I had given orders after the deaths on the raid but when we fought on a battlefield it would be a different matter.

I did not let them simply ride where they chose. I had War Axe ride at the rear of our line of horsemen behind the spare horses. Each spare was led by one of the warriors who had less weaponry. Serpus and I rode as leaders. I needed my friend for each day was a lesson on leadership. While we scanned the hills ahead of us for danger we talked. There were words we would share with the others but we needed to know each other's minds. I felt as though I was walking into a dark room in a place I did not know. My mind was assailed with many questions. Was I doing the right thing? When I took the hunter's trail through the small wood was that the correct decision? Had I chosen the best camp site? Were we pushing the horses too hard? Not hard enough? Serpus did not know the answers either but when I asked the questions our talks helped me to formulate my plans. In that way we covered the four hundred miles in ten days. We might have done it quicker but the men were learning to be horsemen. There were accidents and injuries but those events helped to make them better riders. As we neared Gades we looked and rode like horsemen. We had learned many things on the ride. Two horses had not been tethered well enough and had fled. We had lost another four that went lame. We were learning that being horsemen was not just about staying in the saddle. It was about looking after your animals.

Chapter 2

The city had gates and guards and we were not simply allowed in. Thirteen horsemen armed and horsed were a threat and guards prevented our entry. The first problem proved to be the language. We had avoided contact with most people on our way south. Since leaving the ashes of our home we had not spoken to anyone and I did not understand a word that the guards spoke to us. We could clearly not enter and we had used up most of our supplies so we could not simply camp and wait.

"Here is a problem I did not anticipate."

Serpus said, "Let us dismount and use that water trough for our horses. I am sure that the guards will send for someone who can make a decision about us."

We headed to the water trough that lay close to the road but was outside the walls. We watered our horses and nibbled on some of the salted meat that still remained. We had coins taken in the raided village and I planned on using them in the city. None of us spoke.

Eventually I said to Serpus, "Did War Hammer give any indication of how he would join this army?"

Serpus shook his head, "It was a short conversation one night. I am not sure that he knew how to do this. I think he pined for his dead family and this would have been one last adventure and taking me with him would make me a better warrior."

Just then a soldier strode towards us. He had with him a slave and two of the four guards from the gate accompanied him. He was clearly a soldier, and he looked to be a senior soldier, for he had a sword and wore a breastplate. He had no helmet upon his head and that marked him as different from the guards who all wore leather helmets. Instead, he had a conical hat upon his head. Before he spoke he seemed to be studying us.

Serpus and I turned to face him but there was little point
in speaking to him as I doubted he would understand our
words. He said something to one of the sentries who
pointed north and then spoke. I did not understand any of
it but I deduced that he was ascertaining the direction we
had taken. Then he spoke to the slave. He spoke
carefully and slowly.

The slave was a youth. He did not look like the
soldiers. He had the colouring of someone from this land
and not from Carthage. The curly black hair and beards
of the Carthaginians marked them as different. I also saw
that they shaved their upper lip. They seemed to be the
opposite of us. We shaved our beards but valued our
moustaches.

I could understand most of the words spoken to us but
not all. The slave said, "My master is commander of this
city." I did not understand the word he used but when he
gestured with his right hand at the walls I worked it out.
"His name is General Mazheus and he wants to know
what brings you here."

I nodded to show that I had understood. I spoke
slowly and carefully. I suppose I sounded like an idiot
but I wanted no misunderstandings. All of our efforts to
reach this place would be wasted if I failed. It was a test
of my leadership. "I am Bruneus of the Clan of the Lone
Wolf and we are here to hire our swords to the
Carthaginian army."

I saw the youth frown at a couple of words but I saw
him nod when I had finished. I learned a lesson that day.
It was clear to me that the slave did not simply repeat the
words I had spoken. He summarised them for they were
rattled out quickly.

I saw the smile on the face of the Carthaginian
general. He spoke again and the slave said, "What makes
you think that you are worthy to be hired?"

"Tell the general that most of the horses we ride and
the weapons we have came from a village we raided. We

slew the warriors and took their horses and destroyed their village. Tell him that while we look young we have killed men in battle. Tell him that we will become better soldiers."

I saw Serpus nod and grin, "Well said."

Serpus' words drew a look from the general. The slave translated and the general nodded. The slave then said, "Wait here. The general will return."

The sentries went back to their sentry post and the general headed back inside. While we had been talking others had arrived at the gate but as they were clearly merchants they had been allowed to enter. I wondered if we should have arrived in smaller groups and without weaponry. It was too late for that now.

The slave was still there and I said, "What is your name?"

"Pucco."

"You are a slave?"

"I am. I was taken with my family ten summers since. I can speak in both my language and that of the Carthaginians."

"The general is your master?"

He shook his head, "I serve the garrison. I clean and I fetch and carry. I normally do all the jobs that everyone else can avoid."

"Do you think the general will take us on?"

He shrugged, "I am not certain and I would not wish to raise your hopes. I know that there are ships in the harbour and they are due to sail to reinforce General Hamilcar Barca who is fighting the Romans in Sicily."

It was late afternoon when a messenger came. It was not the general but an officer who wore a helmet and carried a sword while wearing a breastplate. He spoke to Pucco who said, "The general wishes you to enter the city."

I asked, "He wishes to hire us?"

Pucco shrugged again, "That I cannot say but I suspect so for you are to go to the harbour where the general awaits. You are to walk your horses."

I turned to the others and could not help but keep the smile from my face, "We are to enter the city."

The smiles from the others were reassuring. We had almost passed the first test set to me by the gods.

We had rarely seen towns on our way south but this one was big. There were paved streets and stone buildings. The place also smelled differently. There were exotic aromas in this place that lay so far to the south of our own home. As we led our horses through the streets I noticed that there were many who had the same features as we did but the ones in richer garments and the ones who were armed looked more like the general and the sentries. They were Carthaginian. We were stared at by both local and Carthaginian alike. We wore our hair long and braided our moustaches. We looked like wild barbarians. That was clear from the looks on their faces. The clothes we wore stank of horse sweat and dirt. We had no other clothes to change into. We would look to the Carthaginians as wild and primitive warriors. We led horses that looked as rough as we did and we had weapons that were unlike those on the Carthaginians. We were different and so we were scrutinised. Pucco and the officer led us to the quayside of the harbour. There were many ships there. Some were at anchor in the sheltered harbour while others were tied up. I saw General Mazheus. He was talking to what looked like other senior officers. When we reached them the officer with us spoke to Pucco who said, "You are to wait here." The officer said something else and I saw Pucco's face fall. His voice was flat when he spoke, "I am to stay with you when you board the ship. I will be leaving my home."

"Why?"

"I speak your language and Carthaginian. I have to go with you. They need a translator and I am the one they have chosen."

Eventually the general and the officer came over and spoke to Pucco. He translated the words of the general. "You will be paid as mercenaries and are now part of the army of General Hamilcar Barca." He pointed, "You will be sailing on these ships. You now serve under Captain Bomilcar." After gesturing towards the officer with his hand he paused, "I am to go with you to translate the words." I looked at the officer. He looked to be young to be a captain.

I said, looking at the young officer, "And where are these coins that will bind us to you?" In truth I was not that bothered about pay but I thought that, as the leader, I should ask.

Pucco asked the question and I saw that it was the right thing to do for the general nodded. He spoke to Pucco. "There will be food for you and your horses. If your weapons are lost or damaged then you replace them at your own cost. You, as the leader, will be paid ten tetradrachm a month." I frowned for I had no idea to what he referred.

Pucco added, seeing the look on my face, "It is a silver coin." He paused, "It is good pay. The general expects you to pay your men."

I nodded, "Tell the general that we accept his offer and look forward to serving with him."

Pucco shook his head, "The general will not be going with you. You are commanded by this officer, Captain Bomilcar." I saw that the officer was much younger than the general whose trimmed beard had flecks of grey. I took him to be in his twenties. It was as I compared the two men that I saw they had beards but no moustaches. They shaved their top lips. It was not just the ones at the gate who looked that way. I soon recognised it as the fashion in Carthage. "It is he who will pay you and

41

direct you in battle." He added, quietly, for my benefit. "He is a noble."

I bowed to the officer. When I saw him smile then I knew I had done the right thing. I asked, "When do we board our horses?" All of my men had been at sea at some point. We all learned to fish as well as to fight and hunt but the horses had never been on a ship. The warships I saw had three banks of oars and towered over us. The merchant ship we would board was just as high but had no oars.

Pucco asked the question and then he gave us the answer. "We sail on the morning tide." I frowned at the word *'tide'*. I had heard it and I knew it was to do with the sea but that was all. Pucco explained when he saw the frown. "The sea is higher twice a day on this side of the straits. You will load the horses in the night."

"And food?"

He pointed to the slaves bringing bread and fish for us. The general and Captain Bomilcar left us. All the questions had been answered. I think it was a measure of our position. We would not be considered as worthy of the interest of the nobles. We were mercenaries and, as such, expendable. Words need not be wasted upon us.

I turned to the others and told them what would be happening. Serpus had been at my side the whole time and heard everything. I wanted no confusion.

War Axe asked, "So does that mean our pay depends upon you?"

I shook my head, "I will be paid for all of us."

War Axe looked relieved and then said, "And if you are dead?"

Serpus laughed, "We are not yet aboard the ship, War Axe, and already you have our leader dead!"

War Axe looked confused, "I did not say that, Serpus." He shook his head and looked like a bear trying to rid itself of a fly that was annoying it. "Do not confuse me."

I said, patiently, "Whoever takes over from me will be paid for the men. That may be you, War Axe." He looked surprised at that. "Pucco here is to be with us and translate. I think it would be useful if we learned some words from him." I looked at the slave, "Would that be alright with you?"

He stared at me with his mouth open, "No one has ever asked if I want to do something. Of course, I will help you. Until Captain Bomilcar has done with me I am, effectively, your slave. I do whatever you want me to do."

The slaves bringing the bread, fish and wine arrived. We would have preferred beer which was more refreshing in the heat but wine was acceptable. I said, "Before we eat, take the saddles from the horses. The horses have worked hard and it will be a hard time for them boarding the ship. We need to keep them calm." The men were all better riders, thanks to the journey from our home, but Serpus and I were still the horsemen. The ride from the north had allowed me to become a leader. I knew that I still had much to learn but Barcas' death, the disaster at Barcenis, not to mention the hundreds of decisions I had made on the road south, had honed me.

The fish was good. It had been cooked over open fires and was both tasty and fresh. The bread was more than welcome. Alerix commented on its quality. The last breads we had eaten had been the supplies we had taken on the raid. That was many men's lifetimes ago. Once the slaves with the food had left us we were almost ignored. Perhaps they were fearful of our horses or, more likely, us. War Axe had tattoos on both his face and arms and his hair was wild. When he wore a helmet it was not as noticeable but here, in the open and close to the sea it seemed to double the size of his head. I made sure that Pucco ate. He was reluctant to at first. He saw us as his masters. I did not view him as a slave but as a teacher. In the short time since I had met him I had learned some words already. I knew that the more words I understood the better the chance I had of surviving. Our single raid had shown me how parlous was the life of a warrior. That the young ones had survived and the veterans died still puzzled me.

As we ate, Pucco taught us some more words. I saw his shortcomings when it came to the ship. He did not know what all the words were. He shrugged, "If the crew name them I might be able to translate them but..."

"Do not worry. We can point, can we not?" When we had eaten I said, "You had better get some sleep while you can. I, for one, am not looking forward to the loading of the horses."

Bellerix asked, "Who will keep watch?"

I said, "Serpus and I, along with Pucco. Do not worry, Bellerix, you will have your chance but not yet."

They curled up and used their saddles as pillows. Serpus said, "Barcas would have made them stand a watch. Why do you inflict this hardship on yourself?"

I shrugged, "I was still being given lessons in being a leader when my teachers died. I am still learning. You are right, Barcas and my father would have enjoyed a sleep while others watched but I do not know these men well enough yet. We are a small band and it seems to me that the longer we stay whole and without losses the better. If I have to sacrifice a night of sleep to do that then I will."

We spent the watch learning more words.

The ship's captain came down to speak to us not long after moonrise. He spoke to Pucco but I paid close attention to his words so that when Pucco translated I managed to pick up a few new ones.

"You can load the horses now." Pucco pointed to the sling above our heads. Two men were close to the captain and holding a rope. Another two were on the vessel.

I said, "Wake up." I turned to Serpus. "I will supervise this end. When the men have put their saddles and war gear on the ship keep half of them to help you unload the animals."

"Right." He headed to the gangplank.

I shouted, "Take your saddles and war gear aboard. Serpus will tell you what to do." As War Axe passed me I said, "Take my saddle, mail and helmet with you."

He was as strong as an ox. No one else could have managed to carry his load aboard. As I watched him climb the gangplank I wondered how our warband could exploit that strength.

Pucco said, "Master, can I be excused for a short time? I have few possessions but as I know not how long I will be away..."

"Of course."

I knew that the loading of the horses would need all our attention and I doubted that we would need a translator, especially as Pucco did not know all the words we might need on the ship. "We load mine and Serpus' first." Our two horses were the best but the real reason was that I knew the two horses and that, despite the strangeness of the task, they would not baulk. I wanted the other horses to see them.

I fastened the sling around Stormbringer. I stroked his head and spoke to him gently. I hummed a lullaby as I did so. The two sailors gave me a strange look but said nothing. One of the words I had learned was 'pull'. When I was happy with the sling I shouted, "Serpus, War Axe, I am sending up Stormbringer." They leaned over and waved. I turned to the four sailors holding the ropes attached to the yard and the pulleys. I said, "Pull!" They looked at me blankly. I had clearly said it incorrectly so I said it again and mimed pulling on the rope. They grinned and nodded. They began to pull. It was fortunate that none of our horses were large, heavy ones. The yard creaked alarmingly as they hauled on the rope. Stormbringer did not seem to be put out by the movement or the creaking. It was night time and that might have helped. The port was quiet and it was just the sound of the pulley that could be heard. I knew no more words and so I used my arm to slow them down although, to be fair, they knew their task and Stormbringer cleared the gunwale. Serpus and War Axe had taken over from the waiting sailors and used the rope to swing Stormbringer aboard. Serpus waved to me and I motioned for the sailors to lower my horse.

"Clear!" Serpus leaned over, a smile as wide as a sunrise on his face.

One of the Carthaginian sailors leaned over to shout something and the men with me lowered the sling. After that it became easier. Crow happily followed Stormbringer and by the time Pucco had returned we just had four horses to load. I was confident enough in the sailors and my men to look around as he approached. He had little enough with him. There was a small bag around his neck and he had a blanket tied around his body. I saw a beaker hanging from his belt and that was all. The life of a slave was hard.

The captain also looked pleased when the last horse was loaded and came over to speak to us. Pucco said, "He is pleased but now he says to board the ship. We wait just for the return of Captain Bomilcar."

I nodded and turned to the men, "I for one will enjoy making water here for I know not how long we shall be at sea."

When we had all relieved ourselves we boarded. The horses were all tethered on the open deck at the bows. Serpus and War Axe had already made a nest for us. This was not a war galley but a merchant ship. There were no oars. The cargo that had already been loaded was beneath the deck. I saw the hatches. There was one large square sail. Our sails on the fishing ships had been lateen sails but we were all familiar with the sight of merchant ships sailing along our coast. As the rest of the men sorted out their own beds I saw Pucco take out his few possessions. The most precious looked to be the small wooden figure. When he put his hands together and prayed I knew it to be his household god. It would be his most precious possession because he could speak to his god during the voyage and the sea could be a dangerous place. Mine hung around my neck. It was even closer than Pucco's. While we waited for the captain Pucco told us all that he knew both about the captain and the Carthaginians. He did not know a great deal. We would be learning together.

Captain Mago Bomilcar came aboard almost at the last moment. He had with him four men. They were his bodyguards and they had mail shirts, helmets and spears as well as large round shields across their backs. They were warriors but armed so differently from us that I wondered how we would fight together. Their muscled arms showed that they were strong and well fed. The captain of the ship showed his displeasure at the tardy arrival for our leader had still to load his five horses. It was lucky that War Axe and Serpus were so well practised and were able to help the sailors but, even so, one of the horses became agitated as the sling was raised. No one seemed to know what to do and so I began to sing. I did so loudly but my voice, so I had been told, was quite melodious. It had an effect for the horse quietened a little and the sailors hauled even faster to load the horse. I saw the ship's captain nod his approval while our new leader just looked at me curiously. He said not a word. The horses boarded, the sail was unfurled and when the ropes tying us to the shore were thrown we began to head out to sea and we all tried to sleep while it was still dark.

The men I led had all sailed on the sea but we had rarely sailed to a place where we could not see land. When we awoke we found the movement of the ship more dramatic and there was no land to be seen all around us. There were other ships that were taking men and supplies to the conflict. Ours was, probably, the one with the fewest men because we had many horses. There were two of the warships guarding this handful of ships.

We had made water and eaten the food that had been brought on board for us the previous night when an officer came down and spoke to Pucco. The slave had the hint of a smile on his face as he pointed to the dung beneath the horse's hooves, "The ship's captain says that must be cleaned as soon as the horse has..." I saw him struggling for the word.

I nodded, "Pissed and shat. I know." I turned to the men, "Right, boys, find buckets and haul up seawater. We have a deck to clean."

I suppose we could have objected to the duty but I eased my mind with the thought that they were our horses and we would not want to be walking in dung for the whole voyage. We had no idea, at that time, how long the voyage would last. I asked Pucco to speak to a sailor and he said it would take between sixteen and eighteen days depending upon the winds. When I discovered, four days into the voyage that we would be sailing close to our home I wondered if the gods were toying with us. The first seven days we were left to our own devices. We learned to muck out the animals twice a day. It kept the captain happy, the smell was less unpleasant and the task occupied us. Our Carthaginian leader kept to himself at the stern where he sat with his bodyguards under an awning. When we had free time, and we had a great deal of that, we sat with Pucco and learned more Carthaginian. Serpus, Alerix and Bellerix, like me, proved to have a natural ability and we picked up the words and, more importantly, the pronunciation, quickly. War Axe and some of the others were slower on the uptake but they knew the basic niceties and could answer questions. Perhaps Captain Bomilcar was waiting for the right time to speak to the men he would lead. A week into the voyage he came down with one of his bodyguards. We had given the four men nicknames for we were not introduced to them. It was the one we called White Scar for he had an old wound running the length of his left arm. He must have suffered the wound after losing a shield.

The Carthaginian did not look at Pucco but me and he addressed me in his language. I actually understood a couple of his words but I waited for Pucco to translate before I answered.

"How are the animals coping with the voyage?"

"They are happy enough."

"And the men?"

I smiled as I answered. I had learned the word and I said, "Good."

It brought a look of surprise to the man's face. Pucco said, "He said you have not wasted your time while aboard."

As it had not been a question I took it upon myself to ask him one, "Are there more men like us waiting?"

The answer did not come immediately. I saw the young officer selecting his words. "You are the only Gauls. There are some Numidians under his command."

I did not tell him that we were not Gauls. We looked like those warriors who lived further north, beyond the mountains, and we knew their words but we were not Gauls. It seemed the officer had learned enough and he turned and we were left alone once more. I asked Pucco about Numidians. He did not know the whole answer, "Numidia is the land that is close to Carthage. They do not wear armour and they throw spears. That is all that I know."

Serpus pointed to the line of ships that followed us. "We are the only horsemen being sent to reinforce this Hamilcar Barca. Perhaps they have enough there already." I nodded. He went on, "It would explain why we were recruited so quickly. We are few in number but we must be needed."

I looked at the other ships. There were six merchant ships in two lines and two war ships one on either side, like a pair of sheepdogs. It showed our importance. I wondered if I should have asked for more money. I had not negotiated at all. War Hammer would have asked for more. It was too late to do so now but when it came time to renegotiate I would think a little longer.

It was a day later when we were attacked. We knew something was amiss when the lookout sitting at the top of the mast shouted down and we heard the alarm in his voice that needed no translation. We watched the two warships as their oars bit into the seas and they both raced to the north. We could see no danger there but the reaction of the two naval vessels told us that there was a threat.

"What is going on?"

War Axe did not expect an answer from anyone but like the rest of us he was fearful for this was unexpected. We saw the three ships a few moments after the warships had taken down their sails. The three ships looked similar to our warships but they were all a little smaller than the two pentēkónteroi who were our guards. The captains of the merchantmen were trying to get away from the danger. We were at the mercy of the wind and we turned to flee. We watched from the side of the ship as the battle began. No one said who the enemy were, there was no need. They had to be Roman. Pucco had told us that we were sailing to a place called Sicily and there the Carthaginians were fighting the Romans. The three ships chose to use their speed and attack one of the higher and more ponderous Carthaginian warships. They darted in from two sides. It was almost silent for they were some distance away. We watched as oars were run in. I had not seen a naval battle before but that made sense. Splintering oars would cause injuries and deaths. The three ships had surrounded one vessel and we thought that the battle was as good as over. The second Carthaginian did not race in to help its consort. Then we saw something that was burning leave the Carthaginian's deck. A huge column of flame leapt up from one of the Roman ships. We could not see the damage but we did see the Carthaginian that was not under attack begin to build up speed as she aimed her bows at one of the Roman ships. Until the crash, as she rammed the Roman, it had been a largely silent affair. The splintering and shattering of wood and crack of the collision was augmented by screams that we heard. Just as suddenly as it had begun it ended. The one undamaged Roman fled. The one that had been burned followed, smoke rising from the damaged vessel and the one that had been rammed was now a pile of sinking wreckage. We had all fished and knew that the waters would be filled with the thrashing hunters of the sea, sharks.

The six merchant ships reefed the sails and we slowed as we waited for the two warships to rejoin us. They wasted no time in doing so and the one that had been attacked was still dealing with the damage when it took its position to larboard. It had clear damage. There were fewer oars on the vessel and the gunwale displayed signs of battle. Blood was being washed from the decks. We saw it as it was swabbed down the scuppers. Then we saw the bodies as they were flung overboard. We knew which bodies were the crew for they were set over the side with some respect. As darkness fell we heard the keening from the ship as they mourned their dead.

The next day saw the land appear on the horizon for the first time since we had left Gades. The battle had woken me up. "It is time we prepared ourselves for the land. We need to bathe and to make ourselves look a little less wild. Fetch pails and strip off." I knew that we would need to acquire spare clothes. We had just the clothes we had taken on the raid. Everything else had been consumed in the fire when we had burned Barcenis. When we were naked we poured water over our bodies and combed each other's hair to rid ourselves of the wildlife that gathered there.

Serpus nodded at my face and said, "You do not look like our leader."

I put my hand to my face and realised that he was right. My father and my uncle had both been clean shaven apart from their moustaches which they both wore long. It was a sign of nobility. It was alright for the others to have beards and be unshaven but I had a duty to my family. My moustache was not long, yet, but it needed to be braided and chin scraped.

I handed him my dagger, "Hone the blade and shave me. Alerix, it is time to plait my hair."

As the coast of Sicily drew closer so we transformed ourselves from the wild warband who had tried to enter Gades to the mercenary warriors who would fight for Carthage. We cleaned our clothes as best we could and then spent the last hours of that long day sharpening swords, axes, daggers and spears before repairing and cleaning the long shields we bore. I knew that I should have taken the opportunity of repainting the design on mine but it was too late now. When time allowed and I had the materials I would repaint the design that marked it as the shield of Bruneus, war chief of the Clan of the Lone Wolf.

When we woke we could see the harbour which Pucco said was called Drepanum. It was busy and ships were waiting for a berth. Captain Mago Bomilcar was clearly an important man for we were the first to be landed. He and his men went ashore and we were left to unload their horses and then ours. The captain was important but we were not. Having loaded the horses in Gades we found unloading them easier. For one thing the horses were eager to leave. The days we had taken in crossing the sea had taken its toll on the animals. They need to be grazed and to be able to recover the strength in their legs. I waited on the quay as the horses were lowered. I had Bellerix and two others watch over the five horses of the captain and his bodyguards. The rest waited with me as War Axe and Serpus supervised the unloading of the horses. I wore my mail shirt and had my helmet on my head.

Pucco looked nervous. He waited with me. He said, "You will not be needing me much longer."

Stormbringer had just been landed and I was seeing to him when the slave spoke, "What do you mean?"

"You now have more of our words. I notice how you have picked them up."

"Then do you want to return to Gades?"

He said, "It is not up to me. I am now the property of Captain Bomilcar."

"Here, hold my horse's reins." I took Crow's reins and examined him to see if he had been damaged. He had not.

Pucco said, "In any case once you begin to do that for which you were hired, fight, then I will not be there."

I knew that he was right. I smiled at him and took the reins of my horse as well as Crow's. I began to walk them along the quayside. "I shall miss you. We all will miss you."

He walked with me and nodded, "Until I was assigned to you I led a lonely life. You and the others have been kind to me. I have enjoyed the conversations and the laughter."

"If you serve the captain then we will still see you."

He shook his head, "It will not be the same."

He was right.

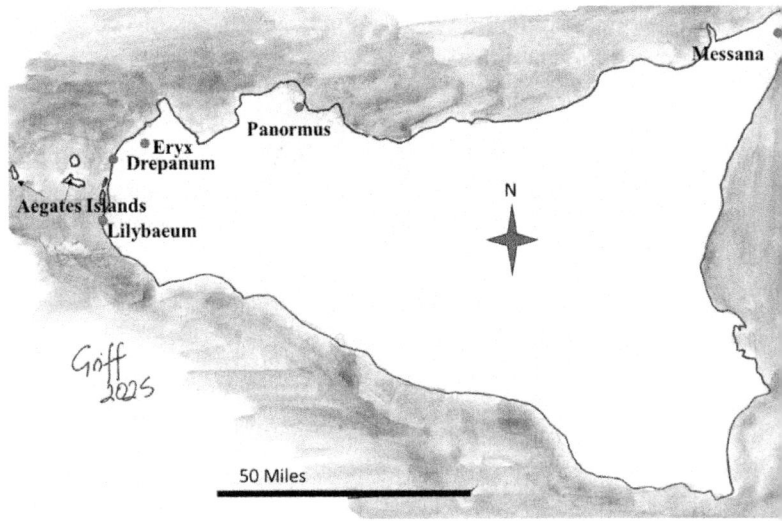

Figure 2 Sicily

Chapter 3

When Captain Bomilcar returned the change in him was obvious from his manner and his tone. He spoke directly to me and almost ignored Pucco. He obviously chose his words for he spoke slowly and was measured. I understood almost every word and his meaning was clear.

"You and the men will mount your horses. You will ride side by side behind me and my guards. You will ride quietly."

I nodded to show I had understood. I pointed to Pucco, "And Pucco?"

He looked at him as though he was an afterthought. He said to him, "You will ride one of the spares. Do not fall off."

"Yes, Master."

The officer turned and went to mount his horse, Aeneas. I saw that he and his bodyguards had their helmets on their heads. I said, "Don your helmets. We ride in pairs and there is to be no noise." I smiled, "We are now part of an army."

Pucco said, "I have never ridden a horse."

"Do not worry. The saddle will hold you in. Alerix, Pucco is to ride a spare. Lead his horse for him."

"Aye, Chief."

On the ship there had been no need for orders but now there was and I was addressed as chief for the first time. I had given an order and Alerix had responded. I did not feel like a chief but I knew that the honour had been thrust upon me. I hung my shield from one of the pommels and I mounted. "Serpus, you had better ride next to me."

Our officer waved his arm and we headed out of the port. The other transports would have to wait for a berth so that they could unload. We did not have far to go for the port was under siege. That came as a shock to me. I knew little of either the Romans or the Carthaginians but I had assumed that we were coming to help conquer the island. When we stopped just half a mile from the port I realised that was not the case. We were here to cling on to the parts of the island still held by the Carthaginians. When the captain halted us we were close to a wooden defensive barrier that had been erected beyond the city walls. I saw a variety of soldiers including some who looked like Gauls. They had the same moustaches as we did and some were tattooed like War Axe.

The officer said, "Dismount and fetch your weapons." He was keeping his commands simple. "Guard the horses."

I said, "Alerix and Bellerix, guard the horses, all of them. Keep Pucco here."

"You may need me."

"Stay here."

We followed the officer to a cluster of other officers. Wild Eyes, another of the bodyguards we had named, held up a hand. He said, "Stand here." To emphasise his meaning he pointed. He and the others went with their officer. Three of the Gauls who were lounging nearby came over. They were not from our part of the world, they had the colouring of those who lived beyond the mountains but we shared many words. They came from north of the village we had raided.

Thanks to my shaven face and my mail I was recognised as a leader and the man who approached me was also a leader; he had a torc around his neck as well as a long moustache. His hair came out of the top of his helmet. "I am Autaritus and I lead a band of mercenaries. This is my lieutenant, Cai."

"I am Bruneus and I lead this warband." I liked Autaritus from the first moment I saw him but not so Cai. There was something about him that jarred with me.

It may have been the lack of smile. Autaritus had a genuine smile. Cai seemed to sneer. Whatever the reason we disliked each other from that moment on.

"There are not many of you. Have you been in Carthage?"

I shook my head, "We came from Gades." I hesitated. Should I be honest with this man or not? I realised that we all looked young and any lies on my part would soon be discovered. "This is our first time as warriors for hire."

He just nodded, "You were lucky to make it through the Roman blockade."

"We were attacked but there were just three Roman ships and one was sunk."

"You are the first convoy to make it for three months. We need the supplies that you bring." He shook his head, "We are clinging on and holding two places, this one and Lilybaeum to the south. Luckily for us their leaders are not as skilled in the ways of war as Hamilcar Barca. He is a clever man." He pointed to the officers and it was clear to whom he referred. Captain Bomilcar and the other officers were all standing around him.

"Where are your horses?"

He smiled, "You don't need horses here."

"Then why were we brought here?"

He shook his head, "I do not know but it is interesting is it not? The officer who brought you, he is a noble."

"You know him?"

"No, but if you look at the other officers they are dressed the same way and our general likes to surround himself with such nobles. Not only does it provide comfort to have the support of noble families, but it also helps to have others to blame for failure. If this island is lost then someone will have to pay. Hamilcar Barca is a good general for he has cunning and guile." His voice became serious, "He is also ruthless. He had some mercenaries executed for failing to stop some Romans from taking an outpost."

I began to wonder if our decision to hire our swords had been a wise one.

"Watch out. Here he comes." Autaritus and the other Gauls began to look busy as the general, our captain and the bodyguards approached. I said, "Serpus, go and fetch Pucco. We might need him."

I saw that Hamilcar Barca was only a little older than the young captain. That surprised me. My father, uncle and War Hammer, had all been older warriors, veterans. They were leaders who had experience. It was hard to see what experience these two young men could have had.

The general spoke. Luckily he used words I understood.

"You are the leader of these warriors?"

"I am."

"Do you know why you are here?"

I wondered if this was a trick question. Had I misunderstood him? I said, slowly, "We are here to fight for you against the Romans."

He smiled. Serpus and Pucco approached and the smile disappeared. The captain said, "This is their translator. He is a slave."

The general said, "I would speak with you. I will speak slowly. Let the slave listen in case there are misunderstandings." I nodded as did Pucco. "I have been waiting for your arrival. Captain Bomilcar was sent to find horsemen. You are little more than boys but..." He waved a hand as though to dismiss the doubt, "We have few horses on this island and we will have to make do with you." He pointed to the mountain we could see in the distance. "That is Mount Eryx and there is a Roman garrison there. The mountain helps them to besiege this town and they have taken the Carthaginian city of Eryx."

I nodded my understanding. Thanks to Pucco and the words I had spoken on the ship I knew what a siege was.

"I need you, under the command of Captain Bomilcar, to slip through the Roman lines and discover the number of Romans who are there."

"And return here?" I asked.

"And return here."

"When, General Barca?"

He smiled, "Tonight."

I had hoped for some time to build up the strength of our horses but that was not to be and I gave him the answer he wanted. "Yes, General."

"Eat and then you will leave as soon as it is dark." He and the captain, along with their bodyguards left us.

Autaritus hurried over, "Spoken to by the general, eh?" It was clear that he wanted to know the reason.

"We are to sneak out tonight and scout out that mountain."

"Getting out is easy enough but I am not sure you will be able to return as easily."

"What are these Romans like?"

"When they fight as they have been trained, they are formidable. They have three types of soldiers. There are the lightly armed and younger warriors, velites. Then there are the more experienced ones who fight with locked shields, hastati or principes, and finally there are their elite troops, the triarii. They are older warriors and they are hard to beat. When you see mailed warriors then try to avoid them."

"Horsemen?"

"They have a few, called equites." He shrugged, "We have not seen many of them. They use them as scouts."

"The general said something about eating first."

Autaritus nodded, "Come to our camp. Now that the ships have arrived there will be more food."

"How have you managed up to now? No ships for three months suggests that you would be starving to death."

Autaritus smiled, "We raid the Romans. They are well supplied but there is little meat in their diet. What we have we will share."

"Why are you being so generous to us?" I could not help but be suspicious.

He shrugged, "When you leave the city there may be an opportunity for you to raid. If you do then you would share with us, would you not?"

I nodded, "Aye."

His lieutenant stood. He had a scar on his face which gave him a permanent look of disdain. That was not his fault but he was also a most unpleasant man. I noticed that his arms were also scarred and he had many battle rings upon his arms. The man had won many combats. I did not like him before he spoke. Afterwards there was a barrier between us. He said, "Why do we waste food on these boys? The are fodder for pila and will soon be dead."

"Because, Cai, I am captain and I say we share."

Giving me a look of irritation, he stormed off. "Cai is a good warrior and he leads well but…" I was not really sure what he meant for I had no men like Cai serving with me.

He was right about the food. There was no meat but it was flavoured with something that tasted hot. We ate. While we filled our bellies we learned more about the Romans. Unlike the Carthaginians they did not use mercenaries. They had good weapons and powerful machines that could throw a bolt or a stone. "If you defeat them then they have armour and weapons that are worth taking." Autaritus' lieutenant, Cai, had a mail shirt he had taken from a dead Roman.

Autaritus said, "But first you must defeat them and you are going to need all your luck just to stay alive. If you come back…" He let the words hang in the air. It was suggesting that we might not return. "And if you do not," he pointed to the spare horses that had been brought closer to us, "then we shall look after your spares."

I was going to say no then I realised what he meant. If we did not return then it would not matter if we gave permission or not. "Of course, but I hope to return."

After we had eaten we prepared to leave. Darkness would descend and then we would slip out of a small gate in the defences. To help us to leave there would be an attack on the far side of the siegeworks as a distraction. I had contemplated shedding my mail shirt as I thought it might make a noise but as the captain and his bodyguards would be wearing more metal I decided to keep it on. The jingling metal might be heard but I wanted its protection.

"Pucco, you stay with the horses and with Autaritus. If we do not return…" I shrugged.

Captain Bomilcar strode up, "It is time. I want you and half of your men to lead and half to be at the rear." To emphasise his words he pointed. "There will be no talking and we shall use hand signals." In the short time I had been in the camp I had picked up more words that would be useful. Autaritus had helped. He knew many words that were unfamiliar to Pucco. We were to protect him. It was his eyes that would gather the information for the general.

We waited behind the gate and listened to the silence. There were eight archers, they were Cretan, who waited with string bows. They were there to prevent any cries of warning. Autaritus had said that the evenings were quiet. If there were raids either from the defenders or the besiegers, they came at dawn. General Barca had planned well. The distraction began. On the far side of the defences we heard the cries and the clamour as men rushed from our defences to slay unsuspecting sentries.

The gate opened and the archers with nocked arrows raced out. I led Stormbringer out. The archers were scanning the Roman defences, more than two hundred paces from us they were formidable. They had built a rampart and placed wood there. This was a moonless night and we could see no movement. I guessed that any sentries would be listening to the noise of battle further along the wall. I knew there was no point in mounting my horse yet. It would only attract attention. I concentrated on heading along the gap between the two sets of defences. Luckily it was wide and we could keep to the ditch to our left. The mountain was a dark lump ahead but until we passed the last of the defences then I just had to keep to the land that divided the two armies. I could hear the shouts, screams and clash of arms but they seemed far off. What I did not hear was the twang of a bowstring.

The ground began to rise and I was aware that we had left the walls of Drepanum behind. I glanced to my right and saw the last wooden Roman tower. I did not mount my horse but led him towards a stand of trees that had managed to avoid being used for either walls or firewood. Once there I waited until the rest of the men arrived. The captain nodded when he reached me and mounted. I waved my arm to signal my men to mount and I mounted. I had not brought a heavy spear but I had a throwing spear. I held it in my right hand. My shield still hung from one of the pommels on my left. The captain pointed for me to move and I kicked Stormbringer on. The town of Eryx had been visible during the hours of daylight but all we had to guide us in the dark were our noses as we headed towards the smell of woodsmoke. The ground rose gently. One does not build a town on a steep slope. The mountain after which the town was named towered over the town and Roman camp. We worked our way up a hunter's trail that wound up through rocks and scrubby undergrowth.

When I had raided with my uncle I had been a novice but the experience of the raid was etched in my mind. I stopped and held up my hand. I knew that there were men ahead of me. I handed my reins to Serpus and turned to the captain. I pointed at me and then the path ahead. He nodded. After taking off my helmet and hanging it from my saddle I headed off through the thin undergrowth. I was careful not to brush the bushes with my legs or javelin. Such sounds could alert an enemy. I remembered how the creaking of the gate in that first village had caused the raid to end in near disaster. I stopped when I saw the camp wall. There was a ditch and a wooden wall with towers guarding the gates. I could hear the sentries talking. I had done what I intended and now it was time for the captain to take over. I walked backwards, watching the gate until I reached a place that I could turn around. When I reached the captain I mimed success. He nodded. He pointed at Serpus and me and the path. I saw Wild Eyes shake his head but the captain was adamant. He did not want his bodyguards. He took off his helmet and handed it to Wild Eyes. He drew his sword and pointed towards the path. Serpus had taken off his helmet and he held his javelin. I went back along the path with the two men behind me. It was much easier the second time. This time I knew when I would be near to the walls of the camp.

When I stopped I waved the other two forward but I continued to scan the walls for danger. The captain, I deduced, would need to see more than the gates and the walls. I saw a depression that ran to the left. If we used it we could move along and around the wall and yet remain hidden. I saw the captain studying the walls. I pointed to the depression and he nodded. I led. My eyes had become accustomed to the dark and could make out shapes. I was aided by the voices from the walls. The captain arrested my progress a couple of times while he studied the wall. Each time he did so I looked ahead. I saw, after one such stop, that the depression no longer followed the line of the ditch. What there was, instead, were some scrubby spiky bushes. They would have to do. When the captain tapped my shoulder I mimed crawling and he nodded. We crawled until we reached the bushes. They turned the corner of the camp and ended at a drop. The camp had been built to use the natural defences, the rocks. We could go no further. The captain pointed back the way we had come and we made our way back. I was keenly aware that time was passing. The sun would soon rise and we would have to hide. Did the captain intend to stay out all day?

It took a long time to get back to the horses and the others. I saw that the sky to the east had the hint of light about it. Dawn would not be too far away. No words had been spoken and the captain was not going to break that silence. He pointed back to Drepanum. He was not going to hide but we would attempt to break back into our besieged port. It was a risk. I donned my helmet and mounted. I waved for Serpus to ride next to me. When we had scouted then single file was the best. With dawn approaching I needed someone next to me. Autaritus had said that raids took place at dawn. After the distraction of the late night attack men would be wary as they watched on the walls. Not a single word had been spoken since we had slipped from the gates and when the single command was given it sounded to me, like thunder.

"Faster!" The captain did not shout it but hissed it and yet it made me think of the creaking gate. That innocuous sound had cost Barcas and War Hammer their lives. I urged Stormbringer on. I led my men but I was under the command of another. As we moved faster so the hooves of the horses sounded louder. They did not exactly thunder but they would be heard in the silence of the night. The single word might not have been heard but a man would have to be deaf not to hear the sound of hooves as they rode over a path which was covered in rocks and stone. I glanced to my left and saw that the false dawn had now been replaced by the start of the real dawn. Ahead I could see the start of the two defences. When we had left in the night we had travelled for four hundred paces before we had passed the end of the wooden Roman walls. We would have to endure four hundred paces of danger. I reached down to pick up my shield and slipped it over my left arm. I then transferred my javelin to my left hand. My right hand would have to guide my horse. What I worried about was my men. They had learned much since we had taken the horses but none of that learning was natural. They fought better on foot than they did when mounted. In addition not all of them were good riders yet. Green Eye and Cestrus did not seem to be able to make their horses move as fast as we did. It had not been a problem on the road to Gades but here it might be crucial.

The Romans used horns for signals. That morning, as the sun's rays peered over the eastern horizon, was the first time I heard them. Their noise told me that we had been heard. We were still hidden slightly because the sun had yet to rise but the land was lighter. I kicked Stormbringer on and Serpus did the same. Alerix and Bellerix emulated us and I heard the hooves of the heavier horses of the captain and his bodyguards as they rode faster. The general would have men waiting for us but I knew that the advantage would lie with the Romans. They could line the walls and use stones and arrows to shower us. Our service to Carthage might be brief and end in disaster. Was I cursed to lead men to their deaths?

The command that came from the walls to my left were not words I had heard before but I knew what they had ordered as I heard the whirr of slings and the twangs of bows. A stone smashed into my shield with such force that it hurt my hand. I ducked my head down and urged my horse on. We could do nothing in reply. If I tried to throw my javelin I would have to expose my chest. Behind me I heard cries as men were hit. They were my men but I could not turn around to view them. I saw the gate opening and the Cretan archers sent their missiles at the Romans on the walls. We were the target and not the archers. The arrow that slammed into my shield broke through the leather and wood. The metal head was close to my leg. I had been lucky. I clutched at the horse amulet I had taken in the raided village. Stormbringer and Crow were the best horses we had and as we neared the gates I was aware that they had opened a lead. I whirled around as I passed beneath the gate and pulled up my shield. Alerix and Bellerix galloped through. I saw the captain. He had survived but only two of his bodyguards were with him. Two riderless horses followed. White Scar and Wild Eyes were not on their animals. I counted my men as they passed through the gate. War Axe had survived as had Aed, Hostus, Sercix and Wal. The other four horses, like those of the bodyguards, were riderless. It was Serpus who shouted, as the last horse passed me, "Bruneus, inside, now!"

I turned my horse and, as I did so, the stone struck my back. It was only my mail that stopped me from having a bone broken. I had been wise to wear the mail and the padded undershirt. My luck had held but Galm, Tadgh, Green Eye and Cestrus had none. Perhaps Green Eye and Cestrus had been slow and the other two had paid the price. My warband had shrunk. A third of my men had perished the first time they had been used.

I had not been the only one to be hit by a stone. Hostus had been hit on the leg by one of the egg shaped lead balls the Romans used. He was lucky that the bone was not broken but he limped for some days after.

The captain looked shocked. He had lost two bodyguards, just Snake Eyes and Scarred Nose remained. I dismounted and, after pulling out the arrow, hung my shield from my saddle. I checked Stormbringer but he was unharmed. Pucco ran over. He saw the riderless horses. "They died."

I nodded, "They either died or fell. I did not see them."

Sercix said, "I was at the back and I saw them fall." He held up his shield. Like mine he had an arrow sticking from it. "They were slow to raise their shields and Green Eye was moving too slowly. I began to overtake them." He shook his head, "I wanted to live." I nodded. "Tadgh was held in place for a few strides by his pommels but then he fell. They are all dead."

"The bodyguards?"

Aed said, "Stones struck their helmets." He shook his head, "I thought a helmet would protect against such weapons."

The captain had recovered. His voice, whilst not exactly cold, seemed to ignore the six men who had died, "I do not need you. Join the other Gauls until I send for you."

He and his bodyguards headed for the general who was striding towards them. Pucco said, "Autaritus has food cooking."

I shook my head, "First, we tend to the horses and honour our dead."

He nodded.

We took the saddles off the horses' backs and dried them with the blankets. The food captured from the Romans suited our horses too and we fed them grain and watered them. That done I had the men gather around me. "Today we have lost men, friends and brothers in arms. They did not die with swords in their hands but they died as warriors. We will honour them and each night we drink to their memory." They all nodded. I would never forget Barcas and War Hammer. They had died in battle. It was how you honoured the dead whose lives had been ended abruptly. As we stood in silence I wondered if I had made the right choice. Had we taken the wrong path? We could have stayed in our homeland and made a life for ourselves. Our decision to become swords for hire looked to be a poor one.

We ate with Autaritus and the other Gauls. They had lost brothers in arms and knew that silence was needed. No one spoke while we ate. I said, after the men had eaten, "Sleep while you can. I know you need it."

War Axe smiled, "Aye, I am weary and yet I wish I had hewn some heads. I like not this scouting. I want to fight."

Autaritus said, "And you will. I have heard a rumour that the general has made plans. Your scouting expedition will have given him the ammunition he needs. It was necessary."

"And yet four men lost their lives. I could have gone with just the captain and his bodyguards. My men were not needed."

Autaritus sounded sad, "And if just six of you had ridden then you all might have died. Six men died did they not? That is war."

I did not want to sleep. I did not lie down for I feared that, if I did, the faces of the dead would haunt me. They would reproach me for my poor skills as a leader. Pucco followed me around. I smiled, "Let us use the time well, Pucco. Teach me some more Carthaginian." While the others slept I learned more words. Concentrating on the lesson kept the faces from filling my head.

When he rose, just before noon, Serpus came over to us. Pucco had fallen asleep for he had waited for us in the night. The slave's head rested on my saddle. My oldest friend said, "You did not sleep?" I shook my head and Serpus sighed, "A warrior needs sleep."

"There are four warriors who now have eternal sleep." I lowered my voice, "Was it a mistake to come here?"

Serpus sighed, "We all wished for this, even Bellerix. What was the alternative?" I did not answer for I could not think of another solution. "We could have all died on the raid along with Barcas and War Hammer but you held us together. The life we have had since that day has not been that bad. The bones have been cast, Bruneus. You cannot go back and change the past. Only a fool tries to change what has already happened. We become better warriors. The hole in your shield shows that you could have died but you did not. The ones who were slow to raise their shields have paid the price."

"What about the bodyguards? They were struck in the helmet."

Serpus said, "Just because they wear fine armour does not make them good warriors. Did they have shields?" I nodded. "Then they made the same mistakes as Tadgh and the others."

He was right and I resolved to put such thoughts from my head and make sure that the next time we went into battle we were better prepared. We were left alone for a whole day. While Autaritus and the other mercenaries did their duty on the walls we did nothing. As there were no attacks then we had a peaceful time. I made sure that we all learned more Carthaginian words as well as practising with shield and spear. We did not use them from the backs of horses. While we were besieged we would be fighting on foot.

Autaritus, who I learned was the captain of the Gaulish mercenaries, was summoned to a meeting the next day. He came back late. Apparently there had been wine.

The captain and his two remaining bodyguards returned the day after Autaritus's meeting. They had been in the port with the general. He seemed to be a different man. He had lost two bodyguards and come close to death himself. Alerix had told me that the captain's horse, Aeneas, had a wound to its rump.

For the first time since I had known him he actually smiled, "How are the lessons in words coming along?"

I did not recognise the word lesson but I worked it out from the rest of his words. I said, "Better."

"Good." He waved over Pucco who translated his words. "You and your men, or most of them, are to bring their weapons and blankets. We are sailing with the general."

I saw Pucco's face as he translated although I had picked up half of them. He looked surprised. Why were we leaving and why not take all the men? "Leaving?"

"Yes. You just need to leave two men to watch the horses and they will take their orders from the Captain of the Gauls, Autaritus." When those words were translated he added, "You are to leave now." He turned and left.

I saw that the men had all been studying us. Autaritus walked over and said, "I did not have time to speak to you last night." He gave a weak smile, "To be truthful I had too much wine. I am to watch over two of your men and your horses."

"What are we going to do?"

"The general is a clever man. He has sent for men from Lilybaeum. They are waiting in transports in the harbour. They managed to sneak in yesterday. He intends to launch an attack on the garrison at Mount Eryx, the camp you scouted out the other day. You and your men will be fighting with them but on foot."

Serpus and the others had been listening. War Axe said, "Who are you leaving here?"

I pointed, "Hostus, you were wounded. You will stay and take orders from the Gaul, Captain Autaritus."

"The wound is healed. I can come with you. Do not leave me here alone." Hostus always seemed younger than his years.

I smiled, "I have to leave someone. Wal is your friend as well as being family. He can be the other. The rest of you get your war gear and follow me. We are going back to sea!"

Chapter 4

The majority of the transports were already standing off shore. There were just two left. Men were boarding them both. I saw Snake Eyes and Scarred Nose at the foot of the gangplank leading to one of them and I headed for it. While Wild Eyes and White Scar had not liked us and made it clear that they did not, the two remaining ones seemed indifferent to us. Snake Eyes said, "This is our ship. The captain is aboard. You will find a place." He grinned, "It will be crowded."

He turned and led his companion aboard. War Axe said, "At least there is no horse shit for us to clean up."

The ship was already crowded but War Axe used his bulk to push us to a corner close to the larboard bow. There were only seven of us and Pucco. We did not need as much as most of the units. Having travelled on one ship already we knew how to make it comfortable. I had carried my mail, helmet, javelin, spear and shield and now I laid the shield against the gunwale along with my spear. I fastened my helmet to a stanchion using the leather thongs. I then laid my blanket out. What we really needed were cloaks. Although they were not needed for warmth they made good tents and offered protection from the sun. If we had spent longer in Drepanum I would have sought some.

Pucco looked worried I asked, "What is the matter?"

"I heard men talking. We go to fight and I am not a warrior."

I shook my head, "You will stay at the camp. I order it so."

"And if you do not return?"

I sighed, "I cannot answer for the future. If I had the ability to look into the future then life would be so much simpler. Let us take one day at a time."

War Axe said, "And at least we will have the chance to fight. I have not had any opportunity to use the war axe since I took it in the village raid. I want to cleave skulls."

Sercix said, "And there may be treasures to be taken if we win."

I said, "Autaritus told me that the ones with the mail will be the best soldiers. The ones they call," I looked at Pucco, and said, "Triarii, is that right?"

He shrugged, "I do not know the word."

A Carthaginian solder had been listening and he said, to Pucco, who translated, "Velites are lightly armed young warriors. They swarm before their hastati, their spearmen. Then come the principes who are more heavily armoured and finally the triarii, who are the veterans." He laughed, "I do not think you virgins will get much beyond their velites, but as you are mercenary bodyguards for a noble then I do not think you will have to fight." The problem with translations was that the man had turned to speak to his friend by the time Pucco had translated. We had no chance to argue with him.

I saw, as I stood, that there were some of the imposing warships that had brought us here and they were waiting beyond the small islands. When we were loaded then the sails were hoisted and we edged our way out of the harbour. The general led and we were relegated to the rear. It was slow going for the winds did not cooperate. The warships sailed to the seaward side of us as we headed north. It took until the middle of the afternoon for us to negotiate the land which jutted out into the sea. The mountain we had scouted looked to be hard to climb. Perhaps we had taken the easiest route. When we turned the winds were in our favour and as the afternoon slipped by we headed towards a small natural harbour to the west of Mount Eryx. The warships positioned themselves out to sea while our transports edged gingerly into the beach. The gangplanks were not run out from the side but over the bows. It allowed the ships to stay afloat. Although our captain had been relegated to the rear of the column of ships, he was clearly a senior officer on this ship and we were the first off. We jumped into waist deep water and then moved up the beach. The general had landed first and he sent some men up to ensure that we were able to land unmolested, although I saw no sign of anyone.

Captain Bomilcar said, "Wait here with me." He sent Snake Eyes, who I learned was called Bodoster, to hurry up the other men he would be leading. It was only then I realised that we would be fighting alongside Carthaginians for the first time. We would all be on foot. The general had brought no horses with him. There was no settlement to be seen. No woodsmoke drifted down to us. Hamilcar Barca had found an empty part of the island. We were hidden from the Roman camp and the Carthaginian settlement of Eryx that the Romans had taken.

By the time the scouts had returned, the ships had landed the soldiers and the food. It was deemed safe enough for food to be cooked. We ate with the captain and the Carthaginians. I quickly realised that the men he led were from his family lands. They were his retainers. None had mail but they each had a helmet, shield and spear. The food was not what we were used to. It seemed to be more peppery than ours but I did not mind its taste. I found that we could now understand far more words than when we had boarded that first ship in Gades. We were able to listen to conversations between Carthaginians and understand them. After we had eaten I went to the sea to make water and it gave me the opportunity to see the different types of soldiers as they made their camps. There were heavily armed and armoured spearmen. I wondered how much use they would be on rough terrain. There were many ordinary spearmen like the captain's retainers. There were men with dark skin and wild hair. Pucco came to make water too and I asked him about them. He did not know but he scurried off to ask someone. When he came back he said that the ones with the round shields and the single greave were called Adyrmachids. They had cropped hair and contrasted with the Garmentian warriors who had no shields but carried javelins, spears and a curved sword. The men were of a similar colouring but looked totally different. I recognised the slingers and found out that they were from the islands that lay off the coast close to our home. A group of them had passed by our village on their way to fight in a local war. I had been a young boy and they had made an impression on me. There were archers with the horned bows that could send arrows through metal. My uncle had been badly wounded by such a bow. Then there were the levies from the southern part of our land. They had curved swords, neat conical helmets, a small round shield and throwing javelins. All in all we were as different as we could be and according to the Carthaginians, the Romans were all, roughly, the same type of soldier. There were another five hundred men like us. They were Gauls and had the same kinds of swords and shields that we did.

When I returned to our camp the others had also been observing the rest of the army. Serpus said, "Well, War Axe, it looks like you will get your battle after all."

War Axe was honing his axe and he grinned, "I cannot wait. I hope the men we kill have full purses."

We all laughed at his confidence. I just wanted to survive. I had lost four men and I wanted to lose no more. Scarred Nose came for me just as we were about to turn in. He waved for me to follow him. Pucco came with me. The captain spoke and, for the first time seemed to actually see me, "Bruneus," I realised it was one of the first times he had used my name. "Tomorrow we will be following the general to attack the Roman camp. You and your men will be with the other scouts and the slingers. I will lead the rest of our band with the main army. Your job is to find the enemy camp and fix their attention. You will be the bait that draws them on to our swords and into our trap. General Barca will have the rest of the army close on your heels and when the Romans come from their camp to rid themselves of you, you will fall back and lead them back to us."

It sounded like a dangerous task but, then again, we were being paid to fight. I just nodded.

"Bodoster will wake you and take you to the start line. Do not let me down."

I nodded, "We scouted the camp out, Captain, but I have no idea how many men are within it."

"Probably three maniples, that is roughly three thousand men." He said the numbers slowly and made a mark of the numbers in the soil with his dagger. "They must be drawn from their camp."

As I went back to tell the men I realised that the only way I could guarantee that, was if I risked all. If I did and I died then I would not care what he thought of me. Somehow the thought made me happier. My fate and that of my men was in my hands.

I sat them around me. We were just a small part of the men who would be sent. The others were all mercenaries. If we did not return then Hamilcar Barca would have saved Carthage money. Autaritus had told me that the war had already cost both countries much gold. If you did not have to pay a dead man then so much the better. None of us wore much armour. As I looked at the others who had been selected for this task I saw that I was the only one who wore mail. That would draw the attention of the Romans to me. They would see me as a leader. My handful of men, however, all had a helmet and a good shield. The slingers had neither. The levies from our homeland had a helmet but their shields were small and round. Their swords were curved. The African javelin men had no helmet and a handful of throwing spears. I saw the captains of the other men doing as I was doing and giving instructions. The difference was that the others looked to be experienced men who had done this before. This would be my first battle. The raid now seemed a distant memory. That night I had not led. All I had done was to salvage what we could from the attack.

"We are bait." There was little point in disguising the facts and they needed to know the truth. "We are being sent to lure the enemy from their camp and make them attack us. I will speak to those who come from our land to discover what their plans are." It was clear to me that the general wanted a piecemeal attack to give the impression that we were disorganised. Our breaking and feigned flight would confirm that. "While I am gone prepare your weapons. I will take my sling and my javelin. The spear I will leave here with Pucco."

Their silence told me that, like me, they were worried. Even the normally confident War Axe was silent. I headed to the camp of the levies. Their leader had spoken to them. There were forty of them. I had heard them speak on the transport and I knew that we spoke the same language.

"I lead the men below." I pointed.

"I know and I command these men. You have instructed them?"

"I have but I wondered what your plans were. You do not intend to die for our masters do you?"

He smiled, "No. We are being used, I know that." He pointed to the Africans, "They are wild men and they will try to get close to the Romans." He gestured to the slingers, "They will stay at extreme range for they are more skilled than the Roman velites. My plan is to sneak as close as I can get to their men who are collecting kindling. The Romans do this every day no matter where they camp. I intend to chase them back to their camp and as soon as we are seen, flee." He tapped his shield,

"Their bolt throwers can penetrate these easily and are more likely to hit flesh. Your shields afford more protection but a bolt will still smash through them. When we run we will be like hares."

"My men will approach at the end of your line."

He shrugged, "As you wish. There are, with the Africans and the slingers, less than one hundred and sixty of us but your handful are just a tiny part. I do not think that you will make a difference one way or the other. I wonder why you have been included."

As I went back to our camp the same thought rose once more in my head. When we had been asked to come I had wondered at the reasoning. Losing four men had seriously weakened us. Leaving two to watch the horses had also been unnecessary. I thought that the captain was relying on us trying to impress him and thereby garner praise from the general. I would obey orders but I would do all in my power to save all my men.

The six of them were talking when I returned, Pucco was watching them.

"Well?" Serpus looked up at me.

"We are the bait but there is hope. We will be raiding their work parties as they collect wood and forage for food. We sneak up on them and try to kill them. We will accompany the levies. That was my decision. They are not the largest number, they are the Africans, but those men are wild and reckless. The levies will fall back quickly and we will accompany them. Get some rest."

I took off my mail and padded undershirt before I laid down on my blanket. I clutched the horse amulet I had taken from the raid. That raid was supposed to have been my initiation as a warrior. My father had commissioned the smith to make me a torc and amulet. I had seen the work in progress and had been keen to be given them. They now lay with the ashes of my family. Someone would eventually find them and take them. I would never get to wear them. The horse amulet was poorly made in comparison but it was all that I had and so was now as precious as the golden torc would have been. I spoke to the dead as I held it. I prayed that they would hear me and that my father, Barcas and War Hammer would watch over me.

I was awake before Bodoster touched my shoulder. I had heard his footfall and my eyes opened as he looked down on me. He started but said nothing. It was dark but dawn was not far away. The bodyguard had been thoughtful by waking us early. We would have time to make water and eat before we left on this mission. I made water and then donned my padded undershirt and tunic. Pucco helped me to don my mail. I also had Barcas' helmet protector which I wore beneath my helmet. Before I put on my helmet I fastened my sword belt. I slipped my dagger into my boot. Serpus and I were the only ones with boots. They reflected the fact that we had been the horsemen. That done I put on my helmet and slipped my shield over my body using the long strap. I took my javelin and then looked at my men. They were all dressed and ready. All but War Axe had javelins. War Axe held his weapon two-handed. I rammed the javelin into the earth and took the bread Pucco proffered. I ate although it tasted like sawdust. He had used the last of the salted meat to give it some flavour but I ate it without taste. I used the ale skin to wash it down.

Bodoster said, "It is time."

I lifted my javelin and pointed it up the slope. To the east I saw a glow. We would be moving through the gloom of pre-dawn for a short time. As we neared the levies I heard a Roman horn in the camp. They were waking. Behind us Hamilcar Barca and the rest of the army were preparing to follow us and get into position. The levies had moved at the same time as us in a long loose line. We were the extreme left of it. The slingers were to the right and the Africans were in the centre. They were almost invisible in the darkness. The white of the slingers' tunics and the light colour of the levies also made them easier to see. Our duller browns helped us but the metal of our helmets would be picked out when the sun rose.

I studied the ground as we climbed the slope. There was no rush and better to reach the Romans unhurt than slip and carry an unnecessary injury. Serpus was on my right and War Hammer to my left. There was the length of a man's length between us. When we were seen the longer line would suggest more men than there actually were. The land rose and then dropped before rising again. The camp was hidden from view by a ridge. When the sun suddenly flared from the east it bathed the mountain in sparkling light. I saw the smoke rising from the village that lay above the camp, the village of Eryx. I could not see the houses. Hamilcar Barca was a clever man. He had found a bay where he could land unobserved. His speedy attack might catch the Romans by surprise. Their eyes would be on Drepanum and not this uninhabited side of the mountain.

I saw movement to my left. It was just in the corner of my eye but I slowed and studied it. I was rewarded by the sight of a Roman tunic. There were legionaries moving through the undergrowth. I hissed at the levy closest to me, "Romans!" and I pointed. He passed the word along and I saw the levies shift. The Africans and the slingers were too far away and I saw the flaw in the general's plan. We now became two groups of men and our mutual protection was gone. There were more than a hundred men to our right and we had less than fifty. The captain would expect us to do our job. I jammed my javelin into the ground and laid the shield next to it. I took out my sling. I could not load the sling one handed. The others, War Axe apart, copied me. When we were ready I slung my shield over my back and held the javelin in my left hand. We were all crouching as we moved, as were the levies. The land had dropped a little and I had lost sight of the Africans and the slingers. As we started to rise and climb through the scrubby trees and the thin undergrowth I was able to pick out the Romans. There looked to be less than twenty of them. I noticed that none wore the small breastplates that would mark them as hastati. They were velites. They wore wolf skins on their heads and carried slings and javelins. They were young warriors. I knew all of this from my talks with Autaritus. Being young meant that while they lacked experience they would be keen to impress and would fight.

We managed to get to within a hundred and fifty paces from them before we were seen. One of them had just bent down to pick up a piece of kindling and when he rose he must have seen the flash of the levy tunic. He dropped his wood and shouted. I saw him reaching for his sling and I whirled mine. He was an easier target than the horse guard had been in the village we had raided and his wolf skin afforded him no protection at all. He dropped like a stone. Even as the others sent their stones at the Romans and the levies drew their swords to run at them I heard a buccina far from the right. The Africans and Balearic slingers had been seen. The first part of the general's plan had succeeded. Our stones hit three men in total. The velites whirled their slings as we pulled our shields around and ran at them. Our shields afforded protection. We knew from Hostus' injury the effect of a lead ball. I held my shield before me and, when the stone slammed into it, the ball merely cracked against the wood as opposed to my helmet or flesh. We were running as fast as the ground would allow and I risked peering from behind my shield. The Romans were running.

We were like hunting dogs chasing prey. We stopped them from heading to our left and the levies to the right.

They were driven back up the slope to the camp. We could still not see the camp but the horns we heard told us that men were manning the walls. War Axe had not used a sling and, fool that he was, he had not swung around his shield. His luck had held and rather than being behind me he was ahead of me and running like a stag. He was gaining on a velite who looked to be tardier than the rest. The blood I saw on his leg suggested that he had slipped and been cut. Whatever the reason War Axe was catching him. The young Roman made a cardinal error. He turned to look behind him. War Axe must have presented a frightening sight. He was so close to me that I saw the terror on his face. As he turned to run he slipped. War Axe was on him so quickly that the youth had no chance. Our wild man gave him a merciful death. The axe split the wolf skin and skull in two. The slope rose once more and as we reached the top we saw the camp. They had cleared the ground before it and as it sloped down we and the levies were able to run faster. I saw that there were about forty other velites and they were all running for the gates. The walls were manned. As they were within sight of the walls the velites turned to show the officers their courage. They were going to each send a stone at us.

This was the first time that the rush of blood that comes from battle had entered my head. When we had fought at the village survival had been all that I could think of. Now we were hunters and our prey was within a hundred paces. We ran at the velites. We were aided by the levies. They were easier targets and the velites sent their stones at our allies. I pulled back my arm and hurled the javelin when I was just twenty feet from the nearest Roman. He was pulling back his arm to send a stone at the levies and the javelin struck him squarely in his middle. I reached him and pulled out the javelin. He was dying but his eyes were open and they stared at me.

I grabbed his bag of lead balls. They were better than the river stones I had.

I saw that we were below the level of the camp. I knew that there would be a double ditch. I had seen them when we had scouted. The levies had also stopped but the Africans were racing at the walls. The cracks from the walls were something I had never heard before. I did not see the machines that made the noise but I saw the bolts. I watched, in horror, as one took the head from an African and then continued as though it had passed through parchment. It struck another two.

The captain of the levy shouted, "Back. We have done what was intended."

I said, more for War Axe's benefit than anyone else, "Back!"

The order was too late for some of the levy. A bolt smacked into two of them. Then I heard the sound of the Roman buccina. We were labouring up the slope down which we had just raced and, as we neared the top, I looked around. The Romans had sent out some cavalrymen and they were heading in a long line. I knew that they would catch us. Behind them I saw the gleaming spearpoints as the legionaries, armoured and with shields left the camp. The plan of the general was working. We were leading the Romans into his trap. It would not matter to him if we failed to survive. We were a small enough sacrifice.

I shouted, "Whatever happens, stay together. That means you, War Axe!"

The Roman horsemen spread out in a line that allowed them to pick their way thought the obstacles that barred their way. As we dropped below the crest I saw that the levy were slightly ahead of us. Perhaps the bolt had given them wings. The frightening weapon had impressed me. We had barely reached the bottom of the next gulley when I heard hooves and saw the four horsemen at the top of the ridge. They had spears and shields. They would catch us. I made a decision. The infantry would take some time to reach us but even four horsemen could take us. "Turn and make a shield wall." I turned and held my javelin above it. Serpus locked shields but War Axe still had his behind his back. "War Axe, shield!"

"I need two hands for the axe."

"Shield!" He obeyed and we presented our shields to the horsemen.

The Roman cavalrymen had committed themselves and were charging down the slope. It took nerve not to turn and run for while the horses were not big we were all familiar with hooves and teeth. We had been told that horses would not willingly ride into men but this was not the time to discover if that was true.

"When I give the command throw your javelins. It matters not if it hits a horse or a man just long as it hits something." We liked horses but none of us would have any compunction about killing one to stay alive. When they were twenty feet from us I shouted, "Throw!" The five spears flew at the horsemen and their mounts. One hit a horse which bucked and reared. Another hit and killed a Roman. His body was held in place by his saddle. A third stuck in the shield of a Roman and as it dropped a fourth javelin hit his arm. We learned that day the truth about horses. They tried to avoid us. War Axe used his axe one handed and when it smashed into the skull of a horse the animal died and the rider fell beneath it. I drew my sword and slashed at the wounded Roman. Sercix and Aed ran at the Roman whose horse had bucked and, attacking from two sides, slew him. I saw that the Roman I had killed had a long sword and I took it.

Serpus shouted, "Run!" I looked up and saw a line of legionaries at the top of the ridge. We ran. The undulating ground and the rocks helped us for the Romans were trying to keep their formation. At the next rise I saw that the levies, or some of them at least, had been caught by the other horsemen. Unlike us they had tried to outrun the horses and they were paying the price. The spears found unprotected backs and the levies died. I had no idea where the ambush was to be but I remembered that there was just one more ridge before the land descended to the beach. For the moment the horsemen were finishing off the levy but then their attention would turn to us, the Africans and the slingers.

"Whatever we do we fight as one."

We ran together in a wedge with me at the fore. The next rise appeared and I saw the ships in the bay. I spied the camps with the fires preparing the food but what I did not see were the men who were waiting to ambush the Romans. I followed the fleeing levies who headed down the path we had used to ascend. It led to the camp. The general had left men to guard it. There were a hundred or so heavy infantry with spears and shields. When they saw us they sounded horns and formed a thin line. The Romans would sweep through them.

"Make for the beach."

To our left I saw that the slingers had almost all survived and they were nearly at the beach. The Africans had been decimated and the survivors were rushing to the sand. There were less than fifteen levies left and I did not see their captain. As we neared the thin line of infantrymen I saw that Captain Bomilcar and his two bodyguards were in the centre. Behind him I saw the rest of his men, the ones without armour. We would have less than two hundred men to defend the camp.

As we neared I heard Pucco's voice and realised that he was standing close to the captain. "Bruneus, you are to go to the left of us."

I nodded and veered in that direction. I heard Bodoster give a command and the single line of heavy infantry became a double one. It meant, when we joined the line, that we were closer to the captain and with retinue we

had four ranks deep. We were a solid square that would
be picked off by the Roman velites.

We had outrun most of their infantry but knew that
they were coming. We could hear their hobnails. I said,
"Double line." I saw the slingers form up behind our rear
rank. They had the protection of four ranks and yet their
slings could still hurt. The levy formed up on the right
but the Africans kept running. There were so few of
them left that I understood their reasoning but as the
transports were two hundred paces off shore they would
have been better off joining us.

The Romans reached the ridge and then formed up. I
saw their velites in a long, loose line before them.
Behind them were the hastati. They were the bulk of the
warriors. The third line, with their distinctive helmets,
were their elite, the triarii. Twenty horsemen had
survived and they were positioned to the right of the line.
There had to be two thousand men on the slope above
us. There was no way we could survive. The velites
moved first and then the ponderous two lines of heavier
armed legionaries followed. The cavalry waited. The
captain had chosen the highest piece of ground above the
beach. It was better footing than the sand would have
been but it meant when we were pushed back we would
be below the legionaries and in soft sand. Our graves
would be easy to dig.

The difference between the Balearic slingers and the
velites was the difference between boys and men. They
were both armed with the same weapon and the velites
outnumbered our slingers but the difference was that
ours had the greater range and the ability to send the lead
balls faster.

Bodoster shouted, "Shields!" We raised our shields.
The velites sent their stones at us and we used our
wooden shields and metal helmets to stop them doing
their worst. Our slingers aimed at men without helmets
and armour. Soon the numbers of stones being sent at us

thinned and our slingers broke the hearts of the young
velites. They began to pull back from the duel which
they were losing. Their hastati came on in their
immaculate lines. The centurions and optios urged them
on and the signifers held their standards aloft. They
came steadily and did not break step. The order to charge
must have been given for the front two ranks of hastati
ran at us. They each had two pila and when they were
within twenty feet of us they hurled their first one. The
lead balls our slingers sent meant some fell short and
none hit my men. I heard the spears as they slammed
into some of the shields of the men to our right. The
Balearic slingers thinned them a little but it was at that
moment that General Barca sprang his trap. He had
waited until his bait had drawn the enemy away from the
rocks and he charged them in the rear. The line of hastati
that struck us had no support. Their triarii were fighting
for their lives. I thrust my javelin at a legionary who
easily blocked it. They had not thrown their spears, their
pila, but they were trying to drive us back. The spears
that came at me scratched and scraped along my helmet
and drove through the top corner of my shield. War Axe
came into his own. Holding his axe one handed he swept
it into the side of the head of one of the legionaries. Even
one-handed War Axe was a strong man and the axe head
drove through the helmet and into the skull. As the dead
Roman dropped I darted my javelin into the face of the
man behind. In that moment we had a hole. They had
been two ranks deep and two men had fallen. I hurled
the javelin into the side of the head of the man fighting
Serpus and drew my sword. It was shorter than the
Roman cavalry sword I had acquired and easier to use.
The two men fighting Alerix and Bellerix had their
attention on my two warriors and when I drove my
sword into the ribs of one of them he was not expecting
it and he fell. War Axe hacked the head from another for
he had slipped his shield around and was using it two

handed. He carved his way through men who were terrified of the tattooed giant. Serpus was also now in the second Roman rank and he and Sercix slew another Roman. Although the rest of our line was fighting, our enemies had gone and with the other hastati and triarii having to fight the rest of our army, we simply turned and began to hack down the line of Romans. We had been on the left and that meant there were only pila and gladii to be faced. Their shields were on the wrong side and that was crucial. In a short time the Romans tried to flee. It was then that the Africans who had taken shelter behind our line and the slingers raced up. The front two ranks of hastati were being slaughtered and that meant plunder.

Captain Bomilcar tried to restore order and make the line move towards the main battle but it was forty paces from us. Men grabbed swords, helmets and daggers from the dead and dying. By the time there were none of the Romans we had fought left alive, the rest of the Romans had broken and fled back to their camp. Had we had horsemen then the victory would have been complete. As it was this was just a prelude to the battle for the mountain, the battle of Eryx.

Chapter 5

The general had lost another bodyguard. Only Bodoster was alive from those who had first followed him. Five of the men who had fought alongside the captain, his levies, were also dead. The captain seemed in a poor humour. I could not tell if he was angry with us because of the deaths of his people or because we had not obeyed him at the end. It did not seem to bother Hamilcar Barca who came to congratulate the men who had been bait. In a rare feat of generosity we were paid. Serpus was more cynical than the rest of us and he commented that it was cheaper to pay the survivors than pay the men before they attacked. Less than half of the bait had survived.

We had taken from the dead Romans and it meant Sercix now had a good helmet. I had taken a helmet but I still preferred mine. War Axe and Aed had each managed to take a bronze breastplate. It only covered their chests but it afforded them better protection than nothing. The ones I had killed had not worn armour but the shield of one of them was in better condition than mine. My original shield had been weakened too many times to repair. All that I needed to do was to put my design upon it. I had decided to paint a wolf upon it. The long sword I had taken was a good weapon and when we rode again would give me a longer reach than with my sword. While we fought on foot then my old sword would suffice. The caligae, gladii and pugiones were all welcome. The pugio I had retrieved had a finely decorated scabbard. All in all we were pleased with the outcome but, as we sat around a fire and Pucco served us food, there was some unease about the way we had been used. No one seemed concerned that so many had died. The results, it seemed, justified the means.

Bodoster had gone with the captain to a meeting with the general but some of the retainers who had fought alongside us had drifted over to our fire. They could not understand our words and, as we talked, I noticed them asking Pucco to translate parts.

"We know our worth then." Alerix did not hide the bitterness in his words.

"We are fodder for arrows." He and Bellerix had become as close as Serpus and I.

War Axe had taken a gladius and he liked weapons. He was sharpening it, "So long as we have finds like this I do not care."

"But we were almost overwhelmed," Alerix persisted.

I was the leader and I saw those like Sercix and Aed looking to me for my opinion. "First, Alerix, we are paid to fight and obey those who pay us." I held up the bag of coins. "Secondly, we were told that we would be the bait that would draw the enemy on and thirdly," I smiled, "we won and defeated the Romans. We have a clever general and I like that."

Serpus, as usual, backed me up, "Bruneus is right. This is not a bad life, Alerix. The food may not be the best but if we are here for a few more days that we can hunt. I saw the droppings of rabbits."

I said, "And did you not find it easier to fight on foot?"

Bellerix gave a grudging nod, "Aye, it felt good to be on the ground and if I am honest, I never felt that we would lose. Once War Axe killed his men we were the ones who, although outnumbered, were driving through them."

Serpus said, "There, then!"

"Yes, but what might have been?"

I sighed, "You cannot worry about what might have happened. Had it gone badly then we would all be dead and enjoying ale with our forefathers."

There was silence and one of the Carthaginians asked Pucco something. The slave said, "This soldier asks, if you fight this hard for Carthaginian, how hard would you fight for your home?"

I smiled, "A good question, Pucco, but tell him that we have no home." I patted the sand, "For the moment, this is our home. If we go to Carthage then that will be our home. We are a band of brothers and our weapons fight for each other and Hamilcar Barca."

When the words were translated, the man, whose name we learned, was Daco, smiled and nodded.

We were not given long to rest. When the captain returned he told us all, mercenaries and retainers, that we would be marching back to the Roman camp but this time we would be going as one army. There would be a battle. There was a change, however. The Carthaginian levy had been badly handled. Their leader had been killed and just fifteen remained. They were given to the captain who made another change. He made Bodoster the one to command the levy and his retainers. He wanted us to be his bodyguards. He did not give the reason but I believe it was because he saw the way we fought. Bodoster was happy to lead men and I think he now respected us. In terms of the battle it would mean that we would flank him. The captain asked for War Axe to guard his right. He had seen the effect of his mighty weapon. I guarded his left side. It also meant that Pucco would be with us. The slave would be going to war. I knew, as we packed up and prepared to head back up the mountain, that he had mixed feelings. He liked the idea of being with us but feared for his own safety.

"Do not worry, Pucco, when we fight then you stay as far back from the battle line as you can and, if we lose or look like losing, then you run, as fast and as far as you can."

He shook his head, "If you lose then where is there to run? The Romans control all the island but for Lilybaeum and Drepanum."

War Axe had been listening and he put a mighty mitt around the slave's shoulders, "And after the next battle we shall have Eryx! The Clan of the Lone Wolf will be the difference and we shall take this island, rock by rock if we have to."

I smiled. War Axe was a like a child in a man's body. He never saw problems and believed that his skill would always see him victorious. I was glad that he was on my side.

General Barca had no intention of being ambushed as we had ambushed the Romans. Once more the bait led the men up the mountain for we knew it, but this time the army was right behind us. The Roman camp was manned but when we arrived we could see fewer men. However, what we did find was another army that had marched from the siegeworks around Drepanum. The Romans clearly intended to use the camp to anchor one side of their line. The rest of their army stretched down the mountain and was angled towards Drepanum. I recognised some of the land from our scouting expedition. I could just make out, for we were to the left of centre, the sea and Drepanum. That was how close we were to our horses and my other two men.

I was new to battle but the contrast between the way the Romans fought and the Carthaginians astounded me. The Romans were set up the way they had been when they had attacked us in the bay. Their different troops were all dressed and armed almost identically. The feathers they wore in their helmets seemed their only difference. They stood in lines that were very straight and their leaders were all in the same place. Our army looked like twenty different armies all joined up together. Some of them, the ones who fought like Greek Hoplites and heavy infantry, stood in reasonably straight lines but many units just milled about. Some leaders stood out because they wore helmets and armour that were nothing like their men but others were dressed identically. Captain Bomilcar now led us, but we were just a handful along with his retinue and levies. The only armour worn by us was my mail shirt, the captain's breastplate, Bodoster's breastplate and the small bronze breastplates taken by War Axe and Aed. Our helmets and shields were all different. My men had oval ones and I now had a Roman one. The captain and Bodoster had larger round ones while the rest had smaller shields that varied from little more than a buckler to one almost as big as the captain's.

General Barca had no cavalry with him and that meant he was not mounted either. To make up for that he stood atop a rock to help him survey the battlefield. Our numbers looked to be evenly matched. This time our general appeared happy to let the Romans come to us. The slingers and the African javelin men were arrayed before us. When the Romans, seeing us squat there, decided to advance, a duel between their velites and our missilemen ensued. As with the previous encounter it was men versus boys and the Balearic slingers drove the velites from the field. This time no one fled from our side and when the hastati advanced they were not met with a wall of spears and shields but javelins, arrows and lead balls. As we had discovered when we had fought them, their small bronze breastplates were not very effective. The first maniples of hastati did not even reach our lines. The buccina sounded the retreat and the Romans pulled back. We lost a handful of men and they had suffered significant losses. Their leaders were not willing to risk their triarii against an unbroken enemy.

As the afternoon waned so the Romans decided to head back to their siege lines at Drepanum. They had brought enough cavalrymen to discourage us and they still had their ballistae on the ramparts of their camp. By the time darkness fell we were alone on the battlefield. It was then that Hamilcar Barca showed what, to me, was brilliance. The whole army moved, under cover of darkness, to pass the camp and head instead for the former city of Eryx, now a Roman stronghold. The Romans in the camp knew that we were moving. You cannot disguise the noise of an armoured army but the bolts they sent, blindly, killed just two men. That was a small price to pay. We stopped at dawn and found ourselves looking up at the city of Eryx.

Fires were lit and food was cooked. We had no siege lines yet but the city was surrounded. The men at the Roman camp could have tried to dislodge us but we had trounced them already. Some Roman deserters had surrendered to us in the pursuit after the battle and they spoke of the shock of their defeat. That first day we just rested and ate. Both were welcome activities. I studied the walls we would have to assault. It was a formidable fortress. Built into the rock there appeared to be few places where men could attack it. However, as I studied it I realised it lacked that which made the Roman camp below. There were few machines of war. I saw one onager and one ballista. Either the Romans thought that they were not needed or they had been too difficult to bring into the fortress.

I returned to the men. Like me they were in good spirits for we had outwitted the Romans. For the loss of a handful of men we had managed to send the reinforcements back to the siege of Drepanum and make the men in the camp hide behind their ramparts.

That evening, when we were well rested, the captain returned from his meeting with the general. We had our instructions. The captain did not like to speak to large numbers of men. I was not sure he actually liked to be close to them. He seemed to me to be a cold man. Perhaps I was misjudging him. I was used to men like my father and Barcas. They had been just as happy to speak to the man who tanned hides and always stank of piss as a noble. I had not seen the captain smile except when he spoke to another noble or the senior officer. The other thing about him was that he hated it when people were too physically close to him. He spoke to me, Bodoster and the man who had led the Carthaginian levy after their captain had died.

"We attack this night. We have a section of the wall to climb and then we kill the guards." Something in the way he spoke told me that he would be doing no climbing and from the look on Bodoster's face neither would he."

"Which section, Captain?" It was the Carthaginian who spoke. Pucco was close by and he whispered the translation into my ear although I had understood. Learning the language was like becoming used to a song that you sang. Once you were into its rhythm it became easier.

The hint of a frown told me that the captain was not happy with what we had been asked to do. His voice, however, was just as commanding as always. "You are to take the south east corner. There is a single tower."

I was new to this but the speed of our attack seemed too fast for me. I asked, "What time will the attack be launched?"

"Take the men there now and Bodoster will come when the general commands. Stay hidden until then." The last command was obvious. I could understand attacking at night. Shadows suited us and their war machines could do little damage. However, we needed to begin at the same time or else the first ones to try to ascend would alert the defenders.

The Carthaginian had more men to brief. I went to my handful. "We climb rocks and become spiders. Spears will encumber us and we will need our shields upon our backs."

Aed said, "There is but one fear in my heart, Bruneus, and that is a fear of heights."

Tadgh had been Aed's friend since childhood and Aed's voicing of his fears showed the effect of the death of his friend. War Axe said, "Climb up before me and I will help you."

"We are not alone in this but I will not rely on others. I will lead. Let us go now and see, before it gets too dark, what is the size of the problem." I decided to use the Roman helmet I had acquired.

The city rose above our camp but the camp was hidden by some trees. We moved through the trees and ascended the rocky outcrop. The ground fell a little before rising again. The hollow hid us and allowed us to get closer to the city unseen. We found a rock behind which we could shelter and see the rock wall and then the stone tower that was our target. It lay just eighty paces from us. Those eighty paces to the rock wall would be as dangerous for us as scaling the rock. It was not sheer. I saw handholes. It was the tower that presented the problem. It was old and the mortar was not the best but the handholes there would be difficult perches. I realised that the wall to the right was an easier option. While the tower rose twenty feet above the rock wall the stone wall was just ten feet and there appeared to be a ledge where the first stone blocks had been laid on natural stone.

I turned to the others, "When we climb then we aim for the wall to the right of the tower. War Axe will be our ladder. We climb him and slip over the wall."

"And how do I get over, Bruneus?" My bear of a man asked a reasonable question.

Pucco had come with us and while he would not be attacking he could still be useful. "Pucco, go back to the camp and find us some rope."

He turned and ran. I realised, as he headed back to the camp, that I could see the glow from the fires through the trees. If we had to fall back to our camp we had a beacon to guide us. The Carthaginian levy arrived. In the short time we had been observing the wall and tower, darkness had fallen. There was less to see. I guessed that their leader had endured even more complaints and questions. We moved slightly to the right to allow them to see the tower. It would make it easier for us to use the lower wall.

I examined the tower and wall while we waited for Pucco. The Romans liked order. I counted the sentries and saw that they all followed a regular pattern. There were four sentries in the tower and just three on the wall I intended to attack. There would be more men close to hand and ready to be roused if the alarm was sounded but if we could make the walls then we had a chance. Pucco arrived with a coil of rope. I handed it to Aed. He would be climbing ahead of War Axe. Having a task to perform might take his mind off his fear. I took a drink from my ale skin and handed it to Pucco. He would guard our things and wait for our return. As the night became even darker I clutched the horse amulet. It was a connection to my past. I had won it in war and I hoped that the gods would protect me so long as I wore it.

It seemed an age before Bodoster and the captain returned. They said nothing but I saw that the captain was not looking at the walls but back towards the camp. I looked back and saw at the same time as the captain, the brand that was covered and uncovered three times. It was the signal. He said, "Now."

Bodoster simply said, "Take the tower."

While the Carthaginians hesitated I did not and I led my men towards the section of wall I had chosen. I knew it was selfish as it forced them to take the tower. I knew that if we made the wall unseen then we had a much better chance of taking the tower. I was counting on my six men being better than the Carthaginians alongside whom we would attack. I also thought that my handful of men would be quicker. We moved like scuttling spiders and as there was just a handful of us we stood a better chance of evading observation. We were aided by our dark clothes for the Carthaginians all wore lightly coloured garments. We reached the rocks unobserved. I had seen our route before dark. I was the leader and I led. I put my hands on the two handholes I had spotted and I began my ascent. I was aided by the men who had built the walls many generations ago. They had chosen a section of wall that had an angle, perhaps it helped them to build or it may have been that the gods made the rocks the way that they were. Whatever the reason it made it easier than I had expected to climb the twenty feet to the base of the wall. There the natural edge gave a better foothold. The attack was spotted before we reached the defences themselves. I heard shouts from the walls and looked up. It was not we who had been spotted but the Carthaginians. Voices in the city were raised and feet pounded along the fighting platform as the sentries from above us ran to the tower. Had one of them looked over then we would have been seen. They did not. Inside I heard the Roman buccinas sound as the alarm was raised. All around the fortress General Barca's men were attacking. He was relying on our speed and the fact that the Romans were not expecting us. If we could gain the wall before the garrison was roused then we had a better chance of success.

I stood on the ledge close to the base of the wall. Once more the builders had aided us. It was only wide enough for my feet but I was able to stand. When my men were all up I took the rope from Aed. The grin on his face was one of relief. War Axe stood with his back to the wall and he cupped his hands. I placed my hands on his shoulders and my right foot in the cup of his mighty paws. He propelled me upwards with such force that I was able to reach the top of the walls easily. I rolled over and drew my sword. Two legionaries were coming from my right and running down the fighting platform to reach the tower. Looking back I think that they thought I was a sentry for they did not shout an alarm. My Roman shield and my newly acquired helmet helped with the illusion. They did not see me as an enemy. That would change when they neared me. Serpus landed next to me and I gave him the rope. Swinging my shield around I stepped to meet the two legionaries. It was my movement that alerted them but there was so much noise in the city already as orders were shouted and men ran to man the walls that their small cries went unheard. I held my shield before me as I ran at them. The wall was on my right and meant I could use my sword easily. Their shields were on their left. The drop from the fighting platform to the city was less than eight feet but when my shield connected with the man on my left and I punched, he tumbled to the ground below. His companion made a cardinal error. He glanced to his right and in such moments men can die. I rammed my blade under his bronze breastplate. I saw more men coming down the fighting platform. I sheathed my sword and picked up the dying Roman's pilum. It was a well balanced weapon and could be thrown as well as used as a thrusting weapon.

War Axe was just being drawn up the wall. I said, "Are we all here?"

Alerix said, "Aye, we are but the Carthaginians are struggling."

"Then let us take the tower. War Axe, lead!"

He took his war axe and grinned, "Aye, for I have been a ladder for long enough. Now I become a warrior once more."

"Serpus, guard our back."

The fighting platform was wide enough for two of us and I ran with War Axe. The door that led to the tower could be bolted from inside but the Romans did not yet know that the foxes were in the henhouse. We opened it and entered. There was a ladder from below and a second one that led to the top of the tower. The head that emerged from the ladder below was too tempting a target and when War Axe swung his weapon there was but one outcome.

I saw a door leading to the other fighting platform. I ran to it and dropped the bar in place. "War Axe, hold here. The rest of you with me, up the ladder." I realised that there was enough noise from above to disguise ours.

My helmet was a Roman one and my face might be mistaken in the dark. In addition, the first thing they saw when I rose through the opening was my pilum and that was a Roman weapon. When first my spear and then my helmet emerged through the opening, no one noticed or seemed to notice. I was able to stand and a Roman said something. He did not look back but I guessed it was an order for me. I stood to the side to allow the rest to ascend and I counted. There were twelve Romans and one of them was raising a rock to hurl down. We needed to kill as many as we could and that would allow the Carthaginians to climb. The tower was crowded. The only space where you could swing a weapon was close to the entrance we had just used. We also had the advantage that the enemy had their backs to us. I rammed the pilum into the back of the man with the rock. He was leaning over and he fell, clutching the rock. The man next to him turned and when he saw that I was not a Roman, he opened his mouth to shout something. He did not get the chance for I rammed the pilum into his neck. There were now ten men but there would be just five of us to fight them. It was all about speed and I thrust my pilum into the side of the officer. He wore a better breastplate and while my spear found flesh he was able to slash down with his gladius and break it at its weak point. The pilum was rendered useless. I drew my sword. My men were all up and I heard the sound of swords clashing. My men were fewer in number but we had the advantage that we were together and our arrival was totally unexpected. The Romans were attacked in the rear. I punched the officer in the face with the boss of the Roman shield and he reeled. My spear had wounded him on his right side and it made his shield arm weaker. I slashed with my sword above his drooping shield and hacked into his neck. By my count there were just nine men left and when Alerix stabbed one and Bellerix another then the odds were improving.

Serpus gutted a Roman who tumbled through the opening. Serpus called out, "War Axe! Ware above!"

I heard a maniacal laugh as War Axe shouted up, "A dead Roman killed a Roman!"

Aed shouted, "Watch out, Bruneus!"

I had almost made a fatal error. Instead of concentrating on the fight I had become distracted. The legionary with the pilum almost managed to spear me. The fight with the dead Roman officer aided me. My sword slashed at the same place that the officer had when he had damaged my spear. The wood behind the head cracked and the spear merely scraped along my leg rather than stabbing me. I punched at his face with my shield for his momentum brought him close. The short sword ended his life. He was an easy kill. Suddenly there was silence for all the defenders were dead. At that moment the moon appeared from behind a cloud and it was as though a brand had been lit. We could see everything much more clearly.

"Serpus, take Aed and help War Axe."

"Aye, Bruneus."

"Alerix, you and Bellerix make sure that they are all dead." I leaned over the wall and shouted, in Carthaginian, "The tower is ours!" I pointed, "Use the wall!" As the leader of the levy waved his acknowledgment I saw the white tunics of the bodies. They had lost twelve men and not even managed to reach the base of the tower. Pucco waved from behind the rock.

Alerix said, "They are all dead."

I nodded, "There will be a time to search the bodies for treasure but it is not now. Let us help the others."

When I reached the floor below it was eerily quiet. War Axe said, "They have learned that we hold this tower." He leaned back as an arrow was sent blindly up. It slammed into the roof beam.

I said, "Alerix and Bellerix, fetch some of those stones from the walls. Let us discourage them."

War Axe asked, "Do we not continue our attack?"

Serpus shook his head, "There are six of us. We were told to take the tower and we have taken the tower. Do not try to win this war on your own, War Axe."

I pointed to my right, "The Carthaginians are coming. Aed, stand by the door to the fighting platform and let me know when they arrive."

When he opened the door it allowed a little moonlight in and I saw that the room had six beds in it. It was a guard room. I saw that there were chests and I opened one. Inside was a bag of salt, a small statue of a god, a dagger and a bag of coins. I picked it up. It was not heavy but if the other guards had such treasure then we might profit. I also saw a cloak. I said, "Serpus, search these chests. Whatever we find we will share out later."

Alerix and Bellerix returned and began dropping stones down the ladder. No more arrows came our way.

"The Carthaginians are here." On hearing Aed's cry I went out to the fighting platform. The Carthaginians were using the rope we had left for War Axe and were now not only filling the platform but racing towards the gate.

The captain smiled and pointed his sword, "Captain Bomilcar has decided to join us now that you have succeeded."

I did not catch all his words but I worked out the meaning when I saw Bodoster and the captain coming. I also saw, to my dismay, that Pucco intended to join us or perhaps he had been ordered by the captain.

I nodded and said, "Now is the time to search the dead on the tower before the captain comes."

By the time the two men had climbed the wall we had taken everything from the dead Romans on the top of the tower. We had left the breastplate on the Roman and the helmet on his head. I guessed either the captain or Bodoster would want them.

The captain had that rarest of things on his face, a smile, "You have done well, Bruneus. Hold this tower while we take the city!"

"Yes, Captain." He and Bodoster hastened to the Carthaginian levies and the main gate. He would lead his men and when the general and he met he would think that Captain Bomilcar took the tower and not the six mercenaries. I did not mind. We had profited and none had been hurt.

As Pucco arrived I said, "Let us make ourselves comfortable. Bellerix, light the brands and see what food these Romans eat."

War Axe said, "And I will dispose of the bodies. I do not want the stink of the dead to put me off my food. I have a mighty appetite."

Chapter 6

We had taken the city on the mountain by speed and surprise. The Romans must have been expecting a long siege but Hamilcar Barca gained the initiative by attacking them so quickly. It was he and his chosen men who stormed and took the gate. The captain was praised for his taking of the tower. I was not there but I guessed he did not tell the general who actually took it. For our part we did not mind. We had the bronze breastplates from the hastati who had guarded the tower as well as their weapons. What we did not keep we sold to other mercenaries and those without armour. We were all now well equipped and we each had a Roman cloak, even Pucco. The Roman cloaks were well made and almost as useful as the bronze breastplates. The salt, coins and food were shared out. Pucco was surprised when I gave him some denarii for he was a slave and unused to such gifts. I made him hide them. As I had expected the captain wanted the officer's equipment. The man had been a centurion. By sporting the breastplate and helmet the captain was suggesting that he had killed the man. Our coins were growing. The four who had died had not spent a denarii of their pay. It was the rest of us who would benefit. We all knew that if we died in battle then the others would benefit.

We stayed in the fortress for a week and then the general had us escort the inhabitants from Eryx. We were to march them back to our beach and then they would be taken by ship to Drepanum. The humiliation of the loss of the Carthaginian stronghold was expunged by its swift recapture. Before we left the general made it indefensible and we sneaked past the Roman camp at night. We were left on the beach while the inhabitants of Eryx sailed back to Drepanum. The captain and Bodoster went with them. We had taken weapons and helmets for Hostus and Wal who were still in Drepanum and I did not want them to feel left out. The attack on the tower meant that, with our pay from the Carthaginians, we were all rich men. When we had lost four men in such a short space of time I had rued our decision to become swords for hire. Now we all thought it was a wise one.

As we waited for the transports to return it became clear that the general was not going to return to either of the two besieged cities. He intended to cause as much trouble to the Romans as he could in the land to the west of Drepanum. I confess that I fretted for I had few enough men without having two of them stuck in Drepanum. I also worried about Pucco. We no longer needed him for translation. I had learned how to ask for clarification and then to understand the answer. There were still words I did not know but the functional words I did. I knew that it pleased the captain not to have to go through an intermediary.

When the single transport arrived in the bay with a warship as escort I wondered what was happening. Captain Bomilcar and Bodoster soon provided the answer. "You and your men are to return to Drepanum. The general needs not only your horses but other horses to enable him to raid. The mercenaries in Drepanum would be of more use here. We are to sail back."

I nodded at Pucco, "And Pucco?"

"You do not need him." It was a statement and not a question. "I will keep him as my body servant."

When Pucco was told I saw the disappointment on his face. He felt valued by us. We had never treated him as a slave. The captain would. We boarded the ship and left at night to slip back into the blockaded harbour of Drepanum. While the captain and Bodoster went to meet with the senior officers in the city we were sent to be reunited with our friends. We had not been apart for long but Hostus and Wal had heard nothing of us. They knew not if we lived or died. "Autaritus had us standing duties with the rest and we looked after the horses but we are pleased that you have returned." Wal shook his head, "Lieutenant Cai does not like us and he gave us unpleasant duties. We are glad to be back with you, Bruneus and Serpus."

I had another reason to dislike the Gaul. "And your injury is healed, Hostus?"

"It was healed before you left." I heard the resentment in his voice. It was understandable but someone had been needed to care for our horses. I knew that not all of my decisions would be welcomed.

We shared out the treasure and Autaritus came to speak to me. I told him of our battles and the retaking of Eryx. "You have done well. I now see why it was so quiet here. The Romans were given a bloody nose and could not venture forth."

"And we are to return to the general but this time with our horses."

"While we stay here." Autaritus shook his head, "Disease is always a threat when you live in a besieged town. You are better off being camped in the open."

The next morning the captain returned and he spoke to both Autaritus and me. "Bruneus, you have spare horses?"

He knew we did and there was no point in a denial. "Aye, Captain."

"Then, Captain Autaritus, choose men who can ride and they will return to the general with Bruneus. Two others can ride my horse and Bodoster's as well as the others from my bodyguards."

I asked, "Are we not to return on the transport?"

He shook his head. I think he was irritated by the question but I thought it a perfectly reasonable one. "Your band of Gauls, Captain Autaritus, will board the transport. General Barca needs your men too."

Autaritus showed that he was pleased. He smiled broadly.

His form of transport was clear but what about ours? "And how do we get there?"

"The Libyans and the Gaetulian horsemen are wasted here. You, Bruneus, will lead them the way you did when we scouted. You will leave at night. I would have said tonight but you will need to speak to them and explain your plan. You will command until you reach the general."

In the blink of an eye I had gone from commanding a handful of men to all of the Carthaginian cavalry. Was I ready?

"Captain Autaritus, choose your men for Bruneus and then have the rest leave for the transport. There is a Roman fleet approaching and we need to be with the general before morning. This city will be blockaded by even more ships soon and we do not know if the port will still be usable."

He turned and left. I said, "Have you men who can ride?" He nodded. "And what do you know of these Libyans and Gaetulians?"

"The warriors are both composed of good horsemen. They will be eager to leave as they prefer riding to fighting on foot. The Gaetulians ride without reins." He shook his head, "I do not know how they do it but...I will send you the men. Good luck."

Thankfully the men all appeared happy to serve under me. I was glad to see that Cai was not amongst them. Whenever he spoke to us it was with such arrogance that I felt like drawing my sword to challenge him. Autaritus realised this and kept us apart. I had Serpus and my men give them instructions about the horses. Thanks to our time on the ship we knew the nature of the horses of the captain and his bodyguards. The Libyan captain and the leader of the Gaetuli did not speak Carthaginian well and I barely spoke it. However, we managed to communicate and I told them we would be leaving the next night at midnight. I explained to them that we would walk our horses until we were clear of the walls. They seemed happy enough. Their names, to me, appeared unpronounceable but as words would not be necessary during the night it was immaterial. Hand signals would be the order of the night. The lessons learned with Captain Bomilcar had been good ones.

When the other horsemen appeared there were more than a hundred and forty of them. Our horses had not fared well having spent a few days without grazing but the others looked to be in a much worse condition. It was no wonder that the horsemen were eager to leave the city and find grass for their horses. It was time to leave for we had been waiting for their arrival. This time there would be no diversionary attack and we would have to be silent. My men and I had learned from the first venture. We hung our shields from the right of our horses and we walked on the left. That way we would have some protection from stones, arrows and javelins. I nodded to the guard who opened the gates. They had been oiled and opened silently. The clouds that threatened rain hid the moon and when we were just a hundred paces from the gates the rain began to fall and it came down as hard as I could remember. It bounced from the ground. While it was unpleasant walking in the rain and the footing became treacherous, I knew that it would keep the Romans occupied. Men on sentry duty would find shelter beneath the roof of the guard towers and keep their cloaks close about their heads. When we passed the last of their siegeworks we mounted and I led my band of horsemen towards the Roman camp. I had passed it so many times already that I knew where it lay and this time, with the rain splattering up from the ground, I felt confident that we would not be seen. It was dawn when we climbed the last ridge that led to the beach. By then the rain had stopped. We were soaked but not a man nor a horse had been hurt. I waited until the sun rose before I risked venturing closer to a sentry who might be nervous. I saw the transport was still in the bay with its attendant warship. I also saw that tents had been brought. We would not be sleeping in the open. I had wondered if the general and his officers would have been soaked but it looked as though they had enjoyed a dry night.

The men behind me maintained their column of fours and we must have made an impressive sight as we headed to the camp for there were cheers. I rode towards the captain. He asked, "Any trouble?"

"No, Captain. The gods sent the rain and we were safe."

"There is a tent for you. Pucco will show you where to pitch it."

I was more concerned about the grazing. When we had been here before I had spied a dell that was sheltered from the winds and looked lush enough to give our handful of horses good grazing. The Libyans and the Gaetuli had never been here before and I saw them lead their horses to the longer but rougher grass that lay closer to the beach. "Bring the horses and we will tether them first." Autaritus' men had left us already and I took the captain's and Bodoster's horse with us. I doubted that they would even notice that we had taken care of their animals but I was now a mercenary and until he stopped paying us I was Captain Bomilcar's man. We took some metal stakes and drove them into the ground. The rains had left a puddle there and we let the horses drink it before we drove the stakes in and tied them to it. I said, "Each night one of us sleeps here with the horses. Tonight is my turn."

Serpus said, "That is not right, Bruneus, you are the leader."

I smiled, "And I lead by example. I am thinking of myself, Serpus. There will be no more rain tonight, see the skies are clearing. Who knows when we can expect another shower?"

I let the men erect the tent while I spoke with Pucco. He had sharp ears and now that he was the servant of the captain he could give us information. "What did you learn?"

"The captain wants more responsibility. The general thinks well of him, especially after the attack on the tower. The horses mean that the general can raid the Romans further afield." He lowered his voice, "There will be no more reinforcements from Carthage. I heard the general tell the captain that Hanno the Great opposes the war and he sees it as a waste of money. Negotiations for peace are already being considered."

"Hanno?"

"The most powerful man in Carthage. He is named Hanno the Great and he is happy to let the Romans have this island."

I nodded and said, almost to myself, "Then why does General Barca try to cling on to it?"

"Because we are trapped, Bruneus."

I looked at him and pointed to the two ships in the bay. "There are ships."

"And they are the last two. There was a battle, we witnessed part of it when we sailed back. We lost and the sailors told us that the Romans now have more ships than Carthage. When those two ships sail they will take messages back to Carthage and the treasure that the general has accrued. They will take a message to General Gisco at Lilybaeum and a letter to General Barca's family in Carthage. There lies hope for the Barca family is a powerful one. Captain Bomilcar's family support the Barcas."

"Then why does he not sue for peace? The Romans would surely be happy to have this burr removed from their saddle."

Pucco's smile was a sad one, "Carthage takes a dim view of leaders who surrender. Most are executed on their return to Carthage. The general wants to cause as much damage to the Romans as he can. When he returns to Carthage he wants to be seen as a man who won despite being hamstrung."

"You are clever, Pucco."

He shrugged, "I am a slave and cannot fight with my hands and so I use my mind."

It gave me much to think about. I took my new Roman cloak and a jar of indifferent oil we had found in Eryx. As I sat and watched the horses I oiled my cloak and thought about our predicament. If the general was trapped then we were in an even worse position. We were mercenaries and the general could not only save money but rid himself of an embarrassment in peace talks if he chose not to pay us. From what I had heard the Romans did not use men like us. At best we might have our weapons and animals taken from us and be sent back to our home. That was not a bad prospect. However, I thought it more likely that Rome would simply execute all the mercenaries. By the time the sun rose I had devised a plan. Captain Bomilcar was our only hope. We had to make ourselves invaluable to him. Regardless of what the general did, if we could become as important to Captain Bomilcar as we could then he might take us with him back to Africa. The prospect of Africa did not thrill me but it was better than death.

The horses had emptied the pool of rainwater and I had the men take them to the stream before returning them to our own patch of good grazing. As we ate our breakfast I spoke quietly to Serpus and gave him my thoughts. He concurred, "You are right. This is an island and if there are no ships…" he suddenly looked out to the bay. As I had already noticed, it was devoid of ships, "they have gone already."

"From what Pucco said they will be lucky to get back to Africa."

"Then we fight as well as we can for this cold captain."

The general, it seemed, was not willing to rest on his laurels. Captain Bomilcar came at noon to see us. While the infantry tried to take the Roman camp we would be riding to raid the supply lines to the Romans at the siege of Drepanum. We would be fighting on horseback. The captain would lead all the horsemen we had brought from Drepanum but we would now be his bodyguards. Bodoster's star had also risen and he was given command of Autaritus and his Gauls. I hid my smile when I heard that. Autaritus would not like to be given orders by Snake Eyes. He did not respect him and certainly did not like him. I had feared that the captain might want his slave with us but he saw sense and left Pucco at the camp. I asked him to watch over our remounts. We still had four and I knew that they could not be replaced. We were told to take supplies as we would be camping overnight in order to come as a complete surprise to the Romans. We knew we no longer had any ships bringing us either men or supplies and we would be reliant on the Romans doing so. I saw the sense in the attack on the Roman camp. It would draw their eye to Eryx and if it was successful would give us not only a base but their food.

We took just throwing javelins. We needed to limit the weight our horses carried. Our mounts were the best in the detachment. They had enjoyed better grazing than the other mercenaries but we still needed to husband their strength. As we headed north Captain Bomilcar thanked me, "My horse has been cared for. Was that your doing or Pucco's?"

"We made sure that all our horses had grazing and water. My horse and Serpus' apart the horses cost us friends and relatives. That increases their value to us."

He asked, "What do you mean?"

I told him about the initiation raid and the deaths of my uncle and War Hammer. I left the plague from my story.

"So when you offered your services to me you had only been on one raid."

There was no point in lying and I said, "Yes."

He laughed and that was so rare that my men all reacted with surprise. "I thought that as you were young you must have begun life as warriors early."

I shrugged, "I think, Captain, that you needed us."

His face was serious as he nodded, "We had lost men and I knew that the general was desperate for horsemen." He studied me, "Perhaps I am a better judge of men than I think. You have done well and impressed me in the taking of the tower."

I lowered my voice, "And can we win here on this island?"

"Victory comes in many ways, Bruneus. The longer we can survive here the more we hurt the Romans. General Barca is a good general. If Hanno the Great would send more men then we could retake Sicily. It is a rich island." It was a slight warming and began a change in the way the captain and I worked. We would never be friends but I now knew that he trusted me and I enjoyed that he had confided in me. Perhaps Africa might not be a bad place to go.

We headed along mountain trails to avoid any Roman patrols. Panormus lay to the north of us and that was one of the ports the Romans used to supply their men. Messana in the east was the other port. I knew, from talking to Autaritus, that when the Carthaginians had ruled the seas the Romans had been forced to use Messana to supply their troops, for it was a shorter crossing. The journey from Messana to Drepanum was a long one. Now they could use the shorter supply lines from Panormus. General Barca intended to make life difficult for the Romans.

It was the horses that chose our camp site. We needed grazing and water. When we found the bubbling stream and grass fed by the recent rains we stopped. We ate cold food for we wanted no woodsmoke drifting in the air. This was not farmed land. There was a swathe of land to the north of us that was farmed but we had avoided that area. I was given the responsibility of ensuring that we had sentries. The leaders of the Libyan and Gaetuli seemed happy enough to obey me despite my youth. I think the fact that I had ensured their safe passage through the Roman lines had helped. I knew that was not my doing. We had been lucky and the rain sent by the gods had hidden us.

There was no fire and we had no tents. My newly oiled cloak would be my shelter. I sat with the captain. He used a stick to draw a map in some bare, damp soil close to where we sat. "The main road from Panormus lies just five miles north of us. Tomorrow we find somewhere we can watch for their wagons." He smiled, "If General Barca is successful then, who knows, they may need to send infantry to reinforce them but we do know that they will need food. We took Eryx and destroyed a garrison. By now they will have had the time to do something about it. We need the wagons and the food they carry. When we are successful we will head back along the main road. I will want your men to act as scouts and prevent us from being ambushed."

"Why us, Captain? Surely the others are better horsemen and have more experience."

He lowered his voice, although there were only my men close by, "You have shown me that you are reliable men who obey orders. That is what I need. I do not need men who go chasing off after treasure and glory. I need reliable men that I can trust."

The road we found was not a straight one. The men of
Syracuse had built it and the Carthaginians maintained it.
It twisted and turned and rose and fell. The captain chose
a section of the road that had a turn in it as it climbed up
a steep slope. It then descended to a plain and rose again
for the last rise. Wagons would not be able to do so
quickly. The rocks and ridges would afford us cover and
the Libyans and the Gaetuli had both bows and javelins.
The captain's plan was a simple one. When we saw the
Romans, Serpus would lead half of my men and ten
Gaetuli to cut off the last wagon and the rest of my men
would take the head of the column. The other warriors,
led by the captain, would eliminate the guards caught in
the middle. It seemed a foolproof plan. Once more we
camped and did not eat hot food. We consoled ourselves
with the fact that if a column of wagons arrived we
would have first choice of any food that was on offer.

It was late in the afternoon when Hostus, who was
watching from the easternmost point, signalled with his
blade. He used it to flash and attract our attention.
"Captain, someone comes."

Captain Bomilcar frowned, "I thought it was too late
in the day."

I pointed to the flatter area before the next rise. There
was a small pool there. We had already used it to water
our horses. "Perhaps they intend to camp there and then
try the ascent in the morning when the animals are
fresher."

"Perhaps. Get your men mounted. I will inform the
Libyans and Gaetuli."

I turned but saw that my men had mounted already in
anticipation of action. I climbed on the back of
Stormbringer and hung my shield from my foremost
pommel. I donned my helmet and then used my javelin
to marshal the men to our ambush position. We rode
along a path that was between the rocks. The rocks hid
us and it brought us out on the other side of the small

rise. The slope was steep and then dropped down. By waiting there we would be hidden.

"Alerix, take off your helmet, dismount and see where they are." He handed his reins to Bellerix and then scurried up to lie just below the top of the ridge. After a few moments he said, "I see the wagons. They are pulled by bullocks." That was good news. When we had finished with the wagons then the bullocks would be slaughtered. The bad news came a heartbeat later. "They are escorted by infantry and there are ten riders too."

I had great responsibility for it would be me who initiated the attack. When my handful of men rose from the rise in the road then we would draw every eye and, hopefully, their cavalry to us. It would allow Serpus to sweep from behind and the other horsemen to attack the sides of the column of wagons and men. I moved us forward until we were still below the rise but closer to the crest.

The news continued to worsen. "There are fifty infantry and they are on both sides of the wagons."

The twenty five on our side of the road would not be a problem but there would be guards on the wagons and the twenty five on the other side of the wagons would be able to use the wagons for cover.

"How many wagons?"

"Seven, no, nine. I can see another ten riders at the rear." There was a pause. "The riders who lead are looking to make a camp. They are slowing."

I was right and our plans had been based on them trying to climb the rise. I made a decision. "Alerix, mount. Let us draw their eye to us." Even as Alerix mounted the thought drifted into my head that perhaps their turning the wagons might work to our advantage. Whatever happened the gods had made life interesting for us.

As he mounted I dug my heels into Stormbringer and we crested the rise. The sun was dropping just behind us in the west but it would still be another hour until sunset. As the sun flared it must have flashed from our helmets and silhouetted us against the skyline. Whatever reason the horsemen's buccina sounded and the ten cavalrymen rode at us. I used the slope and ordered a charge. There were just a handful of us against ten Romans but the slope gave us added speed. The infantry all formed up into three lines to back up the horsemen. We had done our part and as the Roman equites charged at us I caught a glimpse of Serpus and his men as they stealthily approached the rear. The horsemen at the rear were galloping forward to assist their comrades. I calculated that we would hit the Romans just where the ground flattened. They were twenty paces from us when Captain Bomilcar launched his attack. The Libyans and the Gaetuli were frightening warriors and they appeared fearless. Their war cries filled the air and it made the horsemen charging us falter as they looked to their left. It was a mistake. I hurled my javelin at the officer who must have decided to eliminate us first for he urged his horse on. The javelin hit him in the middle. His pommels held him in the saddle but his hand dropped his own javelin. I drew the longer cavalry sword I had taken. It hung from one of the pommels. My own sword was still on my baldric and around my waist. My men hurled their javelins. Three found flesh and the odds were more even. I pulled up my shield and blocked the javelin hurled by the Roman trooper. I slashed at his middle with my longer sword. His shield was the small round one favoured by Roman horsemen and it was on the wrong side. He wore leather armour and while effective my long sword was honed well and I sliced below the leather and into his middle. I did not need to see him fall to know that it was a fatal wound. I turned and brought my sword over to hit the man on my left who was fighting Alerix. I did not manage to cut deeply but my sword struck the bone close to the shoulder and the scream told me that it was broken.

The ten men were dead, dying or had turned to return to the wagons. My men were whole although I saw that Wal had a nasty cut on his cheek. It was a badge of honour that would tell the world that he was a warrior.

The Roman infantry had formed a shield wall and were now protecting the wagons. The Libyans and the Gaetuli were attacking but the hastati who guarded the wagons had good shields, as well as sound helmets, and all of them wore the bronze breastplate. We had momentum and we galloped down the road. The riderless horses helped us for they fled towards the Romans. They would be a distraction. Captain Bomilcar was rallying the Africans he led but they had not enjoyed as much success as they might have hoped. The wagons were in a half circle and there were velites behind the wagons hurling stones and javelins. There was a mounting pile of bodies. Some of the Gaetuli were duelling with the last Roman horsemen and the hope I spied was that Serpus and the rest of my men were attacking the last of the wagons. They would begin to eat into the Roman rear. We had to make the Romans turn to face us. I was glad that I had chosen the longer Roman sword for it would allow me a longer reach. I led my men towards the left of their line. I held my shield across my body and it proved to be a wise move. Jammed against the frontmost pommels when the pilum hit it, the spear did not drag down my shield. It protruded from the shield the Romans called a scutum and effectively gave me a lance. The end went towards a legionary who dropped behind his shield. I whirled Stormbringer and brought my sword down on his helmet. It was as though I had hit him with an iron bar. He fell to the ground and in his falling the pilum fell from my shield. I rode down the line of legionaries. I slashed again at the man three men from the one I had slain and found the gap between the top of his shield and his helmet. My sword struck bone.

Once at the end of the line I whirled Stormbringer. "To me."

As we turned and I was able to examine my men I saw that Wal's face still bled but it was no longer pouring with blood. None of them had either javelins or spears. The horses would be given a breather and I could decide where best we might be used. I saw that the Libyans and the Gaetuli had made the Romans turn to face them. It left an unguarded gap between two wagons and I saw that ahead of me, towards the rear of the column, Serpus and War Axe were having great success.

"Follow me!"

I charged between the gap so that we were inside the circle of wagons. A carter swashed a wood axe at me but I not only avoided it I also managed to gut him for he wore no armour at all. Some of the other carters, fearing for their lives, began to move their wagons. They were going to head west and try to disappear into the darkness. The bullocks they used made that an impossible task but it suited me. I shouted, "Clan of the Lone Wolf to me!" I needed Serpus and the rest of my men. I said to the men with me, "We will attack the rear of the wagons and get to the Romans." There were gaps between the wagons and I could see the unprotected backs of the hastati. Serpus brought his men to join us and I pointed my sword, "Charge!" We rode in a pathetically short line of nine men but we were attacking men who were looking in the darkening twilight at dark skinned Africans. They thought that their backs were protected. There were three gaps and my men split into three. Our first flurry of blows came as a complete shock and when the men in the rear rank fell, the ones in the front found themselves speared and stabbed by the Africans. Their cavalry dead or fled, the shocked survivors surrendered.

I shouted, "Serpus, take your men and recapture those wagons that are trying to flee."

He was grinning as he saluted and led half of my men away.

I rode towards a bloodied Captain Bomilcar. The blood was Roman and showed that he had fought and fought well. He gave me a rare smile, "You led a handful of the men that I did, Bruneus, and yet you won the day. The gods must favour you."

I hoped that they did. I prayed that the bad luck we had suffered in my homeland had been left there.

Perhaps Sicily and Africa would bring me good luck.

Chapter 7

The lone wolves had lost no men but the Africans had and they buried their dead before we left, the next morning. The Romans were left where they fell. The captain decided to let Rome bury the Romans. The legionaries who would come after us could bury what remained after the carrion crows had done with them. Horsemen had escaped and they would return to Panormus to take the news of the defeat. We captured four Roman horses and as the Africans had not lost a horse, we returned to our camp by the bay with more horses and nine laden wagons. We also had fifteen prisoners. Some of the hastati and velites had managed to escape but it was a victory and, as we rode back along the road, I could tell that Captain Bomilcar was changing his opinion of us. I think he had taken us at Gades because he had been told to bring horsemen and had not found any. That we were not what he sought was clear but now, three dead bodyguards later and with victories at the Roman camp, Eryx, and now the road from Panormus, he saw that we had merit. There had been pay in the wagons. It was intended for the Romans in their camp. The captain would give the chests to the general but he took out our payment for the next six months. He also took the pay for his retinue. It was much smaller in number now but they would be paid. I wondered how they would take to Snake Eyes as a commander.

It was after dark when we rolled into camp. You cannot disguise the noise of bullocks and the caligae of marching Romans. Hamilcar Barca himself came to greet us. I saw the dismay on his face when he realised that he had lost forty horsemen. The captain saw it too and said, "General Barca, we may have lost horsemen but we have their horses. We can mount more Gauls like my Celtiberians."

He looked at us, "You have been lucky with your men. I hope Bodoster has as much success with the men he leads."

"He is not in camp?"

"No, I sent him out yesterday with two hundred men to harass the road between the Roman camp and their siegeworks." He turned to his cook, "Have two bullocks slaughtered. We eat well this night."

Th captain turned to me, "Bring the chests with the pay."

General Barca's smile became even broader, "And you bring gold too? These men who serve you bring you luck. Do not lose them."

The general must have spoken about us to his cook for we were brought some choice pieces of cooked meat after the senior officers had been fed. Captain Autaritus was close by. He sniffed the air appreciatively, "I look forward to our food. It is good that you brought meat. It makes up for lack of pay."

War Axe was about to say something when I stopped him, "Aye, but there is nowhere to spend it even if we were paid."

"That is not the point. A mercenary deserves pay. It is why we fight. If we wanted land we would have stayed at home and taken land from our neighbours. We fight for gold so that we can go home as rich men and have comfortable lives with slaves to serve us." He nodded over to his lieutenant. "Some of my men are becoming restless. They say that if we are not paid then we should join the Romans. The men we fight might pay us to defect."

I said nothing but I disagreed. Taking coins was as binding, in my view, as swearing an oath. In our village coins were valued for we had so few of them. Some even used the silver coins as jewellery.

Their meat was brought and was greeted with huge cheers. The Gauls would be distracted from the spectre of pay…for a while.

We had yet to speak of our own future but, as we ate, Alerix brought it up, "I suppose we could also go home as rich men."

Sercix shook his head, "Our home is gone. If you mean the land of our birth then aye, we could but I would like to live in a land that was not baking hot in summer and freezing in winter. We still have time to travel. When Sicily is lost and we all know that it will be lost, then we can look at Carthage. Their officers all wear gold and even the Libyan officers have gold about their necks. It sounds like a rich place to me. Who knows, we might all choose to live there and be like princes wearing fine clothes."

Serpus began to pick meat from between his teeth with his bone toothpick. He shook his head, "We have been swords for hire for weeks, not years. We are all young men and Bruneus has led us well. Wait until we all wear mail and have plenty of gold before you think about choosing another life. I think we have all learned much but there is much more ahead of us." He pointed the piece of bone he had used as a toothpick at me, "Did none of you notice how it was Bruneus who won the battle for us? If he had not had the vision to summon all of us to attack through their gaps and into their backs we might not have won. We follow a good leader here."

War Axe laughed, "Aye, you are right. If I had been the leader then I would still be hewing heads and slaughtering carters."

You could not help but smile at War Axe. He had the simplest view of life and was as loyal a warrior as I ever knew. The next day we began to sort through the treasure we had collected. We had placed it in one of the wagons. We now had enough breastplates to give each of my men a front and backplate. They were easy to join and it protected the vulnerable backs of my men. My mail was not as good but I did not dare to shed it and adopt a front and backplate. That would have brought bad luck. I was now used to wearing it and it protected the tops of my shoulders and my sides. We had spare weapons that could be sold but only when we needed to. The others chose a good shield from the treasure too and each man painted his own design upon it. The greatest treasure, however, were the pila. These spears could be thrown or used as a thrusting weapon. With a pyramidal point they could tear a hole in mail. I had seen some of the Libyan bodies and the wounds had all been horrific.

The next day Bodoster had still to return and the general sent us out to find him and his men. The captain came with us for they were his men that had been with Bodoster. We found the survivors just four miles from our camp. Their news was grave. Bodoster had chosen to try to plunder rather than to obey his orders. They had been on their way back, heavily laden, when the Romans had caught up with them. The thirty men we found were the only survivors and just five of those were the captain's men. When we told Hamilcar Barca he mounted his bodyguards and we headed for the battlefield. It lay close to the siegeworks and the bodies lay where they had fallen. The Roman dead were not there and our dead showed the ravages of carrion. The general rode to within hailing distance of the walls. He called out, "I would speak with Consul Fundanius."

The Roman leader took some time to arrive and when he did General Barca said, "Your men have enjoyed a victory at our expense. I ask for a truce to allow us to bury them."

"You should request a truce to save your living and leave the island. Let their bodies rot!" He turned, "Prepare a cohort."

We were too few in number to risk a battle and so we turned and headed back to our camp. It soured the mood of the camp but I think it made the general even more determined not to leave. I knew another reason. A small boat had beaten the blockade and told the general that the sea between the islands of Aegate and Drepanum were being filled with stones to complete the blockade and the city was now besieged on all sides. Unless we could do something they would have to surrender or starve to death. The Romans were masters of the machines of war and of sieges. The end of Carthaginian rule in Sicily was in sight. The captain was silent as we rode back and I knew why. Bodoster had been his man. Now all his bodyguards were dead and of the retainers who had come from Carthage with the general, only five remained.

There was a sour mood amongst the men and in an attempt to improve it the general used the money we had captured from the Romans to pay the mercenaries. I do not know if he kept some for himself but the mood did not improve and the Gauls, in particular, wanted more. Captain Autaritus was the one who led the men who complained. We did not join in for we had been paid. We were Captain Bomilcar's men. Our decision cost us the friendship of Autaritus and the Gauls. Hostus and Wal had spent time with the Gauls when they had been left to watch the horses and they were the two who were unhappy. As there were only another five who were from the captain's retinue we became a small, isolated band. In many ways it made us closer. We had our own camp and we ate alone. We no longer shared the cooking pots. Gold had come between us and the Gauls. They seemed to love it more than we. My men were just as happy to secure armour, helmets and weapons as gold.

We still had to raid to feed our army and our success meant that it was Captain Bomilcar who was charged with the task of keeping the army fed. The rest of the army had the unenviable job of skirmishing with the Romans to keep our camp safe and to harass the Romans as they gradually increased their stranglehold on Drepanum and Lilybaeum. They were not battles but men still died. They died in small numbers and the burial of friends gnawed at the hearts of men. Virtually all the soldiers we had were mercenaries. It was said that there were twenty thousand mercenaries in Sicily. The best Carthaginian warriors were still in Carthage. For us those days when we raided were a relief. The atmosphere in the camp was unpleasant. Many of the Gauls made intimidating comments as they passed us. War Axe almost responded on two or three occasions but Serpus and I still had mastery of our men. I did not know how long it would last.

We were now more familiar with the road but the Romans also now knew that we would be trying to take their wagons. It became a battle of wits. We had less than one hundred mounted men. There had been deaths and some desertions. The Romans encouraged desertion and promised repatriation for any who did so. I thought it was a ruse. The Romans did not seem to me to be men that you could trust. However, some of the Africans had taken up the offer. We raided one column of wagons when they were just half a day from the Roman camp on Eryx. We waited in ambush at a familiar place. We had raided the Roman camp there in the early days of this war. We knew the folds and rises of the land and used them. They were now using not wagons but mules laden with supplies. It meant they could travel faster. They had a hundred hastati guarding the supplies. It was not a huge column but they must have counted on speed defeating the ambush. They were almost in sight of the walls of the camp when we rose like wraiths from the ground and charged at them. This time they had no wagons behind which they could shelter. We all now knew how to hurl javelins from the back of a horse and recognised the weaknesses of the men we fought. The hastati locked shields and threw their pila at us but we attacked with our shields facing them and we suffered no hurts. Some of the Africans did not use a shield and they were the ones we lost. The Romans soon learned that we had protection for our backs. The new backplates came as a shock to them. When the hastati who had survived the initial attack saw the gaps in their lines then they knew that they were lost and they abandoned the mules whose drivers had been slain. They ran for the camp. We left them for we had supplies to take. We had to be practical. We could not afford to lose men and the Romans seemed to have an inexhaustible supply. The Roman commander in the camp sounded his buccina and sent his men out to try to recapture the supplies. We managed to take more than half of the mules. The others were recaptured by the Romans but over the next few days our raids secured another fifteen. It fed the army for a further week.

The captain led us from the camp ten days later. Food was becoming scarce despite the rationing imposed by the general. The mood in the camp was becoming ugly, almost mutinous, and we had to take a risk. We rode almost to Panormus and saw neither wagon nor mule. I was sent to spy out the harbour and I saw no ships in the harbour. Captain Bomilcar had grown since we had first met him. He was no longer the young arrogant noble. Too many of his men had died for that. He almost confided in me. The African leaders were largely ignored.

"Bruneus, they must be bringing the supplies from Messana." I did not understand maps but I had seen, on the clear days, the huge range of mountains and the volcano that ran the length of the island. "Until the town of Himera they have to use the coastal road but they can then cut south through the pass and avoid the places we ambush. We will head south and wait at the pass."

I nodded for it sounded like a reasonable plan, "But we may have to wait some time, Captain."

127

"Have you something better to do?"

I lowered my voice, "I am not worried about my men but the Africans…"

He sighed, "If we have to then we take the supplies with just, what do you call them, the Clan of the Lone Wolf?" He was smiling when he said it.

We found a good place for an ambush the next day. The road descended from the pass to the fertile plain. There were farms there but General Barca had forbidden us to raid them. This land had been Carthaginian and the people, technically, were our people. For my part I knew that such men would bow the knee to any warrior but the general was clinging on to the hope that we could reconquer the island and make it Carthaginian once more. We made a camp close to the pass. There was a stream and enough grass to feed the horses. While we used the Africans as sentries I also ensured that two of my men were with each shift of men. We spent three long days waiting for the Romans to come and we were rewarded when Aed rode from his position above the pass. "Captain, there are wagons coming down the road. They are drawn by horses and they have cavalry escorting them. There are twenty horsemen and forty legionaries."

We had been in the area long enough to know that the best place for them to camp was at the foot of the pass where there was flat ground for their tents. They were fifty miles from Drepanum and would need two camps, at least, before they reached safety. The Carthaginian turned to me, "Mount the men. You know the plan. I will speak to the Africans."

As the captain left I said, "Aed, fetch back the scouts. I would not alert the enemy to our presence."

"Yes, Bruneus."

"Serpus, break camp. Whatever happens this day we are done with it."

I donned my helmet and fastened my cloak around me. Its colour helped me to blend in with the land and allied to Stormbringer's coat was a good disguise. The cloak would also help to slow down a spear or an arrow. It would not stop one, my mail would do that, but it would protect my mail. As usual I hung my shield from my pommel. I now had three pila and they also hung from my pommels. With my long sword hanging from them I appeared to be festooned but the shield and the pila hung from the left front pommel, my sword from the right and my ale skin and food from the rear ones. I felt comfortable and my horse was now used to bearing the weight. Stormbringer could manage to carry me and my weapons but I was always mindful not to tax him too much with unnecessary charges. I rested him when I could. My men also used their pommels wisely. War Axe only had one pilum. He preferred his war axe but like the rest of us he would use his pilum judiciously.

Serpus waved as he led his men to take their positions on the other side of the road. The captain would be there with half of the Africans. I would lead the other half, including the two leaders. Thanks to my strategy in the first raid they respected me and obeyed me. I was still young and younger than both of them but they recognised a martial mind. We worked well as a team despite the differences in our backgrounds. We had been successful and success makes men more confident. We sheltered behind the rocks four hundred paces from the road. We had ground that sloped down to the plain before us and it was largely free of both vegetation and rocks. When we needed to we could move quickly.

We heard the creaking of the wagons and the conversations of both the guards and the drivers. That was comforting for it showed that they were not expecting an attack. They were anticipating a camp and hot food. We knew the way the Romans worked. They liked to build a defensive camp at night. A small ditch, a rampart and wood to make a palisade would be erected while fires would be lit. There was still at least two hours to go before darkness and the commander of the column would have his intended campsite in mind. What we knew was that we could move more quickly than either the wagons or the men on foot. We outnumbered their horsemen and so if we could take out the horsemen then the column would be ripe for the plucking.

Wal was lying on the rock and watching the road. When I saw him descend then I knew it was time. "Prepare."

"The first wagons are almost at the flat part. They have ten horsemen on each side."

I took a pilum, "Then let us ride."

If the first wagons were almost on the flat then they were committed. What they could not do was to turn and try to climb up the slope. We had managed to persuade the Africans to forego their normal cheers and war cries in the initial approach. I led forty five men and as soon as we were able I wheeled them into a line and we charged the Romans obliquely. The lack of shouts and the noise from the wagons allowed us to get to within a hundred and forty paces before a driver shouted the alarm. The Roman horsemen wheeled and bravely charged us. They wore mail and had good weapons. They rode good horses and man for man might be better armed and armoured than we were but what we had was experience. Despite our youth my men had fought in many battles and against a variety of opponents. We knew how to fight.

Our horses were well fed and eager. We formed an arrow with Libyans and the Gaetuli on our flanks. I hurled my first pilum at the Roman officer. He blocked it with his shield and threw his javelin at me. I was already drawing my sword as his spear came at me and I did not have time to raise my shield. Such was the speed of Stormbringer that his javelin missed the top of my helmet by the width of a finger. The pilum did its work and the Roman's shield drooped. I slashed my long sword and hacked through his upper arm. The blood that spurted told me I had struck something vital. I turned my attention to the man on my right who raised his arm to throw his javelin. I did the unexpected and instead of turning away I rode at him. In theory I was giving him an easier target but with my sword held before me and Stormbringer snapping already I was a frightening sight. Experience cannot be bought and I had it. The Roman had clearly not fought in many battles for he panicked and hurled the javelin at me almost in blind terror. I did not even have to duck. I drove my sword up under his chin and into his throat. As I wheeled Stormbringer to my left I let my arm pull the sword from the dead trooper's body. The Roman cavalry had tried to stop us and had failed. They had, however, given their infantry the opportunity to form two lines on both sides of the wagons.

I slowed to sheathe my sword and to pick up my shield and another pilum. Alerix, Sercix and Bellerix copied me as did most of the Africans but Wal and Hostus had blood rushing in their heads and they did not slow. They were now the arrowhead but unlike the rest of us they had no shields before them and in their hands they each held a sword and not a pilum. Even as we raised our pila to throw the hastati and velites hurled their first pila. Wal and Hostus had plates on their chests and helmets on their heads but their horses did not. The spears that hit them took both animal's lives but their owners lasted but a heartbeat longer for both were struck by a pair of pila apiece. They might have survived the fall from their dying horses but they were then stabbed and gutted where they lay. The least experienced of my dwindling band of warriors were dead. We wheeled to ride with our shields on our left, facing the Roman spears. If nothing else the sacrifice of Wal and Hostus had cost the Romans eight spears. When I hurled my pilum it was at an optio who was shouting an order. The cry died in his throat. A pilum hit my shield. I let the shield hang so that the end of the spear caught the ground and tore it out. I had it back before me a heartbeat before a stone slammed into it. I wheeled Stormbringer at the end of the Roman wagons to ride away. A stone struck my shoulder a glancing blow. It did no damage but it hurt and it was a warning. I took a second pilum and continued in a long lazy loop. Two Africans had also fallen. I saw their horses obediently following the others. I had to put Wal and Hostus from my mind. There was a centurion who was commanding the men of the escort. He had thrown his pilum and had a sword in his hand. He would be a hard man to kill but if he fell then the heart might go from the rest.

I waved my spear as a signal to the others and we rode once more at the Roman line. The centurion's command had made the line of shields shrink to form a tighter wall. I rode as close as I could to the line. The officer saw me and I saw his shield move a little closer to his body. He shouted something and the slinger who remained sent stones at me. My shield held. I took a risk. I feinted with my spear and the centurion raised his shield. When there was no smack he lowered it again. I was six paces from him and I hurled my pilum. The gods guided my hand and gave me vengeance for my dead men. The spear struck his face. The pyramidal head broke bone and drove into his skull. He fell as though War Axe had hit him.

The men I led had also enjoyed success and the once solid line of shields now had gaps. The Africans could be wild warriors and they charged the gaps. The Romans were brave but even a brave man cannot stand before a charging horse. It is in his nature to move and some of the Romans moved into the way of a second charging horse. Some of the Africans fell but their charge broke the enemy who ran.

When we returned to the column of wagons there were just the Romans who had surrendered to us left alive there. Thirty or so Romans had escaped. Some of the drivers had taken the horses from the traces and galloped off. A few of the Roman soldiers had managed to mount one of the many riderless horses. Some had managed to flee on foot. The news of our attack would reach the Roman consuls and the next time it would not be so easy.

Our repeated charges meant that, despite the need to get the supplies back to the general, we had to camp and to rest our horses. Wounds had to be tended and, in our case, comrades buried. As we covered the bodies of Wal and Hostus with earth I could not help but think again that our decision had been the wrong one. Half of the men who had chosen to follow me were now dead. While I knew that the ones who remained were what I would term the best warriors, the six who had died were good men and skilled warriors.

The captain sat with me. He looked worried, "The general will not be happy, Bruneus, I am taking riderless horses back to him."

I nodded and pointed to the wagons, "But you are also bringing back the food that will keep his dwindling army fed. He cannot have it both ways."

He sighed and lowered his voice, "You are not a Carthaginian, Bruneus. You cannot understand." I could see him wrestling to choose words that would help me, "We have no king. Instead there is a Tribunal of One Hundred as well as a senate. They do not fight and do not understand loss of land. If a general fails then he is often crucified."

"You are saying that you could be executed for losing men?"

He shook his head, "No, but I cannot afford too many failures. I need to go home victorious. I have a son there whom I have not seen since the day he was born but one day he will grow into a warrior and join the Sacred Band. That can only be if I have a blameless record. This war has not gone well for us but General Barca might salvage enough honour for me to share some of that glory."

The next day we used the dozen or so prisoners we had taken to drive the wagons and we headed back to the bay. It would take two days. Even though it was doubtful that any of the survivors could reach Panormus and bring vengeance down on us in the time left, we had to move quickly and be vigilant. I realised that since the death of the bodyguards the captain and I had become closer. That was due to a number of reasons, I knew that. The deaths of so many of his men and our success had forged bonds of steel but I think he had started to like me. I had come to him as an uncouth savage. I think I was still a raw piece of clay but he had seen beneath the strange moustache and the uncultured language I spoke. He saw, I hoped, a loyal warrior.

The general was more pleased with our return and the supplies we brought than he was disappointed at our losses. The cynic in me said that he had fewer men to pay. That pay was an issue was clear for a day or so after our return Captain Autaritus went to the general to demand their pay. He led one thousand Gauls. Thanks to the losses amongst the horsemen he now commanded the largest single contingent of mercenaries. I did not support him when he went with his other leaders to make his demands.

We had been on friendly terms in Drepanum but my service with the captain had driven us apart. He came to me the day we returned to try to convince me to make a joint complaint.

"It is not right that we have not been paid. We are swords for hire and as such need to be given what is due to us."

I nodded, "You may be right but the captain has paid us. He has paid me for twelve men even though I only lead six."

His face hardened, "You are one of us! If we all stand together then we will win."

That was the moment I realised that my loyalty to Captain Bomilcar was greater than it was to Captain Autaritus. "But we are not one of you. We are not your men. You are Gauls and we are Celtiberians. Are you saying we are all the same because we are mercenaries? You are the same as others?"

"No, we are better. We are warriors who can win battles." My face told him I would not change my mind. He turned and stormed off to his men.

Cai pointed a finger at us, "I always knew you were a worthless piece of shit and now it is confirmed. I will have vengeance for this betrayal. I am not as forgiving as Captain Autaritus."

Serpus and the others had been listening. They said nothing at first and so I invited comment, "If you think I am wrong then tell me so."

Serpus shook his head, "No, you are not wrong and besides you are our leader. I think that Captain Autaritus has little honour and that snake, Cai, even less. He gave his word and now he thinks to break it." I was pleased. My men were of the same mind as me.

When Captain Autaritus and the other leaders made their demands I stood with Pucco, Captain Bomilcar and my men. We were standing closer to the general and that was deliberate on my part. We heard the demands. Pucco translated the words I did not understand. He said that the general was in a difficult position. He needed the mercenaries but had no gold to pay them. When Captain Autaritus threatened to take his one thousand men and join the Romans I saw some of the Carthaginian nobles reach for their swords. Hamilcar Barca shook his head, "There is no need for that. I give you my word, Captain Autaritus, that when we return to Lilybaeum I will pay each of you and your men one hundred tetradrachms."

"And if we do not return to Lilybaeum?"

"Then when we reach Carthage you will be paid." The general chose his words carefully.

Captain Autaritus said, "You swear this before us all?"

"I swear by the great god Baal Hammon than when we reach Carthage you shall be paid."

"Then we will continue to fight for you."

I said to the captain, "Why Lilybaeum?"

Captain Bomilcar said, "There is a mint in that city."

"But it is besieged."

The captain said, "And that is why they will only be paid when we return to Carthage."

Chapter 8

The next month saw more skirmishing and our dwindling number of horsemen sought more supplies but it was all in vain. The blockading of both ports meant that the Romans could now supply their garrisons, like the one at Eryx, by sea. They were also able to reinforce them with men so that while we lost soldiers their numbers increased.

We heard that there had been a battle at sea and that a second Carthaginian fleet had been destroyed. Even I knew that was the beginning of the end for Carthaginian rule in Sicily. We looked to the sea each morning for a sight of a Carthaginian vessel. The ship that eventually entered the bay was escorted by a Roman warship even though it was Carthaginian. A Roman official came ashore along with two Carthaginian nobles. While the captain was present at the meeting we were not but we speculated.

Serpus shook his head, "This does not bode well, Bruneus."

I nodded, and gestured to the Gauls, "And how will they feel about a possible end to the war and that they have yet to be paid."

War Axe was a simple man and he shook his head, "I do not understand, Bruneus, what does this mean?"

"If the Romans escort a Carthaginian ship here then it is to give orders to General Barca. Those orders must mean an end to the war. The Romans would not escort an enemy vessel to continue the war."

When War Axe nodded Serpus smiled. He said to me, quietly, "You understand our friend better than any. You are a good leader."

I shook my head, "I am not sure. We came for a future and now not only have I lost half of the men I brought but I have lost us an employer. What will this mean for us?"

The discussions went on all day. We ate but our minds were on the tents that had been erected on the beach. We saw to our horses, did our duty and waited.

Captain Bomilcar came to our camp the next morning. He gestured to me to go with him so that he could speak with me in private away from any prying ears. "The war is over, Bruneus. The council has ordered General Barca to open negotiations with the Romans. He is not a happy man." He smiled, "He upset the Romans when he refused to have our men pass beneath the yoke." My face showed him that I did not understand. "It is an Italian custom that a victor demands an army passes beneath the yoke to show that they are defeated. General Barca refused. He will sail to Lilybaeum and delegate the terms of the surrender to his deputy, General Gisco."

I took that in. It meant that he would not be the one seen as surrendering. The Romans would just be happy to have the thorn that was Hamilcar Barca off the island. "And us?"

He smiled and lowered his voice, "The Carthaginians in the camp are to be repatriated to Carthage. The general will return with the ship and retire from public life. I will take my men and return to Carthage and my home."

I shook my head, "I don't understand. We are to be left here?"

He shook his head and I saw in his face the concern of a leader for his men, "No, Bruneus, you are my bodyguards. You are now part of my retinue. To all intents and purposes you are not mercenaries but Carthaginians. You will return to Carthage but," his eyes darted to the camp of the Gauls, "you must say not a word about this. The general will be away for a day or so and when he returns you and your men bring your horses and mine to the beach. To help the deception take the horses down this morning and for the next days. Exercise them in the sea."

"And Pucco?"

"He is my slave and he will not be left behind."

"The Gauls will not be happy."

"The general will ensure that they are not abandoned here. He knows that they are good soldiers."

"And the promise of pay?"

The captain's face became a mask, "When they reach Carthage I am sure that they will be given what is due to them." In my village when a man spoke there was no smoke hiding the words. The Carthaginians chose their words as carefully as a man selecting the best piece of fish at a feast.

It was when we went to tend to the horses that I spoke to my men. War Axe apart they all understood what would happen to the Gauls. They would not be paid what was owed to them. If nothing else it was hard to see how they could get to Carthage. "We say nothing but start a new routine. It is not a bad idea. Swimming the horses in the sea is good for them and keeps them cooler. We keep that which we wish to take close to hand. When we go we will slip away and leave the tent where it is. Hopefully, by the time the Gauls know what is afoot we shall be at sea."

Serpus asked, "Who will be left here to command?"

I had not been told but I knew that Justus, the Libyan cavalry commander, was well respected by the other mercenaries. "I am guessing that Justus will be given command. Most of the mercenaries who are left are African. A few are horsemen but most are infantry. They now outnumber the Gauls."

"And the rest of the captain's men?"

"There are just five of them, Alerix, and I am guessing they, as Carthaginians, will be given a berth on the last ship back to Carthage."

Captain Autaritus was suspicious that first day. He had not spoken to us since the meeting with the general. We got on well with the other mercenaries and it did not bother us but it was sad as the Gauls had been our first friends. He had some of his men pointedly follow us to the sea. When we stripped off and walked our horses into the water they sat on the rocks and watched us. They were perplexed for to them our behaviour appeared strange. We had all grown up by the sea and had learned to swim at an early age. It was bracing and helped us to clean our bodies. By the third day they stopped following us. On that day we took some of our armour and weapons when we led our horses to the sea. We had collected sacks from the Roman wagons we had raided and we used those to carry them. We buried them in the sand. In that way, over the next two days, all of our surplus weapons and treasures had been taken and secreted. The general returned six days later. His Roman escort was no longer with him.

When he came ashore Captain Autaritus, Captain Justus and the other mercenary leaders went to speak to him. There had been rumours abounding and they wanted the truth. Captain Bomilcar sent Pucco for me. "The captain says that you should come."

The meeting was at the general's tent which had been moved from the main camp to the land above the high-water mark. He was flanked by his bodyguards. He had no smile on his face when he spoke. "I have been ordered by the council to begin peace talks that will lead to the abandonment of Sicily. I am not happy about that and I have resigned my position as supreme leader on Sicily. General Gisco now commands. I will retire to my estates in Carthage."

It was Autaritus who spoke and there was anger in his voice, "And what of us? Are we to be abandoned too? What of your promise for it was you and not General Gisco who promised us our pay."

"And that promise will be honoured. I will speak to the council when I reach Carthage and tell them of their obligations."

Captain Justus asked, "And how do we get back to Carthage?"

"That is another reason that I will be returning to Carthage as soon as I can. I will send ships to bring you all to Carthage where you will be paid, I promise."

His words seemed reasonable and as he had brought supplies from Lilybaeum and the men would be fed, all seemed well. I was going to head back to our tent to tell the men when the captain arrested my arm. "We leave before dawn. Are you ready?"

I nodded, "And your retinue, Captain?"

"I will move them aboard tonight."

I looked at Pucco, "Will you need Pucco, Captain?"

He shook his head, "No, my other men can carry my things aboard. You may use him." He left to give instructions to his men.

I said, "Pucco, come with me." I took him to the part of the beach where we had hidden our treasure. "There are sacks hidden beneath the sand." I pointed to the circle of rocks we had used to mark the place. "When no one is watching move them aboard the ship. I am guessing that we will have to endure the open deck again." He nodded. "Good, then put the sacks where you can get at them easily."

Once back at the camp we began to prepare food. Serpus and I had gone out each day when we were not needed to patrol and brought down doves, as well as hunting, in the evening, for rabbits. We did so that day while the others set to cooking our food. We were watched by the Gauls but as we did nothing out of the ordinary they did not seem to be overly suspicious. We managed to bag six doves and pigeons. They would augment the three rabbits we had caught the previous night. Before Autaritus had fallen out with us we would have shared with them. Now we offered our surplus to the Africans who were more than grateful. They were closer to us than the Gauls. We had fought alongside the horsemen and we knew the worth of the other. I did not expect trouble from the Gauls, not yet anyway, but it was good to know that the Africans would back us if it came to blows. Autaritus and his Gauls were not popular men.

My mail and helmet were buried in the sand but I still had my shield, my spears and my swords. They were on display, as were the shields and weapons of every other warrior. That was a bridge we would have to cross when the time came to leave.

Pucco came to join us for food. He said, quietly, to me, "Everything is aboard and none saw me. I have covered the tracks in the sand."

I smiled and took out a tetradrachm, "Here, this is for you."

His eyes widened, "But I am a slave."

"That does not mean I have to treat you as one. You are a friend and while you may be the slave of the captain, to us you are Pucco the friend."

There was an uneasy mood in the camp that night. The Gauls had managed to get hold of some wine and as they liked to drink it unwatered it usually ended badly. We heard the noise as a brawl began and it ended bloodily. One warrior lay gutted. There would be bad feeling between the friends of the dead man and those of the victor. It took Captain Autaritus's commanding voice to end the commotion. It was good that we had decided not to bother to sleep that night for there was so much noise that it would not have been restful.

As well as swimming the horses each morning we had taken to visiting the animals after dark. We took them to the small stream that tumbled into the bay to allow them to drink. The night of the commotion however, when we had watered them, we continued down the stream to the sea. We walked them around the sand that led to our bay and prepared to board the ship. There would only be ten horses aboard. We had left most of our spares with the African horses. They would be cared for. We had eight of our animals as well as the captain's and his spare. This time they would be boarded from the sea. We stripped off and swam to the seaward side of the ship. War Axe and Serpus were aboard and they would haul on the pulley. Our job was to fit the sling. When we had first taken the horses from the village we had been seen as enemies. Countless battles and many leagues across the sea had bonded us and our eight were loaded easily. It took as long to load the two belonging to the captain as our eight had taken. It was almost dawn when we had finished and General Barca was impatient to be away. He cast a baleful look in our direction. There was little point in telling him that it was his man's horses that had caused the trouble. We dressed on the ship as the sail was let fly and we headed out to sea and sneaked away from Sicily.

Although we had not enjoyed a night of sleep none of us were ready to go to bed despite the pleasant rocking motion of the ponderous merchant ship. We were near the bows with our horses and we stood to calm them but, in reality, we were looking to the mountain of Eryx and the island of Sicily. Six of my men lay there. Two were buried and the bodies of the other four had been burned by the Romans. I do not know what the others were doing but I was saying goodbye. As we cleared the land that jutted out we began our turn. The sail had to be adjusted and it took time. Once we were heading west I looked back and saw the first glow of sun as the new day began. We were heading out to sea. I thought I knew the reason. It was to avoid the Roman fleet which was blockading Sicily.

Serpus came to me, "And now we start another life and another journey."

I nodded, "We sailed east and now we will sail south. Where will our journey end?" Even as I said the words I touched the horse amulet. Since I had learned that one of the symbols of the Carthaginian god Baal Hammon was a horse I had felt a connection to Carthage. It seemed to me that my course was not directed by me or my men but the gods themselves. How else could our survival be explained? When we had been hired we had been raw young warriors. As the Roman velites had shown us, it was the youngest and least experienced who were more likely to fall in war. We had lost just six. Some of the horsemen alongside whom we had fought had lost far greater numbers. Was our course, like the ship, being directed by some celestial captain?

By the time dawn broke we were many miles to the west and had begun to sail more southerly than westerly. One or two of the men had curled up in balls to sleep but Serpus and I had stayed awake. I had noticed that the Carthaginian officers, including the general, had not slept either. In fact they appeared to be waiting for something. It was when the lookout shouted that there were sails ahead that I knew why. It was the Roman fleet blockading the island. It was confirmed when the sail was reduced as the quinquereme raced to greet us. As she passed us I saw the crests on the helmets of the marines. It was a warship and she had weapons of war and many soldiers aboard her. I could not hear the conversation and would not have understood a word as it was spoken in Latin but as it did not sound angry and there was no attempt to board us I guessed that it was pre-arranged. Our course had not been determined by a need to avoid the Romans but was a prearranged meeting. We were not stopped for long but when the sail was allowed to billow free I saw that the Roman warship accompanied us. We passed the line of blockading ships and it was almost noon when the quinquereme finally turned and left us to sail in an apparently empty ocean.

It was only then that Serpus and I made water and, after making a shelter with our blankets to protect us from the sun, we slept. Sleeping on a merchant ship is easy. I had once, as a boy, been out fishing and my father had been forced to stay out at sea for a night. A small fishing ship that stank of fish and was tossed about by even the smallest wave was not pleasant. This was different. The motion rocked a man to sleep. The wind was not helping us and our progress was slow. That too made for a gentler motion.

When I woke I could smell the horse dung. The sun told me that it was late afternoon. I said to Alerix, Bellerix and Aed who were sitting and eating, "The horse dung needs to be cleaned and then we can eat. Come, you do not need Serpus or me to tell you to do the most obvious things."

"Sorry, Bruneus. You are right but this feels like we are leaving war and with it work."

"No Aed, now wake the others. I will help you."

I stripped off so that my clothes would not stink and then took the shovels and began to move the dung and throw it over the side. The fishes would feed and when they did sharks would come. Life was a circle and no matter what man did life went on. Our village was dead but the sea still teemed with fish and until more people came the rabbits would prosper. With the others roused we soon cleaned the dung and then we hauled pails of seawater to sluice down the deck. We completed our task by dousing ourselves.

It was after we had dressed that Hamilcar Barca, the captain and Pucco came from the stern to speak to us. He used Pucco to translate but I noticed that there were now few words I did not understand. Part of that was that he spoke to me as though I was simple, using short words and speaking slowly.

"Tell me about your land. The place you were born and your journey to Gades."

It was easy enough to tell him for I had nothing to hide and, in many ways, it was comforting to speak about a home I had not seen for a long time. Talking about the people who were long dead brought them back to life, however briefly. He seemed more interested in the journey to Gades and the people who lived there. He asked about the towns and cities. I was less useful to him for we had avoided those places but when I had finished he seemed content.

He spoke to Captain Bomilcar after the interrogation was over, "These men will be useful, Mago. Sicily is lost to us and the Romans will not let it slip from their grasp. The land north of Gades, now there is a piece of ripe fruit that can be plucked and we would not need a fleet to do so."

"But Hanno the Great does not look north. He looks south to Africa."

The general shook his head, "There is more desert than treasure in Africa. What is the point of having vast realms to rule if there are no people there to work and to bring an income? No, my family looks north. We have time, when we return home, to enjoy our families but we plan. You will need men. Your family is tied to mine and together we can all profit."

They headed back to the stern. Pucco came later on with some dates and figs, along with wine. "General Barca sent these. He thinks well of you, Bruneus."

As we ate I told the others of the conversation I had overheard. "So, it seems, we shall be returning to our homeland sometime."

Serpus had listened carefully to the conversation and picked up on the fact that we would have a period without war. "And we must become better warriors, Bruneus. There are just seven of us and I do not wish to lose another friend."

"Nor do I."

I expected to rise and see Africa on the horizon but we were roused by the lookout who shouted a warning. I had never heard the word before but it roused me for men ran along the decks and the Carthaginians armed themselves. A sleepy Pucco said, "Cilician pirates. The captain asks you to arm for war."

It took me the longest to don my mail for the shirt was a tight fit over the padded undershirt. The others all looked as sleepy and confused as I felt. We had all thought that the greatest danger was the Romans and the thought of pirates never entered our heads. Of course, we knew about the raiders who prowled our Blue Sea and landed in the night to take slaves but our walls had protected us when our home had not been cursed by the plague. Our fishing ships were too small a morsel for them so this came as a shock.

I had just donned my padded headgear and helmet when Pucco ran to us, "The captain wants you to come to the bows. You are to protect it."

"And the captain?"

"He will join you with other men."

I nodded, "Whence came the pirates and how are they bold enough to attack a Carthaginian ship?"

He pointed to the east, "There is an island there, Maleth, and while it is Carthaginian, the pirates use the islands that surround it to wait and pounce on ships which sail alone. They are bold."

Pucco looked terrified. He was a slave but there were good masters and bad ones. Mago Bomilcar seemed to be the former.

I said, "We will need slings and javelins."

Alerix said, "What about the horses?" Already the movement along the deck and the noise had alarmed them.

I shook my head, "We save the ship first and then think about the animals. If we lose this day then we shall not need horses, eh?"

When we reached the prow we saw that there were other warriors there. Few had mail or armour. I saw the two pirate ships. They were powered by oars and were racing from the east and the rising sun. The darkness and the shadow of the island I could just see had protected them from the lookouts who had been watching for them. They looked to be more than four lengths from us but as they had wind for their sails and the added power of a double row of oars then they would catch us. I saw that Hamilcar Barca was at the stern and was with his best troops, his bodyguards. That made sense for if the stern was taken then we were lost. The ship's captain and his helmsmen needed to be protected.

Even as Captain Bomilcar ran down the centre of the ship I saw the two pirate ships come a length closer and their tactic was clear, they intended to attack two sides at once and divide our defence. Our one advantage was that we were filled with soldiers and they would not be expecting that. Our ship had four bolt throwers, two at the bows and two at the stern. I had seen them used and knew that while they could keep up a steady rate of bolts, with just four of them we could not expect to do a great deal of damage.

Captain Bomilcar had Pucco with him. I had hoped the slave would take shelter for he had no means of protecting himself. The captain said, "Bruneus, you and I stand together." He did not seem to be familiar with the names of all my men. "Have the big one with the axe guard my left and Scrpus too. The others can stand before us." He nodded to the handful of men he had left from his retainers. "Cuneus, you, Daco and the others stand to the right of Bruneus." There were a handful of slingers who had been brought aboard and they would be the ones left to defend the bows. The centre of the ship had a few lightly armed men. I had never seen a sea battle but I guessed that the bows and the stern were the parts where the fighting would be fiercest. The pirate ships were getting closer.

I glanced at the captain. He had a long spear and his round shield as main weapons. This was the first time I had seen him using a shield and it reflected his worries. His sword hung from his belt. It was my six men who had the missiles. Even War Axe had laid his axe at his feet and held javelins behind his shield. I said to Captain Bomilcar, "Will you give the order to send stones and javelins, Captain?"

In the time we had been together the captain had changed. He seemed less arrogant. Perhaps the losses had made him so. He shook his head, "You know your men best. I trust your judgement."

I nodded and laid down my shield and javelins, "Serpus, let us see what we can do with our slings."

I saw that the slingers on our vessel had chosen the slings that would give them the maximum range. They were professionals and had two or three each. Serpus and I just had one each. I took a lead ball. Our victories over the Romans meant that the two of us had good, well made lead balls we had taken from the dead velites. The one I chose had markings on it. The dead velite had written a message or perhaps a curse upon it. I nestled it in the sling. Its slightly oval shape fitted well in the sling.

When I looked up I saw that one pirate ship was heading for our bows. It looked to be slightly faster than the other one or, perhaps, the second one was heading for the stern. I did not know the reason but when the two bolt throwers on our side cracked and sent their bolts at it I confess I jumped. Both bolts hit the enemy and we cheered but it was like spitting into the wind. One hit the side and stuck there while the other slammed into the mast. Neither had killed anyone and they had neither damaged nor slowed the ships which began to close with us. I saw the eight slingers whirl their slings and their balls flew. When only two reached their target then I knew it was too far for us to waste lead. I saw a few archers on the pirate ship. The slings probably had a longer range but Serpus and I would be reliant on Aed, Sercix, War Axe, Bellerix and Alerix for protection.

I was suddenly aware that I could hear a drum beating on the pirate ship and when the beat increased I saw that it was turning slightly to close with us. They were flying over the sea. The slingers found their range and all their stones hit. When the arrows came in reply only two struck our gunwale but it was a warning. I was pleased when my men raised their shields and moved back a little. I said, "Let us see the range, Serpus." We both whirled our slings and then released. I followed the flight of my stone. I saw it descend into the ship but I knew not if I had done any damage. I had the range and we began to rain upon the pirate. When arrows hit the shields of my men then I knew we were rapidly closing. The enemy arrows had hit two slingers and one of the retainers. I saw that the pirate was turning slightly. Their captain did not want to ram us as that would lose them whatever treasure we carried. I saw men with shields move to the side. They would board us. The bolts had continued to hit the pirate but now they were causing more damage. One bolt slammed into a pirate with a shield. It drove through the shield, his body and knocked him into the waiting warriors behind him. The machine took time to reload and its success made it the target of the archers. When one of the men working the machine was hit then the rate at which they could send the bolts slowed.

Captain Bomilcar said, "Move to the side. We will need to use spears soon."

He was right but it took courage to shuffle across the pitching deck as one. One of my lead balls hit a pirate on the head and he fell but when I saw the oars on our side run in I knew they would close and board. They would be relying on their sails but both ships were smaller and faster than the ponderous merchantman. It was time for javelins. "Serpus, shield and javelin."

I dropped the sling, bent down and retrieved my shield and javelins. I now had protection but as the slingers' ranks had been thinned there were less missiles hitting the enemy.

War Axe said, "Bruneus, can I throw?"

My biggest warrior was also the strongest and I said, "Aye!"

He pulled back and his javelin soared. It hit a pirate in the chest and the man tumbled into the sea. The archers tried to send their arrows at him but he had his shield covering him. The arrows that smacked into it would not hurt it.

They were now within thirty feet of us and closing. I said, "Throw when you are confident."

I saw pirates moving to the side with grappling hooks. Safe behind a wall of shields they whirled them over their heads. We had to take out the men with shields. We each threw when we felt we could hit a pirate. I aimed at the helmeted head of a pirate but he raised his shield just in time. When I saw the shield droop a little I chose another javelin. The pirate ship had closed a little and this time my javelin hit him in the face. He fell. The pirate with the grappling hook was now just twenty feet away and he risked all to send the hook across the water. One of our javelins killed him but the hook sailed over the gap and other pirates, hidden beneath the gunwale, grabbed it. To my horror it began to drop close to the captain. It missed him but its metal teeth dug into the back of Aed. He screamed as the pirates pulled. They might have thought they had the wood of the ship. They tore my comrade in arms over the side and he fell into the sea. We had no time to mourn. Bellerix, Sercix and Alerix closed together as another hook bit into the wood of the gunwale and men heaved the two ships together.

"War Axe, cut the rope!"

As my axeman had thrown his spears he was ready
with his axe and shield. He ran to the side as arrows and
stones struck his shield. More hooks bit into the gunwale
but pirates paid for their success with their lives. As I
threw my last javelin I picked up a pilum. Although War
Axe sliced through the rope two others dragged us
together and I saw the pirates waiting to hurl themselves
to our deck once we were close enough. There was one
half naked pirate with a boarding axe and as he jumped I
thrust up with my pilum. I embedded the spear into his
middle and let his momentum carry his screaming body
over my back. The head tore free from his body but it
was no longer true. I could only thrust with it. The spear
that struck Sercix came from the side. He had no chance
to defend against it but his death was swift for the head
found his heart. Alerix slew Sercix's killer. War Axe
was screaming his war cry and using his axe two handed.
None dared to close with him.

Captain Bomilcar was doing well for his long spear
was the perfect weapon to both hurt the enemy and keep
them aboard their ships. The slingers who had survived
the arrow storm sheltered behind our shields and they
now picked off the pirates as they tried to board. Some
attempted to swing across from the yards. Some were
slain by stones, the captain killed a couple and I hacked
the leg of one pirate. He lay on the deck, blood spurting.
Pucco ran and, picking up Sercix's sword, slit the man's
throat. We were doing well but I knew we had to take
the battle to them. I shouted, "Lone Wolf, to me!" I
knew that I was leaving the captain unprotected but our
attack might win this particular battle. Without waiting
to see if they had heard me I ran to the side. A pirate was
swinging across and I was able to leap up and gut him as
he swung. I landed next to the gunwale and I first hacked
my long sword into one of the ropes that tied us together
and, as an axe came down at me, lifted my shield to

block the blow. Had this been my old shield it might have ended badly but it was a well made scutum and had a metal boss. The boss bore the brunt of the blow and as the pirate had used the axe two handed I was able to swing my sword into his neck. The others had severed the rest of the lines and a gap began to appear between the ships. I rammed the point of my sword into the deck and picked up a javelin that lay there. I hurled it at the pirate who was swinging a grappling hook. He was impaled and then the bolt thrower cracked and the angle was such that the bolt flew down the length of the pirate's deck. It struck eight men. That was the moment that the battle of the bows ended. We had inflicted so many casualties that I could see blood coming from their scuppers. The bolt thrower cleared another file of men.

Captain Bomilcar shouted, "Bruneus, the general!"

I saw that the general and his bodyguards were beleaguered. The other ship had managed to board us and they were in the waist of the ship. We ran at them and this time it was a wild War Axe who led us. He had lost two friends and War Axe was determined to have vengeance. He swung his axe two handed and hacked into the backs of pirates who thought they had won. When the rest of us slashed and stabbed into the backs of men who wore no armour and had no protection a wail went up. It encouraged the general who led his men to charge those before us. Every boarder was slain and sailors hacked through the ropes. The second Cilician gave it up as a lost cause. They had thought they were attacking a sheep but it was a wolf in sheep's clothing that destroyed them. They would retire to the islands north of Maleth and lick their wounds. They would choose easier prey the next time.

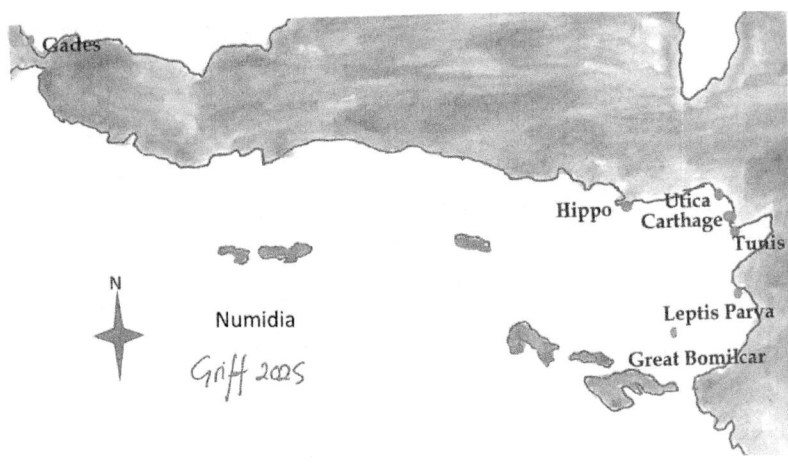

Chapter 9

The pirates' bodies were stripped and hurled into the sea. The sharks threshed around as they tore into the feast. It was for that reason that we did not bury our own dead. We had lost Aed overboard but Sercix could be prepared for his journey to the Otherworld. We would bury him in our new home in Carthage. The sun had passed its zenith by the time the ship had been cleared of the enemy corpses. No one wanted food and so we worked with the rest of the crew to make the ship whole once more. Weapons were collected and placed close to hand in case the pirates came back. That done we went to see to Sercix. We cleaned his body and then dressed him. He would be buried as a warrior. Captain Bomilcar seemed to understand what we needed to do and left us to it. We wrapped our friend in his cloak and then Bellerix and Pucco sewed it up. We placed it by the prow. We would be a guard of honour as the night passed and we neared the land of the Carthaginians.

Captain Bomilcar came to speak to us. Pucco had brought food. We wanted none but the wine he brought as welcome. "Once more, Bruneus, you fought well. That you did not obey my orders worked out well this time but do not make a habit of it."

Serpus could now speak Carthaginian almost as well as me and he said, "With due respect, Captain Bomilcar, if Bruneus had not acted as he did then we would have lost the ship."

The Carthaginian looked at Serpus to ascertain if my friend's words were impudent. He must have decided that they were not for he nodded. "Perhaps you are right. We land tomorrow and then you five will come to my estate south of Carthage. There you will be both my bodyguards and, as they are now old enough, you will train my sons, Mago and Himilco, to become riders and warriors. I would also have you make the retainers and men of my home into better warriors. Rome invaded my land once before and, whilst we were not hurt that time, the recent reverses have made me cautious."

I nodded, "For the same pay?"

He looked at me and I saw him calculating, "I hired thirteen men and now I have five." I said nothing. "You were paid ten tetradrachm. I have seen your worth and I will pay you eight tetradrachm a month. Is that acceptable?"

I looked at my men who nodded. Even War Axe had learned enough Carthaginian to understand the words. As there were now fewer of us it meant a pay rise and I was happy. "We accept. How old are your sons, Captain?"

"My eldest, Mago, is now eleven. My youngest, Himilco, was born just before I left for the war. He will be four or so by the time we reach my home."

"And you wish us to make them into warriors."

"They will need to be taught the basics of handling weapons. Had I been at home then Bodoster and the others would have begun the work already. You, Bruneus, and you, Serpus, are good riders. You will teach them to be horsemen. I want the giant, War Axe, to show them how to be brave. When they are ready then teach the sword and the spear."

"And will we go to war again?"

I knew that the Romans had inflicted a huge defeat on our new employers and I wondered if this would be the end of Carthaginian ambitions.

He nodded, "Our leader, Hanno the Great, wishes to conquer more of Africa. Our general sees the land north of Gades as ripe for the plucking but we first have to get the rest of the mercenaries back from the island. You will have months to get used to Africa and to begin the training of your charges." His orders given, he headed back to the stern where Hamilcar Barca and his other officers were taking advantage of the shade of the awning that was erected there.

That night, as we stood vigil over the body of Sercix, we sang a lament. It was a paean to help him find his way to the Otherworld. There were now just five of us left and we were the last of our clan. My new clan had diminishing numbers. As the sun began to rise in the east, I looked north. If we all died then it would be as though our clan had never existed. I swore an oath, to myself, that I would ensure that my people were never forgotten. Even if I was the last of the clan, so long as I was alive then the memory of the dead would be honoured.

The next day we were told that we had another half day of sailing. We would not be landing at Carthage but, instead, the city of Utica, which lay seventy miles further west. It did not matter to us for we knew nothing of the land but we were intrigued. As we headed into the bay and the port, Pucco was able to enlighten us. He spoke quietly so as not to be overheard. "The news of the terms of the surrender have not yet reached Carthage; that is because they are still ongoing, but General Barca does not want to answer awkward questions about the loss of the island. He fears that would happen if we landed at Carthage. He has estates close to Utica. It means, when we land, that we will have a longer journey to the home of Captain Bomilcar at Great Bomilcar."

That all made sense, at least to me, "And is the captain happy about that?"

"In Carthaginian politics you choose your side and stay with it. He is General Barca's man."

The port was a busy one but Hamilcar Barca was an important man and a berth was made available for our ship. The ships we saw were not warships but merchant ships. The Carthaginians were merchants who traded the seas. I wondered, now that their navy had taken a beating, if they would continue to be safe on the seas? The attack on our vessel was, perhaps, a taste of the future.

We landed and we carried our friend's body off before we brought the horses. I left War Axe with the body while the rest of us returned to bring the horses from the ship. That done we waited at the foot of the gangplank for the general and his staff were leaving the ship. Captain Bomilcar was with them. The general saw me and approached us, "Your men did well in the sea fight."

"Thank you, General."

He handed me ten tetradrachm, "A warrior is worth payment and your actions saved not only the ship but me. I remember such things. Remind me, where is your home?"

I pointed north, across the blue sea, "Almost in the land of the Gauls but this side of the mountains, General."

"Then when I decide to conquer that land I will have your master bring you to serve in my army. You could be useful and there will be rewards."

"Of course." My neutral tone belied the answer I gave for inside I was angry. I had no master. I was a sword for hire.

He and his men left. Pucco and the three retainers who remained were with the horses. I realised that we now had spare horses and the three retainers could ride back to the estates of Captain Bomilcar.

The captain checked Aeneas to see if he had suffered any wounds on the voyage and in the sea battle. I had checked the animals already and they had survived unharmed. He mounted the horse. "You will need to pack the horses and ensure that my men know how to ride. I will go with Pucco. We will stay with a friend of mine. We need supplies for the three day journey to my home. I will send Pucco back with instructions. I go to speak to the officials of the port."

"Yes, Captain Bomilcar." They rode off. I turned to the three survivors. "Can you ride?" They all shook their heads. We had three horses with war saddles and they would be the safest way for the three to ride. While Alerix and Bellerix packed the other animals, War Axe, Serpus and I each took a retainer to instruct him how to ride. It was as I did so I remembered how we had taught the dead lone wolves how to ride on the way back from the raid. I hoped these three men would last longer.

When Pucco returned an hour later, we headed, first to meet the captain and then the market where Captain Bomilcar bought some gifts for his family. That done we headed on the road to the villa where we would sleep. I was glad that we were not staying in the town. It was crowded and noisy as well as stinking. Captain Bomilcar's friend greeted his friend warmly. As we moved through Carthage I began to see what an important man Lord Bomilcar was. Men bowed to him when they greeted him. We were not given rooms in the dwelling but the stable was more than adequate. After we had eaten we asked permission to bury Sercix. The captain and his friend agreed and gave us directions to a suitable burial plot. The captain's friend had been a soldier and understood our need.

That night we found the ancient grove with old olive trees. It lay just beyond the boundary wall of the estate. It belonged to no man and Sercix would be buried in a free land for we were free men. After finding a patch of earth without too many rocks, we dug a grave that was deep enough for the body. It took us a long time but Sercix deserved the effort. We placed the rocks we had uncovered on his body and then showered it with earth. We found a piece of fallen olive wood and we carved the sign of the clan upon it and sang our paean once more. We placed the marker on the grave so that others might know who was buried. None of us knew if we would ever get back there but I knew that we could all find it if we needed to.

What surprised me, the next day as we headed along the Carthaginian road, was how green the coastal strip was. There were verdant forests and many farms. For some reason I had expected desert. The land was divided into market gardens and orchards planted with all sorts of fruit trees. There were many streams of water flowing in channels which irrigated every part of this fertile and fecund land. There were country homes everywhere. They were lavishly built and covered with stucco. Part of the land was planted with vines, part with olives as well as other productive trees. Beyond these, cattle and sheep were pastured on the plains, and there were meadows with grazing horses. When we camped we had plenty of water and food but no tents and so we lay in the open by irrigated farms. The horses appreciated both the water and the grazing not to mention the shade from the trees. It was, however, hot. For that reason and because this was friendly land, I did not ride in my mail. We used two of the spare horses to carry the mail and weapons. The cloak I wore became invaluable. It had a cowl and kept my head cool. We did not enter Carthage but the city, which we saw in the distance took my breath away. Even viewed from afar it was imposing. There were rings of white walls and a citadel rose high above them. I could not wait to visit it.

We headed due south of the city and passed more farms. The captain did not live in a city but a walled estate by a river. It took fourteen days to reach it. We did not rush for we wanted the horses to be fit when we reached our new home. To be truthful I had mixed feelings about the new experience. Until now we had, since we had left home, lived in camps with other soldiers. The only women and children we had seen were the ones in Utica and the villa where we had slept in the stable. It had been a brief glance. I did not know how these people lived. Our people lived in family dwellings where we all slept together under one wooden roof. In Utica I had seen many stone buildings. The same had been true when we had passed through Eryx and the other island settlements. We had not even raided one. How did you sleep in a stone building? Our homes were made by the people who lived in them. When I had lain in my bed next to my brother I had looked up and could see the wood I had placed there and the roof my uncle had woven. I was part of the house and as I had built it I was protected by it. I might be living in a stone house built by another. Would I be safe?

The captain and Pucco rode at the fore with the remaining retainers. I was next to Serpus and the other three led our horses. Serpus knew me better than any. He had been like a brother growing up. Our mothers had carried the two of us the same time and our births were just hours apart. We had lived on this earth for the same length of time. He said, "What is it that worries you, Bruneus?"

I jerked my head around, "Is it so obvious?"

He smiled, "To me, it is."

"We are going to a place so foreign that we might as well be living on the moon."

"We knew that when we made the choice we did on the beach near our home. You were right to suggest we leave and to travel."

"It has not worked out well." I gestured with my thumb. "How many have I lost already?"

"You lost none. Each man made his own decision." He touched the amulet he kept around his neck. "The gods chose to take them. That hook could have struck any of those who stood before us, including our paymaster, Captain Bomilcar, but it was Aed they wished to take. You could have died as could I, and as for War Axe," he shook his head and laughed, "the gods must like a madman for that is how he fights and yet he never suffers a scratch. We are warriors. None of us were fishermen. Perhaps Alerix might have become a baker but he chose to come on the raid. There was something," he patted his chest, "here, that made him choose the way of the warrior. Do not disparage the men you lead. We are good warriors and I would not choose to fight with another." We rode in silence, the breeze from the north making it a little more comfortable than when it did not blow. The shade from the trees which lined the road also helped. Serpus broke the silence. "Why do you think that Autaritus was so keen to welcome us when we first arrived in Drepanum?"

I shrugged, "I know not."

He laughed, "That is because you only had eyes for the men you led. You are a born leader. He recognised that quality in you and saw, in us, warriors who were at least the equal of his and, probably, superior. When we first arrived in Drepanum we were young and we were raw but we moved liked warriors and each time we fought, Autaritus saw that. He wished to command you."

I realised that he was right, "And we have now made an enemy of him."

Serpus took out the piece of dried venison to chew on it. It was now many months old but it would stave off the hunger pangs until we ate. "It matters not for we are to be Captain Bomilcar's men." He lowered his voice, "He changed his view of us and that was solely down to you, Bruneus. For me I am looking forward to the start of a new life. I like being a warrior but I miss the life in the village." He looked wistfully behind him, "Birga is but a dream yet I can still feel the softness of her skin and the shape of her beneath her shift."

Birga and he had been betrothed. He had been saddened by the death of his family but the death of Birga had hurt him more. I had not yet chosen my mate. Perhaps that was as well.

"Yet how will we live when we reach our new home? None of us have lived in a stone building and these Carthaginians seem to need it like a horse needs grass."

"We should ask Pucco."

That night we camped by a small stream in a wooded glade. There was enough grass for the horses and the supplies we had bought in Utica were still enough to make a good meal. After Pucco had finished his duties with the captain he joined us. He had to bathe the Carthaginian's upper body and comb his hair. Our captain also like his upper lip to be bare and Pucco shaved it each night and morning.

Pucco ate with us and Serpus said, "This place we go to, Pucco, what is it like?"

"I have never been here so how do I know?"

"You lived in Gades and that is Carthaginian."

"That was a city built by the Phoenicians and we are going to an estate." He chewed some food, thoughtfully and then said, "When I spoke to one of the retainers, the son of the overseer, Daco the Younger, he said that the estate was one of the richest in Carthage. There is a river and the estate is built on a piece of high ground overlooking the valley. It has a wall and two gates to protect it ensuring that the people are safe from both animals and Libyan raiders. Each day the labourers go to tend the fields. The animals are moved to graze and everyone works."

Bellerix asked, "Everyone?"

"There are free men, the overseer, the master of the vines, the butler, the horse master and the like but there are more slaves than free men. The captain has two sons and a daughter. His wife is supposed to be beautiful. They do not work. They have a Greek slave who teaches the children." That seemed to impress Pucco.

"Teach them?" I saw the puzzlement on War Axe's face. "What?"

163

"How to read and write. How to count. Your job will be to teach the boys how to be warriors but you will not be slaves."

There was silence as Pucco ate for we were all thinking about our own home. There had been just two slaves in the village. Both had been captured in a raid. They were little more than children but one day they would have become women who would have been given tasks to occupy every waking moment. They were not treated badly but with just two of them they were unusual.

"How many slaves?" It was my voice that broke the silence.

Pucco shrugged, "I did not ask but from the way he spoke I am guessing hundreds. If that is true then the place must be big, bigger than your whole village." We had told Pucco about Barcenis and the disaster. He was familiar with the names of our families. The two long sea voyages had ensured that. "The captain has an unpleasant duty when he returns. The retainers were men whose families farmed his lordship's land. He has to tell them that their men will not be returning. He is not looking forward to it."

That night, as I said my prayers to my gods, I thought about the number of slaves. One man's home would be far bigger than the village in which I had spent my life up to now. I knew then that when the village had been burned my old life had gone up in flames with it. Now I was reborn and my home would be wherever I slept. I might not even have the same bed each night. In many ways that was a comfort and I woke refreshed and looked forward to seeing my new home. It might be just until we went to war again but I would embrace whatever the gods threw my way. So long as there was a water that ran to the sea then the goddess Icaunis could take my offerings back across the sea to my home and the spirits of my family.

When we saw the walls of our new home it was late afternoon and, coming from the northwest, the rays of sun made the white walls seem pink and red. They rose above the valley and it looked like a city to me. We reined in and Captain Bomilcar waved a hand and said, proudly, "My home, Great Bomilcar. We have come at a propitious time for the gods like to paint our walls red at this time of day. It is my colour." He pointed to the river, "We have no bridge here but we need none for the river can be forded and it will wash the journey from our horses' legs."

He nudged his horse down the slope and we crossed the river which came halfway up our horses' legs. War Axe's long legs ensured that his boots were also washed clean. To me it was a symbol. The dirt would be taken from us and carried to the sea. That same sea touched the beach at Barcenis. The spirits of our families would know we had landed. The road twisted and turned up to the gates. I could not see any guards but then realised that he might have taken them to war. Now that I was getting closer I saw that the sandstone walls were as high as a man standing on the shoulders of another and painted white. Although the gates were open I saw that they had a design painted upon them. It was an eye on each door. Two men stood at the gates and bowed. They wore hats but their heads looked to be shaved. They wore long white garments and a thin red border ran along the bottom. I now saw what Lord Bomilcar had meant by red being his colour. I had thought that the red trim on his tunic was merely an affectation.

"Welcome, Lord Bomilcar. You were seen from afar and all is ready."

"Thank you Craster. Pucco is my new body servant, find him quarters in the main house. These five warriors now serve me. They can occupy the barracks. Daco, show them where the stables are to be found."

"Yes, My Lord."

The captain, Lord Bomilcar, dismounted and handed the reins of Aeneas to Serpus, "Tomorrow is time enough for you to meet my family. For tonight you can settle in. There is a bathhouse. Make sure that they use it, Craster. They stink and I would not have my wife offended when she meets the men who are to teach my sons the way of war."

He was right, we did stink. You cannot ride a horse for fourteen days and not do so. Horses sweat as do men. Despite Pucco's efforts Captain Bomilcar also had a ripe aroma.

Craster nodded, "Yes, My Lord. Daco, have them dismount and take their horses with them." His voice told me that he liked giving orders and he expected them to be obeyed. Daco nodded.

As Lord Bomilcar, Pucco and the butler, Craster, headed off, Daco, the overseer, greeted the retainer I knew to be his son. We did not intrude and I looked around. The walls had a fighting platform and stone steps led up to them There were two small towers atop the gatehouse. There were no defences within. There were buildings built into the walls but Lord Bomilcar was heading for a building which stood on the highest part of this settlement. It was a villa even more magnificent than the one in which we had stayed, outside Utica. There were pillars at the entrance and a roof which had carved figures upon it. There were two guards standing on either side of it but they each just wore a small helmet and carried a sword and small shield. I had not met them but knew that they were not warriors like us. If they were then Lord Bomilcar's sons would not need us to teach them the ways of war.

"A grand place, Bruneus."

"Aye, Alerix, and somewhat different to our home."

War Axe looked perplexed, "A bath, but it is not yet springtime."

I laughed, "I think that we will be bathing regularly."

It was clear from Daco's expression that his son had told him of our exploits. The look of disdain he had first given the dirty, hairy warriors was now replaced by a smile. "My son has told me how you have saved both him and Lord Bomilcar many times. I will tell the others and you will be even more welcome. First, the stables."

The horse master, Galbas, greeted us at the door. Daco said, "Here are warriors who have saved the life of Lord Bomilcar."

"Then you are doubly welcome. If you wish to leave your horses I will have slaves attend to them."

I shook my head, "These are our animals and we ride them to war. Thank you for the offer but we will tend to them this night."

The horse master smiled. He loved horses, that was clear, and our affection for our animals made us instant friends.

The stables were made of stone and there were stalls for twenty horses. Three work horses occupied the first of them. We unsaddled our animals and hung their saddles from hooks. It was all very organised. I saw that there were combs and brushes. We brushed our horses and used water to cool and clean them before fitting nosebags and putting a bucket of water by each of them.

That done Daco and his son led us to the sleeping quarters. We were laden with weapons and armour. The long low building had twenty beds inside. There was a table and two benches in the middle of the two rows of beds. There were also hooks and a shelf running along the wall. Daco said, "I will go and see that there is all that you need in the bathhouse. My son, Daco the Younger, will fetch you when you are done."

When he had gone and I had hung my mail shirt from a hook and placed the rest of my gear on the shelf, I sat on the bed and looked at my new home. Despite the number of beds and the table it felt somehow smaller than my own home in Barcenis. It would take me some time to become used to sleeping in a stone building.

The young man who had been in Sicily with us and journeyed from Utica with us returned. I asked him, "Daco, what do we need to know about a bathhouse for we have never used one."

He smiled, "I am looking forward to mine but you are honoured for Lord Bomilcar asked for you to use it first. We are lucky to have one for our use. There is a grander one in the main house but that is reserved for the family. When you go in you take off your clothes, all of them. A slave will wash them for you if you wish."

I shook my head, "Apart from our armour these are all that we possess."

Daco the Younger frowned, "Lady Bomilcar will not like that. I am guessing that there will be new clothes for you. I will ask the slaves to beat the worst of the dirt from them. You go into the bathhouse and enter the water. There are sponges for you to use. There are also latrines should you need to make water or empty your bowels. There are separate sponges for that. When you have enjoyed the bath enough then you go to the cold water bath or you can simply dry off and the slaves will fetch your clothes. If you wish there is oil for your bodies and strigils to scrape off the dirt. When you are used to our ways then you might take advantage of them. There are also combs and razors." He smiled, "I know I will need the wildlife taking from my head. Come. You must be hungry and we cannot eat until you are clean."

Serpus asked, "Where do you live?"

"As my father is overseer for the slaves, we have a house attached to the slave quarters. I have my own room!" He seemed proud of the fact that he did not have to share a room.

When we reached the bathhouse we stripped off and while that did not normally bother us the two shaven headed Nubian slaves who waited for our clothes

168

intimidated us slightly. I was glad to enter the water. It was hot. We had bathed in the sea when we had been camped by the beach near Eryx and the water had been warm. This was hot. I sank beneath the water and let the warmth cover my head and hair. When I emerged I saw the lice and nits fleeing. We were dirty. One of the slaves had gone to clean our clothes and I waved over the other. I pointed to a sponge on a stick and a comb. He brought them over. I used the comb first to remove even more of the wildlife. I realised I would need to have my moustache trimmed. A real warrior never cut his hair but while a moustache was supposed to be long enough to be braided it did not do to let it rise into the nose. I then used a sponge to clean the ingrained dirt from my body. When that was done I handed them to Serpus. By the time we had finished I felt much cleaner. I chose the shock of the cold water and, I know not how, but it made me feel much cleaner.

By the time we returned to the sleeping quarters I saw slaves fetching food for us. There was wine too. Two slaves waited on us and I asked them what we were eating. Some of the words I did not understand but through mime and common sense I worked out the nature of the food. Pucco joined us just as we were finishing, I saw that he had a white tunic like the men we had seen. It too had a red border but it was far thinner than the two we had seen. The thickness and numbers of the bands seemed to indicate a hierarchy. I stored that information. He had also taken advantage of the bathhouse and bathed. He smiled, "Lord Bomilcar asked me to come and ensure that all was well and to answer any questions."

He clarified the type of food we had eaten and then Serpus said, "What do they grow here?"

"They have olive trees, fruit trees including pomegranate, almond, fig, and date palm. They have vines and bees are very important to them. They produce honey. They have cattle, sheep and poultry."

War Axe emptied his beaker of wine and said, after belching, "I think I could get used to this life."

I smiled for he was right. We had lost men but we, the survivors, had been rewarded with a life of luxury.

Chapter 10

We woke before dawn. That was the way of the warrior. Slaves brought in olives, bread, oil as well as boiled eggs and ham. It was as good a start to the day as I could recall. As we ate I said, "Now, we need to make a good impression." I pointed my eating knife at War Axe, "No wild hair and no belching. We are meeting the wife of a noble."

War Axe looked suitably offended, "Me?"

I shook my head as he smiled, "Now I know that you have all tried to speak the language but from now on we only speak Carthaginian. I know it will be hard but we look strange enough without sounding like barbarians."

War Axe said, "But we are barbarians!"

Ignoring him I said, "Serpus and I will be the ones to train the two boys and that means you three can work with any others that Lord Bomilcar wishes us to train."

Bellerix asked, "Others?"

"Lord Bomilcar fears that the Romans may decide to invade Carthage and if they do he wants his men to defend these walls. We are being paid well."

I had Serpus plait my moustache and I did his. We tied our hair back. Even with clothes that had been shaken clean by the slaves and combed hair I knew that we would appear as wild men to sophisticated Carthaginian nobles. It could not be helped. Serpus said, "Do we take our swords?"

I thought about it and nodded, "We are warriors and if it causes offence then I will take the blame and remedy the situation."

Pucco came in and I saw that he was now wearing a coned shaped cap, "They are ready for you." He looked us up and down, "Good, you have your swords and your look presentable." He smiled, "The mistress of the house has tunics for you."

Serpus said, "Tell me that they are not white!"

"No, there will be two tunics for each of you and breeches to go with them. The beeches you will reserve for formal occasions are blue and the tunics to go with them are a deep red. The ones you wear each day are lighter in shade and there are two of them for each of you. Lady Bomilcar instructed me to tell you that the tunics and breeches must be washed once a week. Slaves will attend to that for you. There are also hats." War Axe's mouth dropped open and Pucco shrugged, "It is the custom of the people to wear such things and Lord Bomilcar wears one." He tapped his head which was covered in a small, conical hat, "As I do, although Lord Bomilcar's is far grander. Now come or I shall be in trouble."

As we headed out of the cool sleeping quarters and the hot sun hit us I said, "Pucco, I have not had the chance to ask you, how do you feel about this new arrangement?"

He beamed, "I am glad that I fell in with you. Already my life is better than in Gades and Lady Bomilcar is a kind lady." He suddenly stopped, "The eldest son, Mago," he shook his head, "do not upset him."

"Why?"

"I will say no more; it is better that you form your own judgement but be cautious." His words worried me. The entrance to the house was still guarded by the two sentries. Both looked to be little more than boys and I think the only thing they could have prevented from entering would have been a small lap dog. They stared at us as we passed into the room they call an atrium and I saw fear in their eyes. The entrance was open to the skies but there was a pool. I guessed it was rainwater as I could not see any pipes.

Craster was waiting; he looked us up and down and sighed, "Until you can be dressed properly this will have to do. Follow me and do not speak unless someone speaks to you. Do you understand?"

I smiled and said, "Perfectly."

We went into the house and down a corridor that was lit by oil lamps in the wall. At the end was light and we emerged into a garden courtyard covered in quarried stone with a bubbling fountain and surrounded by lemon trees. The trees were cunningly arranged so that they shaded the courtyard from the sun. There were also pots of aromatic herbs and the open space smelled most pleasant. Lord Bomilcar was now dressed in a white tunic with a pair of broad red borders. I also saw his children. The eldest son was dressed like his father.. The younger one was dressed in a white tunic. The daughter had a hat and wore a long white tunic. She had to be older than the younger son but I could not work out her age. It was Lady Bomilcar who attracted and held my attention. She was stunningly beautiful. Her arms were bare and she had blue paint above her eyes and her lips were the same colour as the border on her husband's tunic. Her eyes were the deepest blue I have ever seen. They were almost purple. Her fingers, which were long and elegant, were festooned with jewelled rings and about her neck she wore a golden chain. She looked like one of the statues we had passed in Utica, the ones of the gods and goddesses.

She turned to her husband, "You have brought us real warriors, Mago. These are men and that one," she pointed a finger at War Axe, "could be Hercules himself."

"I told you, my sweet, that these men are the reason we survived and I do not mean just my men and me. But for Bruneus here we might have lost the ship and General Barca."

She smiled and I saw a row of perfect teeth, "Then my sons are in good hands." She turned to look at her eldest son, "Mago, what do you think of them?"

The eldest boy had a sneer on his face. I came to realise that it was a permanent feature. When he spoke he seemed to whine, "They are uncouth barbarians!"

His father laughed, "Aye, that they are but they will make you into a warrior that can fight in the Sacred Band."

He looked surprised, "You are sure?"

"I have seen them fight and know that they have skills which are greater than Bodoster and the bodyguards I lost."

The boy nodded, "Bodoster was a mighty warrior."

"Yet he died and they live." He turned to the little boy, "And you, Himilco, what do you think of your teachers?"

"They look fierce and I would be afraid to fight them but if they can teach me to be a warrior then I will be grateful."

I liked Himilco from that moment. Unlike his brother he was willing to learn.

Lady Bomilcar said, "The lessons can start tomorrow. Craster and Lord Bomilcar's new body servant will instruct you in the ways of this house." She smiled again and it was like the sun had risen, "I am happy that you are here."

It was clear that we were dismissed. I bowed and while Serpus, Alerix and Bellerix caught on and followed a heartbeat later, War Axe looked at us in wonder and only bowed whilst we were rising. Lord and Lady Bomilcar, along with Himilco and the girl laughed but Mago snorted with derision and sneered, "Barbarian!"

Craster and Pucco took us to the atrium where slaves were waiting with piles of clothes. Craster said, "Your hair must be tied back at all times. There are sandals in your sleeping quarters. They will be worn indoors. You will change your clothes every four days and keep your best tunics for such occasion as Pucco here will tell you. I am to be addressed as Master Craster and the family by their titles, my lord and my lady. You may address her ladyship as Domina if you wish. The children's titles are: Master Mago, Master Himilco and Mistress Dido. Are there any questions?"

I did not like the butler's attitude and so I asked one, "And do you pay us or will that be Lord Bomilcar's task?"

The man looked shocked, "His lordship does not demean himself by such acts. I will pay you each week when the other free men are paid."

"And when will that be, for we have worked for fifteen days already?" I could see that I had irritated him and I smiled to soften my request.

"I will bring fourteen days of pay while you dress. Does that satisfy?"

"We are all free men, Master Craster, are we not, and we all deserve our pay. If not then we are little better than slaves."

He waved an irritated hand, "Take them hence!"

Serpus laughed as we stepped into the sunlight once more, "I see you did not take your own advice. Master Craster will not be our friend."

"Serpus, he would never have been our friend." I looked back, "Now Lady Bomilcar..."

"Lady Dido," said Pucco. "She is named after the famous Queen Dido."

"And she is as fair as a queen, a goddess even."

Serpus put an arm around me, "And do not even dream that dream."

I put my arm around his waist, "A man may dream for those are for his own enjoyment, Serpus."

The next day when the training with the boys began, my worst fears were realised. Whilst Himilco listened to

175

everything Serpus and I said Mago chose what he wanted to listen to. The result was that Himilco improved each day whilst Mago's development was in fits and starts. It depended upon if he liked the lesson we were delivering. As we rarely saw Lord Bomilcar it was hard to know what to do. My three men enjoyed their life as the men they trained were willing to learn and they ended each day in a good frame of mind, but not so Serpus. A month after we had begun the training Serpus was almost ready to tell Lord Bomilcar that he wished to quit and find other employment. I persuaded him to stick it out. "The pay is good and we are not spending any of it. If he does not become a good warrior then it is not our fault."

"But I want to make him a good warrior."

"Why?"

He looked at me as though I was an idiot, "Because that is our job."

I shook my head, "Our job is to be warriors. You can only teach if someone is willing to learn. Anyway, we can begin riding lessons next." I could not help but smile. "If he does not listen and falls off then that will teach him, eh?"

He looked up at the sky, "Then I hope he falls!"

"Yes, but just a bruising and not a death. That would never do."

He laughed and already had changed his mind about quitting. I think he just wanted to voice his frustration. "Yet Himilco, who is much younger, improves every day. He will be a good warrior. I see him as a good leader."

"As do I. All we are doing is giving Mago the skills to join the Sacred Band."

"What is that?"

I had spoken to Daco and knew the answer. "They are an elite infantry unit of Carthaginian citizens that serve in military campaigns but only in Carthage. It is an old tradition that has been recently revived. When Rome invaded it made them worry about the defence of their land. They have to be chosen from the noble families of Carthage. I do not think that Mago will have any problem winning a place. They fight with a spear and shield and only fight in Carthage. When Hamilcar Barca tries to invade our homeland he will not be with us."

"So the riding is not necessary?"

"No, but Lord Bomilcar needs his son to be a good rider in case he is given command at some future date."

The young noble had a good horse and that saved him from too much harm when we began the equestrian lessons. A poor horse might have bolted for the youth proved to be heavy handed with the reins and I saw the horse master wince at the pain he inflicted on the animal, for he was free with the whip and used it to punish the horse for his mistakes. His fall, when it came, was of his own making. As luck would have it his father and mother were there watching and the young noble was desperate to impress. Serpus and I showed him how we rode and used our knees to make sharp turns. We demonstrated how to throw a javelin without becoming unbalanced. I knew he was not listening and had selected the parts he liked. He did not use his knees and when he threw the javelin he overbalanced. The pommels were there to keep a full grown man in the saddle and not a youth. He crashed to the ground and lay still. I feared the worst but when we reached him he was still conscious. He had broken some ribs and his arm was cut, quite badly by the edge of a sharp rock. He jumped up angrily and glared at us. Before he could say anything his mother shook her head, "I am not training to be a warrior, Mago, but if I was I would listen to my teachers. You did not and the gods have punished you."

She and her husband then turned their attention to Himilco and left the older youth to limp to his room where the estate doctor tended to him. There was a great deal about the Spartans in the Carthaginian culture. I had learned that already. Himilco, in contrast, heeded every word we said and when he threw his javelin not only did he keep his saddle, despite being smaller and younger, but he also hit the target. His little face lit up when he was praised by his parents.

When the lesson was over Lady Dido came over. She put her hand on mine and I felt a shudder of excitement race through my body. When she spoke her voice seemed to sing to me, "Bruneus, you are a good teacher. I know that Mago tries your patience but persevere. He has that kind of nature. He is not a likeable youth. Himilco is different. Keep doing what you are doing and I shall be in your debt. I would have my youngest child survive the wars that are yet to come."

Her words gave me more confidence in how we should treat the unpleasant youth and we became harsher teachers. He did not like it. He cursed us and promised dire retribution when he became a man but we persevered. Lady Dido had given us permission. Four months after we had begun our training of the two young men two things happened that were to change not only our lives but the life of every Carthaginian. The first was that Mago was summoned to begin his training with the Sacred Band. He was now twelve and that was deemed old enough. Like the Spartans the Carthaginians admired, he was sent with just a slave to Carthage. There were no tears but there were smiles in our quarters. That changed our lives but not that of Carthage. It was Hamilcar Barca who inadvertently caused the war to start. When Autaritus and the mercenaries had threatened to leave the army Hamilcar Barca had promised them payment. General Gisco had sent the men back in small units and they had been deposited in Utica but no one had paid them. We now heard that they had rebelled. We learned all this, second hand from Pucco who had sharp ears and was waiting on Lord Bomilcar when the news was delivered. The twenty thousand mercenaries were not a major problem but the Africans who had joined them and swollen their army to one of over seventy thousand was. The lands conquered by Hanno now rose in revolt. There was a rebel army to deal with.

I was desperate to speak to Lord Bomilcar but knew that it was not my place. Instead we threw ourselves into making Himilco a good warrior. He had advantages that we had not enjoyed when we had been his age. He ate very well and his father maintained a doctor for his estate. Minor ailments did not develop. The result was that he grew well and filled out quicker than we had done. His father also had enough money to have leather armour and weapons made for him so that he was able to learn quicker and not risk as many injuries. It was a delight to work with him for he thanked us each day. Unlike Mago he never tried to curse or demean us. Each time we stopped for refreshments he asked us about our lives and our families. When we told him the story of the end of our village he became upset. War Axe showed a side to him I had not seen before. He took to the boy and became protective of him. When Bellerix was a little too eager during one training session and Himilco tumbled to the ground and was winded, War Axe became angry and punched Bellerix in the face, knocking him to the ground. I had to take him to the side and calm him.

It was Himilco, however, who managed to calm the savage beast that was War Axe. When he regained his breath he took War Axe to task, "If I am to be a warrior, War Axe, then I need to know what pain is. Bellerix did nothing wrong. Now apologise to him."

The giant nodded and said, "Sorry, Bellerix."

Bellerix spat out a tooth, "Now I know what it is like to be struck by a bull and besides," he laughed, "I did not need that tooth. All is forgiven."

We heard more news of the rebellion from Lord Bomilcar himself. The five of us were invited to dine with the lord and lady as well as Himilco. It was Himilco's birthday. We were told to bathe and to wear the better tunics and breeches we had not yet worn. We were both excited and fearful at the same time. We had eaten Carthaginian food before but I knew, from Pucco, that the food the nobles enjoyed was richer in both flavour and variety. That excited us but we were fearful for we knew that they were refined and our upbringing and life in the army had not prepared us for such events. As I inspected my men I said, "Do not simply dive in and begin to eat. Watch how Lord and Lady Bomilcar choose their food and the portions that they take. Copy their actions."

Serpus wagged a finger at War Axe, "That means, War Axe, do not shovel platters of food down your gullet and do not speak while you have a mouth full of food."

He nodded glumly, "And I take it I cannot fart either."

I rolled my eyes in exasperation, "Definitely not and no belching either. Eat less than you normally do. This is an honour. The food does not matter."

A slave came for us, "Lord Bomilcar summons you."

We marched to the villa wearing unfamiliar clothes and feeling as though we had been reborn in a new land. Our lives had changed since we had left with Barcas to raid for horses. We were no longer the same callow youths who had eagerly anticipated our first raid. We were warriors and about to dine with one of the richest nobles in Carthage.

While the days were hot the evenings could be cool and there was a brazier in the room family used for dining. The Carthaginians did not recline when they ate but sat on chairs so that their backs were straight. Lord and Lady Bomilcar and their two children waited for us in the room but they were seated. Pucco opened the door to let us in and then, when it was closed, he stood behind Lord Mago. Lord Mago was at one end and Lady Dido at the other. The two children faced each other in the middle. Lady Bomilcar rose and waved a hand. "Sit, for you are our guests. Bruneus, come and sit at my right hand and Serpus at my left." She smiled, "War Axe, my son has asked for you to sit next to him." The warrior who could charge recklessly into overwhelming numbers of enemies looked terrified as he nodded and pulled out the chair.

We sat and almost by magic Craster and slaves appeared. Wine was poured into the goblets that were proffered. I saw that it was white wine. I caught War Axe's eye and raised an eyebrow. He nodded. He would behave. The slaves then brought out small platters. They had small delicacies upon them, olives, anchovies, and capers. Lady Dido said, "Eat."

I picked up an olive and ate it.

Lord Mago said, "We have been remiss. You should have been welcomed ere now but…"

Lady Dido said, "This is better, my husband, for we celebrate Himilco's birthday and these warriors have already changed our youngest. This is fitting."

I felt obliged to mention Mago, "And have you heard from Mago, My Lady?"

She shook her head and the smile left her face, "No and we shall not. Our son is now a warrior of Carthage, he is a trainee of the Sacred Band." The smile returned and she drank some wine. She wiped her mouth with a napkin and said, "And Himilco will not have to leave us as his brother did for it is only the first born who is allowed in the Sacred Band."

Alerix asked, "My Lord, what is the Sacred Band?"

Lord Mago also drank some of the wine, "It is a phalanx of two thousand five hundred men. It has not fought in battle for many years. It was destroyed at the battle of Crimissus in Sicily a hundred years ago. Since then the Tribunal of One Hundred has decided that the Sacred Band's duty is to defend Carthage."

Alerix was clever and he said, "So it is unlikely that they will have to fight in battle."

Lord Mago nodded.

The platters were empty and they were taken away. The next course came in and was a platter of small fried fish. I saw War Axe's face light up. We had often eaten this in our village and was one of his favourite foods. I suspected this would be better than what we had enjoyed as the oil used to cook it would be the best. Our goblets were topped up with fresh wine.

Himilco said, "Father, did I hear that war has come to Carthage?"

Lady Dido said, "You have sharp ears, my son. Be careful what you listen to. Half a story is worse than hearing a lie."

Lord Mago wiped his fingers on his napkin, "No, my love, it is right that he takes an interest and these warriors who are to guard me in battle need to know what is happening in the wider world."

Lady Dido smiled, "You are right."

Lord Mago wiped his fingers and then sipped his wine, "The mercenaries from Sicily have risen in revolt. They are joined by Numidians and other Africans who tire of the yoke of Carthage as well as our neighbours, the Libyans. Our city is cut off."

His daughter Dido said, "Are we in danger, Father?"

He smiled, "No, for we are too far from the rebels who are in the west but the situation cannot be tolerated. We have lost Sicily and our two other islands are threatened. If we lose the west then Carthage is doomed. Hanno the Great has raised an army and he will quash this rising."

I asked, "And General Barca?"

"He waits in Carthage. You should know, Bruneus, that Hanno the Great and Hamilcar Barca do not get on.

If Hanno the Great succeeds in quelling the rebellion then it means the general's plans to increase our empire to the north will come to naught. If, however, the rebellion continues then we may well be called upon to join General Barca and finish off the enemy ourselves."

I could tell, from his words, that he knew his future was tied to that of Hamilcar Barca.

Himilco said, "Does that mean my training would cease?"

I shook my head, "A good warrior can practise without being watched. My men and I have given you the routines that you need. There are slaves with whom you could spar and if we are called to war then when we return, victorious, we can see how much improvement you have made to yourself."

I saw from the looks on the faces of his parents that I had said the right thing.

When we finished the fish, the plates were removed and fresh goblets fetched. Our appetites whetted, a lamb was brought in. I could see the joy on War Axe's face. As much as he loved fried fish meat was his favourite and his beaming face showed it. Lady Dido recognised the look and laughed, "Craster has chosen the perfect food for our guests. Why, I believe that War Axe could devour the whole animal himself."

The smile left War Axe's face and he mumbled, "I am sorry, I…"

Himilco put his hand on War Axe's, "Mother is teasing, War Axe. Eat as much as you wish. This feast is as much in your honour as it is to celebrate my birthday." He looked at me, "I have never thanked you and your men, Bruneus, for saving my father." He raised his goblet of watered wine. "I do so now."

I saw the pride on his parents' faces.

Our goblets had been filled with red wine and I raised mine, "And for our part we thank his lordship, for he gave my lone wolves a home."

As we ate Lady Dido said, "I have heard parts of your story, Bruneus, but I would like to hear more. Lone Wolves?"

I told her the story from the moment my uncle had led us from our home up to the meeting with Lord Bomilcar. My men and Lord Bomilcar had heard it and they chattered as they ate. Lady Dido and I could have been alone as I told her the tale. It was a pleasure to be so close to her and drink in her perfume. She hung on my every word and when her hand brushed mine as she refilled my goblet I thought I would burst with joy.

When I finished and the lamb carcass was removed, she said, "You have lost all and yet you kept your men together. You are a remarkable man, Bruneus. I know my eldest called you a barbarian but he was wrong. You are a noble and I think that the gods sent you to us."

The spell was broken when the last course was fetched. There were platters of fruits, figs, dates, and plums and there was cheese. There was also a pastry made with cream and lemons. Lady Dido's daughter clapped her hands together, "My favourite." She smiled at War Axe, "You liked the lamb but I could eat all of this alone."

War Axe had such a smile on his face as the young girl spoke to him that all of us smiled. I do not think that I had ever seen War Axe as happy as in that moment.

As we headed back to our quarters I could tell that, although War Axe had behaved himself, he had still drunk more than the rest of us put together. Lady Dido had watered her wine but we had been served the powerful red wine without any water. He was humming a song and staggering a little as we walked. Serpus said, "So we go to war and if Hanno loses we may be facing Autaritus and the Gauls."

I nodded. I had worked that out already, "We are not of any people save our own. We are the Clan of the Lone

Wolf and while there are just five of us we are loyal to each other and the man who pays us."

Alerix said, "I would be loyal to this family even if they did not pay us. Now that the wart has gone this is a good place and I like them all. I feel part of a family. I know that they are not my family but they are worthy of my loyalty."

Bellerix nodded as we entered our quarters. Slaves had already lit the oil lamps and there was a warm glow to the room we now called home. "And it would be perfect but for one thing." We all began to undress and did so carefully so as not to damage the precious garments we had worn.

Alerix said, "You need a woman." Bellerix nodded. "We all need a woman but we are not near a town. We have the money and we could pay for the finest whores but we cannot do that. I fear we will continue to live like this."

He was right. I also had urges but I would not waste my seed on a whore. Besides, what woman could compare with Lady Dido? "I will speak to Pucco on the morrow. He is a clever young man and he may have an answer for us."

Pucco did have an answer. While War Axe allowed Himilco to rain blows on his shield Pucco pointed to the slaves who were heading to the fields to work. "There are slaves there. They can be taken."

I shook my head, "We will not take our women."

He smiled, "Then your men can ask the women if they consent."

"But what if we put them with child?"

"Lord Bomilcar raises crops and animals. If a slave bears a child then that is another slave for the estate." I looked at the young slave to see if there was a lie lurking behind his eyes. He shook his head, "I have enjoyed the company of a slave four times since we arrived. I am not a eunuch and I have desires too."

I got on well with Daco and when I saw him, later in the day, I told him what Pucco had said. He nodded, "Pucco is right. I confess your words relieve me for I feared you were the kind of men who shun women and prefer different company. My son said that you did not abuse the captives you took at Eryx."

"No, we are men with men's desires but we are also mindful that the slaves belong to Lord Bomilcar."

"Let me put your mind at rest. The slaves talk to me for I am not an overseer who overuses the whip. I know that many of the female slaves find you and your men attractive. You are exotic and look nothing like their men. Your paler skin and long hair intrigues them. I will send over five of them this night. It will make everyone happy."

"Just four."

He studied me, "You do not wish to lie with a woman?"

"I do, more than anything but she will be a free woman. I am content. One day we will visit a town and then I can satisfy my needs."

The arrangement worked. I left when the women arrived and I walked to the river. I had not made a sacrifice since we had arrived and this seemed like a propitious moment. I took out a tetradrachm. I kissed it and said, "I give you this, Icaunis, so that you can continue to protect us and I hope that your waters flow to the dead of my family." I tossed the coin into the water and the plop made me smile. I felt better.

When I returned the women had gone for there was a bell rung when all slaves had to be in their quarters. The men were happy. War Axe said, "You do not know what you are missing, Bruneus. They said that they wished to come again and I for one am happy."

I smiled and lay on my bed, "Then I am happy too."

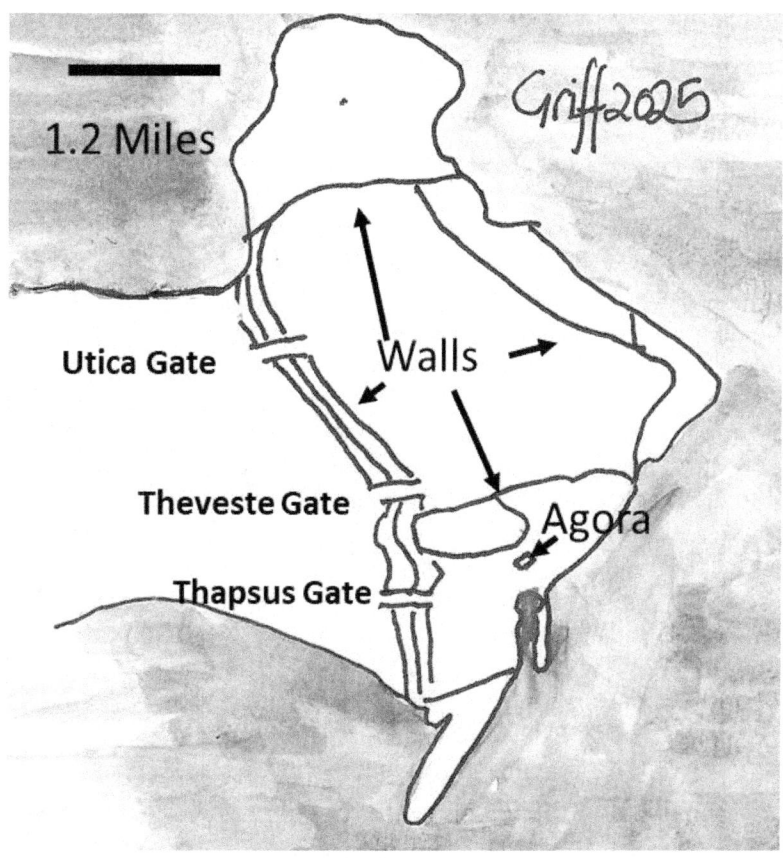

Figure 3 Carthage

Chapter 11

It was two months after the birthday meal that Lord Bomilcar came to speak to me. I had seen the cloaked riders arrive the day before and watched as he had waved farewell to them. They were clearly messengers and the import of their news manifested itself when he took me aside on the morning following their departure. That he had visited me and not sent for me was a first. "Bruneus, there has been a disaster. Hanno the Great defeated the rebels." I frowned and he gave me a wry smile. "That is not the disaster. He thought the war was over and returned to Utica. The men he left at his camp were surprised and defeated. All their baggage was taken and the survivors fled to Utica. General Barca has been summoned to Carthage. I think we will be needed sooner rather than later."

"We are prepared. The horses have not been ridden much and they are in good condition."

He nodded, "You may wear the armour and helmets you brought with you but I want the shields painted red with the sign of the eye upon them." I nodded. That was not a problem although I would be losing my wolf design. It would still be there, hidden beneath the eye. "You will also all be given an exomis to wear instead of your tunic." I frowned at the unknown word. "It is a Spartan tunic with short sleeves. The ones for you and your men will be ready before we leave. The blue breeches you wear will suffice. There will also be red cloaks for you all." He saw the question on my face. "I will wear the same but it honours Xanthippos the Spartan general who defeated the Romans. My father fought alongside him and the colour will bring us luck."

"It will also make us easier to see on the battlefield."

He nodded, "I know. I want to show the Tribunal of One Hundred what I can do."

I prayed that it would not end in disaster for him.

Serpus apart, the others were somewhat disappointed to be leaving. They enjoyed the company of the same four women two or three times a week and as all four were with child they were not as happy as they might have been. War Axe would also miss Himilco. I explained to them all the realities of life. "We are swords for hire and we work for Lord Bomilcar. We have coins in our purses but we are not rich men. When we are then we can think of a life that does not include war."

Serpus understood and said, "This is good. Think of it, War Axe, when we return we may all be fathers. That is not something I thought would ever happen."

War Axe brightened at the thought.

We painted our shields but it was Pucco who showed he had an artistic bent and he painted the eye upon them. I confess it looked effective. He cunningly incorporated my boss into the design. He would be coming to war with us. We had taught him to ride whilst teaching Himilco and Mago. He would not wear mail but Lord Bomilcar had a leather cuirass made for him and a small helmet. For his defence he had a short sword but no shield. I was not sure how long he would last in a battle but as we had to defend Lord Bomilcar, if Pucco died then we would have already led the way to the Otherworld.

The next messenger who arrived and handed a lead scroll to Lord Bomilcar did not stay long. They were orders. I was sent for and told that our departure was imminent. We would join the muster in Carthage.

Himilco, of course, knew that we were departing soon and he became sad. We tried to cheer him up but we failed. The mothers of my friends' unborn babies were also tearful. I understood all of those but the sadness and teary eyes of Lady Dido surprised me most of all. She had endured her husband departing before. Poor Himilco had seen his father for the first time when we had returned with him but the lady was clearly distracted. She sent one of her ladies, a freewoman and not a slave, the day before we were to depart, to ask me to meet her in the fountain garden. I had seen the lady before and she seemed to have a perpetually sad look on her face, as though she was in pain. This was unusual and so I changed into clean clothes and made sure my hair was groomed. I put my red cloak on and fastened it with a small brooch. As I followed the freewoman to the villa I knew that no matter what I did I would still appear like an unhewn piece of rock compared to the finely carved marble that was Lady Dido.

She was seated alone. Himilco and his sister were having a lesson from their Greek teacher. Lord Bomilcar was checking that his overseer and estate workers knew what was expected of them. There was a jug of wine on the table and after she dismissed the freewoman she poured us both a goblet of wine. She gestured for me to sit next to her. She raised her goblet, "I drink to the five men who will bring my husband home safe." I drank but I could not help but clutch at my horse amulet with my left hand. I did not want to offend the gods. She smiled and laid the goblet on the table. She nodded, "It is good that you honour the gods. I have had tokens made for you. I had them purified by the priestess of Isis." She smiled, "My family have connections with Egypt and we have always worshipped the Lady of the Heavens. I have a small temple and my daughter and I, along with my women, worship there. My priestess keeps the temple purified. Lila, the woman who brought you here also worships there. Her husband was one of the men who died in Sicily." That explained the look of sadness on her face. She took out five brooches. They were beautifully made but one was slightly bigger than the others. They were all the same design. She laid the four smaller ones on the table and held the slightly larger one so that I could see it more clearly. "They are to fasten your cloaks but they will also protect you." She ran a finger around the enamelled brooch, "See, this is the face of the goddess, Isis. She was responsible for resurrecting her brother Osiris and she is powerful." I saw that the face was modelled on Lady Dido. The eyes were the same shade as were the lips. The figure was kneeling and had outstretched wings. The metal worker had coated the enamelled brooch in fabulous colours. It looked vibrant and would stand out, even on our red cloaks. "This is the goddess Isis with the wings of a kite. The red you can see is red jasper." Her voice became earnest. "It has the power to protect the wearer. Yours has more than your men's because I sense that it is your fate to protect my husband. I want both of you to return from this war. There is unfinished business here." Her eyes held mine and I wondered what this unfinished business was. I thought it was the training of her son but I did not know for certain. She put the winged brooch down and stood. "Stand." I did so and she stood before me. Her head came to my chin and as she looked up at me her perfume intoxicated me as our eyes met. They were like two pools seen in the moonlight. She said, huskily, "Hold your cloak so that I may fit the new brooch." I did so. I was terrified for I dared not speak and I worried that my body might do something I would regret. It was like a spell that I dared not break. The brooch I had used was high on the cloak and her hand brushed my hand as she unfastened it. I could not bear it. She was beathing heavily and her eyes never left mine. She placed the old brooch on the table and took the new one. She slipped the metal through the cloak but as she did so she pricked herself. Her hand jerked up and I could not help myself. I took her hand and kissed the wound. What had I done? I waited for the rebuke but none came. I stared into the pools that were her eyes. She smiled, "Thank you,

Bruneus. That has sealed the spell and you will be protected by my blood and Isis." She moved her hand away but did so slowly as though she was keeping the contact for as long as possible.

She sat as did I. She picked up her goblet and I saw that her hand was shaking. I picked up mine and saw that I too was shaking. We said nothing but looked at each other. The voice from behind, when it came, made me start for I had not heard Lord Bomilcar arrive, "Ah, I see you have given him the lucky charm."

A frown of irritation came over Lady Dido's face, "It is not a lucky charm! Bruneus knows that. It is you who are the barbarian. It is a holy piece of art that will protect him in battle and as he protects you then both will be protected."

He laughed and poured himself some wine, "She is not my goddess but if she looks after my men and me then I am happy. Is all ready for tomorrow, Bruneus?"

The spell was broken and the moment was over. "All is prepared, My Lord. Pucco has his horse and we have chosen the three horses that we will use to carry what we need. The muster is at Carthage?"

He nodded, "Yes, you will get to see the greatest city in the world. Thebes, Rome and Athens are nothing compared to it. We will wait until Hanno returns. It would not do to leave the city while he was absent."

I stood, "Then I will go and ensure that all is packed and deliver these to my men." I turned and locked eyes with Lady Dido. "I thank you for these, My Lady. We will guard them with our lives."

She smiled, "It is they who will guard you but it is a token only of the love I bear my husband and his protectors."

I left in a daze. I could barely speak when I gave the brooches to my men. They were impressed but War Axe said, "As I am the biggest warrior should I not have the largest brooch?"

I turned and snapped, "No!" He recoiled. He could not know that each time I touched the brooch I would smell Lady Dido's perfume and feel the touch of her hand. I would taste her and that memory would sustain me through long and lonely nights. I would never lie with a woman or spill my seed wantonly. There was one woman who would haunt my dreams and she was unattainable. I was content. Lady Dido would be my Isis and she would be the one I worshipped.

I was lucky that I had much to do. The packing of our bags needed care for the horses that carried them had to be balanced. We left our finest clothes in our quarters but all else was packed. Craster had promised us food and wine for the journey but that would not be available until the next morning. We would rise before dawn and travel when it was cool. The noon sun was too hot for the road to be travelled. That night we sat around the table and drank the wine that had been provided.

Serpus said, "This feels like home now and I shall be sad to leave."

War Axe smiled, "I will be glad to cleave some skulls."

I shook my head, "War Axe, we are bodyguards. We protect Lord Bomilcar. I want no wild charges from you. There are just five of us and we have Pucco and Lord Bomilcar to keep from harm."

"We have all changed, Bruneus, we are not the boys who followed Barcas on the raid." We looked at Alerix who could be quite thoughtful at times. He waved an arm around the other three and said, "We have lain with a woman and left our mark, you have chosen, instead, to become a leader. That you are a good one means that you have chosen the right path. One day, when we have earned enough coins, we four will probably buy the slave who is the mother to our children and become farmers," he smiled, "or a baker, but you…" he shook his head, "you will be a leader and a warrior until the day you die."

I felt uncomfortable for he had almost hit the mark. Had he or the others witnessed the meeting with Lady Dido then they would have had a better insight into me. The silence that followed was uncomfortable.

Serpus broke the silence with a wry laugh, "Listen to yourself, Alerix, you talk of things that are so far in the future as to be the stuff of dreams. Sercix and Aed had dreams too but they ended in the battle with the pirate. We do what we are paid to do and we fight. If we are lucky and the gods smile on us then we return here and you are right, it is a good life. I enjoy working with the men of the estate and Himilco. Laying with a woman gives me more pleasure that I expected but we are warriors and we should never forget that. The Clan of the Lone Wolf was a well-chosen title. There are now five wolves and our enemies should fear us."

Bellerix said, "And look at Pucco. He has changed as much as any of us. He was barely a boy when we first met him and so thin that I thought a stiff breeze would break him asunder. Now he has filled out and has to shave every day. He smiles and carries a sword. We have all changed and that change will continue. I think we will become less like the men they see as barbarians and more like the Carthaginians." He smiled, "But better!"

I did not fall asleep straightaway. My mind was filled with too many thoughts. I was not helped by War Axe's stentorian snores. He was asleep the moment his eyes closed. It must be good to be War Axe and not be assailed by doubts, fears and visions of the future.

I rose early for I needed to make water. I went out to the use the pot that was there. It was better than having it in our sleeping quarters. The moon was just setting. It was a wolf moon and I smiled. That was a good sign. I took out my horse amulet and kissed it. As I did my eyes strayed to the villa. There Lady Dido would be beneath her sheets and sleeping. I pictured myself lying next to her and stroking her hair. I shook my head. Such thoughts led to madness. I went back inside and began to dress. I had seen the moon setting. My movements woke the others and by the time the slave arrived with the food, we were dressed. Laden with our war gear we headed for the stables. Galbas and his slaves had the horses already prepared and their saddles were polished and ready to be used. Even as we led the horses out Craster's slaves arrived with our supplies. We packed the horses carefully to ensure that they were balanced. I was about to send a slave to tell Lord Bomilcar that we were ready to leave when he and Pucco arrived. He smiled, "Good, you are eager. That bodes well. Let us ride while it is cool. We have far to travel."

As we passed through the gates I was disappointed. I had hoped that Lady Dido would have risen to bid her husband farewell. Perhaps that was not their way or they may have saved such intimacies for the bedroom. I was quiet as Lord Bomilcar led us north on the road that passed Tunis and then reached Carthage.

We stopped before noon at a village that had date and palm trees as well as water. The animals were ready for the rest and we needed refreshment too. Lord Bomilcar waved me over and Pucco left his side to join the others. "You should know my thoughts, Bruneus. The messenger who brought me my orders also had orders from General Barca. They were sealed orders and private. The general has not been given enough men to do the job. We have just ten thousand men and only seventy war elephants. The rebels have twenty five thousand to face us. The rest are besieging Hippo. They have taken Utica and General Hanno is attempting to relieve the siege. He still has an army and hopes to end the rebellion himself." He shook his head, "He is doomed to failure for he has lost too many men and their spirits will be low. General Gisco was captured along with many other officers and soldiers by the enemy leader Spendius. The seven hundred are hostages." He shook his head, "I think that General Barca has been given, a poisoned chalice."

"Then why does he accept it?"

He sighed, "Because in the eyes of the Tribunal he lost Sicily. It was General Gisco who signed the treaty but General Barca was seen as responsible. He has to defeat the enemy. I am given command of half of the elephants and a unit of cavalry. It is a small part of the army but I intend to show that I am worthy of the honour. I will lead, do you understand me?"

"Yes Lord Bomilcar."

"And that means I rely on you and the others to guard me." He studied me and smiled, "Lady Dido sets great store by you. She believes you were sent by the gods to guard me." He tapped the brooch of Isis on my cloak, "That is her way of guarding you."

I rode in silence for I was thinking of the task ahead. When we finally reached Carthage I saw the vast camp that lay before the city. Lord Bomilcar found the tents which had been erected for us and then he went with me and Pucco into the city. Serpus could see to the camp easily. We did not take horses into the city. He paused before the Thapsus Gate. "I have enemies in Carthage. They are General Barca's enemies too. Be wary, Bruneus, and view all as a threat. Pucco, walk next to me and Bruneus, behind. Have your hand ready on your sword."

"Yes, My Lord." I moved my cloak to free the access to my hilt. The seal in Lord Bomilcar's hand allowed us to pass through the gate. There were three walls through which we passed, each one higher than the one before. The city had looked formidable from a distance but up close it was truly colossal. We headed through the streets and up a slope that led to the Agora and, as Lord

Bomilcar explained, the Senate Chamber. There were
houses and workshops. The streets were busy but our
armour and swords carved a passage through them. I saw
ahead the mighty harbour of Carthage. With a special
circular bay for warships called the cothon, over two
hundred vessels could be safely sheltered and protected.
Since the defeat of the Carthaginian fleet many of the
bays would be empty.

We passed, as we neared the Agora, a sombre and
dark place. Pucco asked, "My Lord, what is this place? It
is empty and sinister."

He paused and said, "It is the Tophet of Salambô. It is
a place of sacrifice."

I was intrigued, "Animals, my lord?"

He nodded, "Sometimes, but in times of need it is
often children who are sacrificed to Moloch; it is usually
the first born. Mago was sacrificed to the Sacred Band."
He smiled, "Better that way, eh? Come, we must hurry."

We did not enter the Senate chamber. The Tribunal of
One Hundred were debating. We stood outside and
waited with the other officers. We had made it unharmed
to the building but I was still wary. However, Lord
Bomilcar looked relaxed as he spoke with some of the
other nobles and so I was able to study the harbour. I had
never seen anything so awesome in my life. The outer
harbour was filled with ships but the inner harbour, the
war harbour, hid the vessels from view. I saw many
guards on the walls that guarded it. It was below us but I
could hear the hammering and sawing. I did not know if
it was the repairing of ships or the building of new ones.
These people were truly great.

I knew when Hamilcar Barca emerged for silence fell.
He smiled at Lord Bomilcar, "You are here, Mago,
good." He then addressed the rest of the gathered
officers. "My orders are confirmed, let us return to the
camp. Tomorrow we begin preparations to end this
rebellion."

The general had his own bodyguards and they cleared the way as we headed down the slopes to the Thapsus Gate. Pucco and I trailed along behind. As we passed the Tophet I clutched my brooch of Isis. I was the first born. The thought of being a human sacrifice terrified me.

When we neared the camp Lord Bomilcar said, "I have no need of you, Bruneus, but Pucco, you shall attend on me."

When I found our camp Serpus, Alerix and Bellerix were not there. War Axe guarded our gear. "Where are the others?"

He pointed, "At the horse lines, there was trouble."

That was typical of War Axe. He gave the barest of information. What kind of trouble? I headed for the horse lines and saw Serpus stroking Crow who seemed agitated. Alerix and Bellerix were doing the same with their animals. I hurried over. "What is amiss?"

Serpus continued to stroke his horse but nodded to the elephants. "They do not like the smell of the elephants."

I could now smell the animals. Even the smallest were taller than the horses by more than the length of a man's arm. They did not seem bothered by the horses but I knew that we had a problem. I said, "I will see what I can do." I headed over to the elephants. The men who rode them had their camp. They were Numidians. I knew that I would appear as a giant to them and a barbarian. I took off my helmet and smiled, "I am Bruneus and those are our horses."

They nodded and a grizzled Carthaginian warrior stood, "I am Drixus and I command this squadron of elephants."

"Our horses are fearful yet the other horses are calm, why is that?"

He smiled and showed a mouth full of white teeth, "They need to be schooled. They must become familiar with the elephants. When we go to war the elephants will make the enemy horses back away. We do not need that with yours. They are not from this land?"

"They are from the land across the straits, north of the Ebro."

"Ah, bring yours over and sing to him softly while you do so. Layla is my elephant and she is gentle."

I went for Stormbringer, I held his reins and said, "Come, my brave horse, today you need to show courage for you are a leader." I began to sing a lullaby my mother had sung to me. I walked slowly towards the elephant and its handler but kept a tight hold on the reins. My horse was a brave one and he let me lead him but I could feel that he was not happy. He snorted and stamped as we moved.

The handler said, "Keep singing but bring your animal so that his head faces Layla."

I did so and I had to fight to keep Stormbringer's head still. The handler then touched the elephant's ear with his crop and the elephant gently raised its trunk and stroked Stormbringer's head. I feared the worst but it did not happen. Instead Stormbringer calmed.

Drixus smiled and said, "These are fierce beasts in war but they are gentle with other animals. Your horse will now accept them as friends. Bring the others over one by one."

I led Stormbringer back and said, "Serpus, take Crow. Sing as you take him but do everything that Drixus says and all will be well." He looked at me dubiously and I smiled, "Trust me, my friend, I would not lead you or Crow astray. We have endured too much together."

When he led him Alerix shook his head and said, "I will not do that, Bruneus."

"Nor me."

"Then I will do so. That is how a leader leads. He goes where others fear to tread."

Alerix shook his head, "It is a monster."

"It is not. It is as gentle as a lamb. I know that in battle it will be fierce but we make him our friend, eh?"

I was not sure if Lord Bomilcar's horse had been schooled and so, when the others had been greeted and welcomed by Layla I took him. When the horses were all settled and my men were grooming them I returned to Drixus. "Thank you, Drixus."

"We are on the same side and we go to war. We lost, so I heard, one hundred fine elephants when General Hanno's camp was overrun and his men were defeated. We must protect these animals if we are to win."

"But there are more than twice as many enemies before us."

"Have you fought alongside General Barca before?"

I nodded, "I was at Eryx with him."

"Do you think he has the beating of this Spendius and Mathos? A Roman deserter and a Numidian who is disloyal?"

I thought about it. He had defeated Romans and they were well led. While I did not doubt that the men the two deserters led were good warriors, neither of the men struck me as having enough experience to defeat as cunning a general as Hamilcar Barca. "You are right and I must have faith. Captain Bomilcar, who is our leader, tells me that he may be put in command of elephants and horses."

The calm expression that had been on Drixus' face while we had spoken now became frowned, "Then I hope he knows what he is doing. These animals must be used wisely."

I was not sure. His leadership on Sicily had been limited. Had he been promoted too soon?

The next day the army moved from its camp to a flat piece of ground half a mile from the walls of Carthage. I saw men lining the walls. General Barca would have an audience for his manoeuvres. He separated the army into two. The horses and elephants were on one side and the heavy infantry phalanxes on the other. The general did not address us all but while the men and animals were marshalled he gave his instructions to his officers, Captain Bomilcar amongst them. Now that we were in the army Lord Bomilcar had reverted to his military rank. I knew, from our conversations on the road, that he aspired to be a strategos or general one day. Captain was but one step.

He and another officer came over to us. The elephants and horsemen were divided into two groups. I was pleased to see that Drixus was with us. I saw that each elephant had a man who had a crop or stick to guide it and an archer on his back. There was leather protection for the elephants' heads. There were a thousand cavalrymen under the captain's command. They were a mixture. There were Numidians, Libyans as well as a few Gaetulians. We had met warriors like them in Sicily. There were also about forty nobles wearing mail and with long spears.

"Captain Drixus, move your elephants to the right. Horsemen follow."

When we were away the captain marshalled them so that the horsemen flanked the elephants which, the front three apart, were four abreast.

The captain shouted so that all could hear his words, "The general wants us to practise a tactic which we may use in the coming battle. When his horn sounds three times we will pass between the phalanxes." I looked over and saw that there were, as yet, no gaps between the phalanxes. It took some time for the elephants to be organised. In battle this might have sealed a defeat but this was practice for war. Silence reigned, except for the jingling of mail as horses stamped impatiently or perhaps in irritation at the presence of the elephants. Then the horn sounded twice. Some horsemen moved forward but Captain Bomilcar roared out, "Stand fast!" The infantry moved apart and gaps appeared. When the

horns sounded three times the captain had us wheel and
we passed, frighteningly close to the infantry. I could see
why the general had us flanking the elephants. The
infantry had some protection from the huge beasts.
Having done it once we repeated it six times until it
seemed as easy as spreading butter on bread. The horses
and the elephants were then taken to practise the charge.
It was now obvious why they were divided into two
groups for we flanked the infantry when we charged. We
were weary by the end of the day but returned to the
camp feeling more confident about our general and the
men alongside whom we fought.

That night we sat with Pucco, who joined us to speak
about the day. Alerix said, "I would not like to face those
elephants in battle."

War Axe frowned, "They just have a bowman on the
back. He cannot do much harm to men who wear
armour."

Serpus said, quietly, "It is not the bowman who is the
danger. It is the animal itself. When we charged the
Romans then it was Crow, Stormbringer and the other
horses that terrified them, not the smell of your breath.
The elephant has four feet that can crush and smash a
man to a pulp."

I nodded, "Our horses do not like to strike a man but
the elephants are trained to trample. There will only be
seventy of them but they can cut a swathe through the
enemy ranks."

Bellerix nodded, "And our job is to protect them."

"No Bellerix, there are one thousand cavalry for that.
Our purpose is to protect Lord Bomilcar."

The next day saw us refining the manoeuvre. When
we had passed through the infantry we moved to the
flanks and when the horn sounded once then the whole
line moved forward. The day also saw a refinement. The
general had men use flags to repeat the signals. Red flags
were used for the cavalry and elephants and green for the

infantry. It gave us all confidence. One thing that had puzzled us was why the Sacred Band was not with us. The answer was supplied by Pucco who told us that Hanno the Great had ordered the Sacred Band to guard the city of Carthage. Mago Bomilcar would be safe and it would be his father who would be in danger.

Then news came that General Hanno had given up on his attempt to retake Utica. He was camped close to Hippo where the rebels under Mathos were besieging it. We heard this, not from Captain Bomilcar, but Pucco who was serving at the table.

"We are going to war. General Barca has to cross the Bagradas River but the rebels hold the only bridge across that river. The general fears that we could be destroyed if we tried to force a crossing. We march tomorrow but not to the bridge. We go to the mouth of the river."

Serpus said, "He wants to ferry us across? That would be madness. While the horses could swim the infantry and the elephants would need so many boats that the enemy would know what we intended and destroy us."

Pucco shrugged, "All I know is that we leave Carthage tomorrow night and march to the mouth of the river."

"Night time?"

Pucco had changed. His time with us and the captain meant he understood strategy far better than when he had been a slave in Gades. "Yes, Alerix. The general knows that the enemy, whilst many miles to the west, occupy hills from which they can observe our movements. The bridge is five miles downstream and the rebel army is just nine miles from the river's mouth."

Serpus nodded, "Then it seems our general intends to become a wizard and use magic to help us cross the river. It should be an interesting experience."

Figure 4 The Battle of the Bagradas River

Chapter 12

By dawn we had reached the mouth of the river and we all waited for the magic trick the general had promised. In the end it proved to be a disappointment to some. The magic was that the wind which blew from the east and the low tide revealed a hidden sand bar across the mouth of the river. As the sun rose behind us, we picked our way across the sand which threatened to suck us down and crossed to the west bank. While some were disparaging I was not. The general has used his own local knowledge and experience to outwit the enemy. He was using the land itself to help to defeat an enemy. It saved us a battle at the bridge and would, I knew, discomfit the rebels. The sight of an army not before them as they had expected but behind their defences would shake their confidence.

It took the morning to ensure that no equipment had been damaged, eat and to rest a little. The order was then given to head for the relatively small rebel force holding the bridge. We had, of course, been seen once the sun rose. You cannot hide an army of ten thousand men, not to mention the seventy war elephants. The rebels at the bridge almost had parity of numbers with us. There were about eight or nine thousand of them, according to Captain Bomilcar who confided in us. We also saw the rebel army further west, closer to Utica, begin to move. They outnumbered us by two to one. They were nine miles away but we saw the shadow and the dust cloud moving towards us.

Hamilcar Barca had a plan. It was in his head but he knew what he was doing. Before we had left Carthage he had spent hours with his captains. Captain Bomilcar and Captain Drixus knew his plan and their part in it but the men who would fight the battle were in the dark. We knew as little about the plan as the enemy who were just reacting to the surprise move. The general headed for the river crossing. It was a race to see who would get there first; us or the army of Spendius. The infantry were next to the river and the cavalry in a long column to the west of them. The elephants were on the extreme right of our line. I was learning about strategos. One never knows what goes on in the mind of a great general. When we had lived in the village we had not bothered about such thoughts but since we had become mercenaries I had seen how the cleverness and quickness of a general's mind could win a battle even when the odds were against him. As we marched towards the river it became clear that the rebel army was moving far faster than we were. After two hours of marching it was obvious to anyone who could see that Spendius and the rebel army would trap us against the rebels holding the bridge. We halted. I am not sure if this was preplanned or if the general just thought on his feet but he gave the command to about turn. It was the simplest of manoeuvres and we completed it easily. We then began to head back to the sandbar at the mouth of the river. As soon as we turned the men who had been at the bridge began to not only follow us but edge closer to Spendius and the army from Utica. They intended to combine their numbers.

We said nothing but I could hear some of the Numidian horsemen complaining. We remained silent. I think the others were like me and wondering what the general had planned. Serpus glanced behind us and said, "The ones from the bridge are marching to join the larger army."

Even we relative novice warriors knew what this meant. Alerix said, "They mean to trap us against the river."

I saw what Spendius intended. He did not have many cavalrymen but his infantry were numerous and I saw his lighter armoured men moving as fast as horsemen. He intended to extend his line, turn and surround us. Twenty five thousand men could easily defeat our paltry ten thousand. I had my doubts then about Hamilcar Barca. The about turn had put doubt in my mind. Did the general know what he was doing? Was Lady Dido destined to become a widow? Would Himilco be trained by another? I saw that the few horsemen that the enemy had were at the front of the column and at the rear. They would be able to race around our flanks and destroy us by attacking unprotected backs.

I threw back the cloak to free my arms, for when the battle began it would be so quick that I would not have time. As I did so my hand brushed the Isis brooch. Lady Dido's face flashed into my head and I smiled at the memory. My action coincided with Drusus, one of the Numidian captains saying, "This is madness, Captain Bomilcar. We should turn and face the enemy."

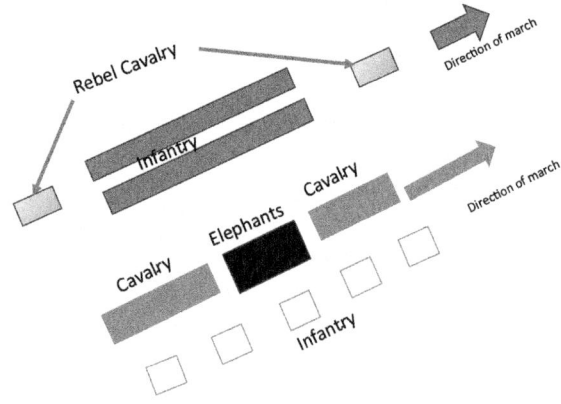

Figure 5 The rebels shadowing the Carthaginians

Captain Bomilcar said, "See the leader of my bodyguards, Drusus, he smiles and he is not discomfited. Take heart and trust to our general. I have fought with him before and even though all looks black he is a cunning strategos."

Almost as though General Barca had heard Captain Bomilcar we heard the two horns sounded and the flags waved. This was the exercise we had practised on the plains before Carthage. The phalanxes allowed gaps to open. They did so with the simple expedient of the ones at the front marching at double time and the ones at the rear using the death march. Large spaces appeared and when the horns sounded three times Captain Bomilcar said, "Wheel!" The elephants and cavalry, which had been marching on a parallel line to the enemy now turned as though one and we passed through the now static phalanxes. To the enemy it would appear that we were running to the river. All that they would see was the dust raised by the animals and the rear of the beasts. As we did so I heard the order given to the infantry. They turned to face the enemy with levelled spears. The slingers and light infantrymen formed a line before them. I knew that the rebels would not see this. The dust raised by the elephants and horses not to mention the sheer bulk of the African bush elephant meant that all they would see were the elephants and cavalry retreating. They would see an enemy running away. They would not see the levelled spears and shields of infantry who were ready to receive an attack.

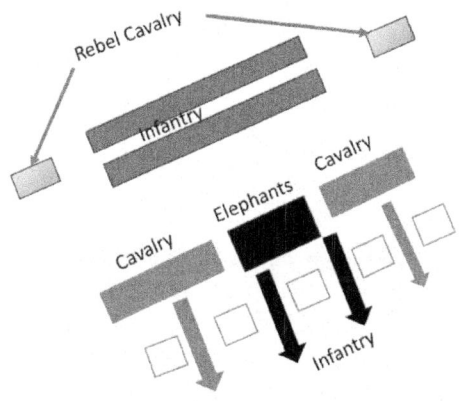

Figure 6 The feigned retreat

Once we had passed the rear of the infantry Captain Bomilcar ordered our column to head to the left of the infantry. As we did so I saw the enemy approaching. The general had tricked them into believing that we were not just retreating but routing and the rebels were racing, without any kind of order, to get at us. It was a disastrous mistake for they would not be attacking a dispirited army but one ready to fight them. As we passed through the infantry, the elephants moved to form lines to the left and right of the infantry and as we were marshalled into our formation we were able to watch the charge of the rebels. These men were not led by leaders. They were rebels and mercenaries who were obeying their own natural instincts. When an enemy has his back to you then you take advantage and they were racing to be the first to strike at unprotected backs and get the treasure that they hoped our men carried. The problem was that we were facing them and these were not the Roman legions marching in precise lines and presenting a wall of shields. These were wild men, some well armoured and some half naked, racing at a solid line of shields and spears. They had forgotten the elephants and cavalry whom they had seen fleeing. When our slingers and Numidian archers sent their missiles they harvested with every strike. We were still marshalling our men on the flanks with the elephants to our left and light infantry to our right and we had time to watch the slaughter unfold. When the enemy line struck the shields it was like floodwater hitting a prepared dam. The survivors of the initial contact, the faster, lightly armoured troops, tried to flood back and in doing so they disrupted and disordered the heavier armoured men who followed. It was then that the signal was given to attack. Our infantry remained like a sea wall upon which the enemy would break but we were the weapons that would deliver the fatal blow.

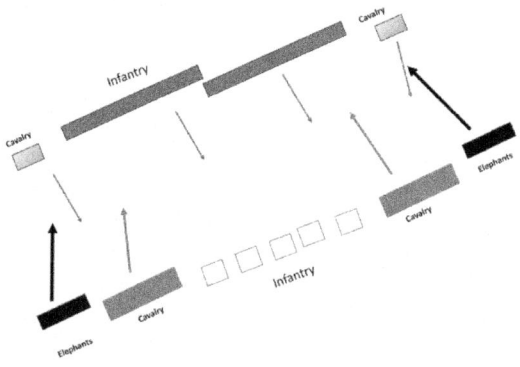

Figure 7 The attack

I had never witnessed an elephant attack before but that day I was privileged to be in a prime position to see what a weapon of shock it was. Captain Bomilcar showed his maturity by commanding the Numidian, Gaetulian and Libyan cavalry that he led to hold the line as we moved into the attack. He intended us to strike at the same time as the elephants. There was no order to the rebels. The eager ones had died or been disheartened and in their flight they had disrupted the enemy line. When the order was given to charge, the elephants had no wall of spears and shields to bar their way. For the horsemen it was even better. The ranks we faced were open. I had to remind myself what our task was and I shouted to my men, "We guard the captain and Pucco!"

The rebels saw the elephants and horses racing at them. The light infantry were hurling stones and javelins at them and they were mesmerised by the sight of the ponderous but deadly elephants charging towards them. They seemed to freeze. War Axe might have been right, a single archer on the back of an elephant does not sound like much but as they were sending arrow after arrow with seeming impunity they seemed a threat to me. The

211

pilum I held had been chosen as I could throw it but also because it could be used as a lance. I had learned that if you avoided armour and aimed for flesh then the spear lasted longer. Captain Bomilcar held a sword but it was more to encourage than as a weapon. He had never used a shield when we had fought and he did not have one now. The infantry we met were either dead or lay cowering on the ground. While that might protect them from horses, it did not stop the elephants. I was witness to the effect of the trampling by the elephants. Armour meant nothing. I saw heads that had been covered with good helmets crushed like a gull's egg. Bodies were pulped into a bloody mass. As the infantry moved forward so the elephants and the horses closed around the back of the fleeing army. Some men escaped. That was always inevitable. They were the faster runners or they were mounted but most ended up trapped. Spendius and the leaders were amongst those who escaped. I did not have to bloody my weapons for the rebels surrendered. The sight of the elephants and the crushed and mashed bodies encouraged the survivors to give up. It was a strange battle but a great victory. We halted and reformed our lines. The horsemen were sent to see if any remained alive on the battlefield. While I watched over the captain, Serpus and the others joined the horsemen. With treasure in their purses and a few more prisoners, they returned. We headed for the rebel camp by the bridge and, with the enemy defeated and the battlefield ours, we rested and celebrated the victory. With the bridge in our hands we controlled the road to Carthage.

General Barca was delighted with the result and summoned his captains for a feast, courtesy of the men who had guarded the bridge. Carthage was now safe and holding the bridge meant that we could protect the towns and villages that lay close to the fertile river valley. As we ate the captured supplies we discovered more from the horsemen who had pursued the fleeing rebels. The bridge garrison had headed for Tunis while Spendius and the men with him had headed for Utica. While we feasted Serpus said, "Now is the time for General Barca to drive north and join up with General Hanno. We can crush the rebels between our two armies and this war will be over." I knew that Serpus wanted nothing more than to return to Great Bomilcar. Impending fatherhood had changed him.

Drixus' camp was next to ours and he overheard Serpus' words. He came over, shaking his head, "You are not yet a Carthaginian, Serpus, and do not know the way that nobles work. If General Barca went to fight Spendius and join with General Hanno then the victory would be General Hanno's. The Tribunal of One Hundred and the Senate would give the triumph to Hanno the Great and he would have even more power. The two leaders have different views on the future of the empire. Hanno looks south to Africa. General Barca looks north to the Blue Sea. General Barca will only join with Hanno when there is no alternative. This war has just begun and we know not the direction the rebels will take."

The next day the prisoners were given the chance to swear allegiance to Carthage or be sold as slaves. Surprisingly some chose slavery. I think that in their position I would have chosen the former. While the elephants enjoyed the river and a rest the cavalry commanded by Lord Bomilcar were given the task of riding the land to secure as many settlements as we could. Our job was to accept the surrender of any who opposed us and to destroy any rebel bases. Not all were friendly. Some supported the rebels but the sight of five hundred horsemen riding towards their villages and farms soon persuaded most of them to accept Carthaginian rule. The ones who fought us paid the price and they were killed. We did not loot from those who were our allies but any opposition resulted in everything of value being taken.

It took some time to subjugate the area. We were there for months but news that Tunis needed to be retaken had us, eventually, moving. It was as soon as we did move that Spendius, reinforced by some Gauls began to shadow us. From the description given to me by one of the Numidians I guessed that Autaritus and his band were amongst the reinforcements. We were a lumbering and cumbersome army because we had prisoners with us. We also had men who had swapped sides and chosen Carthaginian rule; they had to be closely watched. Hamilcar Barca was no fool and he ensured that the new regiments were flanked by two loyal ones. It was painfully slow progress for we had to build a camp each night. To avoid the risk of an attack by our elephants Spendius and his newly reinforced army used the high ground and mountains for protection. The Battle of the Bagradas River had made them wary and fearful of the elephants. They were largely an army that was dismounted and they kept to the rocks and mountain trails.

I knew the threat that the rebel army posed. They held all the advantages. If we tried to discourage them from following us then they could ambush us as we negotiated ground which suited them. For their part they could choose when to raid us. I remembered the village we had raided. We had been callow youths and yet we had slain far more of them than we lost. The advantage was always with the nighttime attackers. General Barca had appointed sentries but I took my four men apart. "The five of us will take it in turns to watch this night. Serpus, you take the first watch. Wake Bellerix and after him it can be Alerix. You wake me, Alerix and War Axe can have the morning shift. War Axe, sleep across the door of the captain's tent." I smiled, "If nothing else a killer will need ropes to scale your belly!" My men smiled. "Sharpen your swords before you retire."

Bellerix shook his head, "And will you be teaching us to suck eggs too?"

"Just do it, eh?"

Pucco had been listening, "Do you think that the enemy will try something?"

I nodded, "I am not a Carthaginian. But if this was in the land close to Barcenis my people would suspect something and Captain Bomilcar told us that General Hanno's camp was surprised and attacked. Spendius has a cunning mind. Besides, the loss of an hour or two of sleep is better than an eternal one because you have a throat that has been cut."

My words did nothing to reassure Pucco. I felt a little guilty for I had clearly terrified him. In the battles thus far he had been safe. I had now put the thought in his mind that he could have his throat slit while he slept. War Axe apart, we made our beds around the outside of the tent. Serpus found a rock on which he could perch and after speaking with him I went to my bed. I did not enjoy a deep sleep. When Serpus woke Bellerix I heard the exchange. The same was true when Alerix was woken and he went to the rock. Part of me was almost ready to get up but I knew that even a few moments of sleep might make the difference. I was already coming to when Pucco's strident voice broke the silence of the camp.

I was up and on my feet in an instant. My sword had been next to me and I rose, bare weapon in hand. I saw Pucco pointing. Gauls were streaming down the rocks and I shouted, "Stand to! Alarm!" If nothing else Pucco's warning had possibly saved the camp. Even as I grabbed my shield and ran to meet the Gauls I wondered why Alerix had not raised the alarm. I looked to the rock where he had been on guard and saw Lieutenant Cai holding Alerix's head aloft. The Gauls alongside whom we had fought were here. They had not been at the battle at the river and that made them dangerous. They had not been defeated. I was the bodyguard of Captain Bomilcar but all thoughts of duty were driven from my mind as I ran to end the life of the man who had murdered Alerix, my gentle warrior. I suppose I also realised that War Axe was now standing in the entrance to the captain's tent, his war axe in his hand. No one would get past him.

Cai's gesture had put him in a weak position. He was standing on our lookout rock and he had to get down. I had time to get to him but first I had to negotiate the warriors who were streaming over the open ground close to our camp. They were clearly intent on hurting the elephants. I had neither mail nor helmet but that actually helped me. I felt lighter and quicker. I ducked beneath the long Gaulish sword that came at my unprotected head and hacked my short sword into the Gaul's thigh. My sword was sharp and bit to the bone. The blood that spurted told me that the wound was mortal and I raised my shield to block the blow from his companion. I recognised the man but I could not remember his name. His blow to my shield was powerful and as I had been ducking when I had slain his companion I was almost on my knees. I used that to my advantage and as I sprang up I pointed my sword above me and drove it under his chin and into his skull. He crumpled as life left his body.

All around me was confusion and the sound of battle as men woke and defended our camp but I had eyes only for Cai. The two dead Gauls had bought him enough time to descend and he came towards me. I would not underestimate the man that Autaritus had appointed as his deputy. He had a Gaulish sword and they were longer than my shorter one. He had a shield which was similar to the one I had first used. My scutum was better made for it had a metal boss. He was, however, mailed. I remembered that he had taken the shirt in combat. It was a longer one than the one I had and came to his knees.

Even as I advanced towards him I was cold enough to
work out how to defeat him. I was now a better warrior
than I had been but Cai was older, and although I did not
like him I knew that he would not have attained his
position without being the one of the best warriors in
Autaritus' warband. In a straight combat, with his mail
and experience, then I would lose. I had no intention of
losing and so I decided to use the land. We had camped
on flat land but there were ropes that tethered the tents to
the ground. I would use those. Our spears were stacked
in fours. I knew where they were and they would
become my allies.

I took the offensive and ran at him. My lack of mail
made me feel as light as a feather and I darted from side
to side like the weaving head of a cobra. I had seen one
in the market in Utica when we had landed and it had
terrified me. I now used the serpentine movements to
confuse Cai. He carried his shield and mail easily but I
knew that the longer the fight went on the weaker he
would become. I made as though I was going to charge
him and to aid my illusion I roared, "Cai, you will pay
for the death of Alerix!" I pulled back my arm as though
I was going to slash across his middle and he moved the
shield to counter the blow. Instead of striking I
pirouetted and he slashed his sword at empty air. I was
now to his right and he had to turn. Before he could do
so I slashed my blade at his arm. His mail shirt did not
cover his lower arm and my surprise move was so quick
that it meant he could not block the blow. Blood oozed
from the wounded limb. A warrior like Cai would shrug
off such an injury but the more blood he lost the weaker
he would become. As he turned, his feet became snagged
in the guy ropes and he stumbled. Although he kept his
feet it was too good an opportunity to miss and I swung
my sword at his head. He had a helmet protecting it but
his hair came through the hole in the top. My sword not
only dented the helmet and made him, no doubt, see

stars but it also cut a hunk of hair which fell to the ground.

It enraged him and he roared, "Boy, I will make you pay for that!"

I laughed. I did not feel like laughing but I knew that it would anger him, "You should pay me as a barber!"

Men like Cai regarded their hair as a sign of their manhood. Losing his hair made him, in his own mind, a lesser man and, his honour impugned, he raced at me. He was still quick. Had I been wearing mail then he might have caught me. As it was I scrambled back and as I did so I used my sword to knock down the stacked spears. They fell in his path and he was forced to stop or risk falling.

The horns that sounded from the slopes above the camp were a signal for the Gauls to fall back. I remembered the calls from my time with Autaritus. Cai had no intention of doing so until he had ended my life. He had more urgency as he came at me. This time I saw him glancing at the ground to avoid any more objects that could entrap him. The horn signalling the retreat of the Gauls also meant that our men raced after them leaving Cai and I almost alone. His advantages were his mail and his longer sword. Mine, as I had already demonstrated, were my speed and agility. He swung his sword in a wide arc to negate my movement. I blocked it with the shield. He had aimed for the middle in the hopes of hurting my hand and weakening my defence but the boss on the scutum took the blow and also took some of the edge from his sword. I darted my hand holding my sword towards his neck. The mail shirt came short of his neck. He reacted quickly but the move was so unexpected that the edge managed to rake the mail shirt and catch part of his unprotected neck. Like the wound to his arm it was not mortal but it would weaken him and, more importantly, damage his confidence.

Blood oozing down from a neck wound could not be comfortable. Where would I strike next?

From behind me I heard Captain Bomilcar shout, "War Axe, go to the aid of Bruneus."

Cai's face showed me that he had heard and when his eyes flickered to the lumbering bear that was War Axe I punched with my shield. His right arm was hurt and when the boss struck his hand I saw him wince. I did not hesitate but raised my sword and hacked down at his neck. He tried to raise his shield but he was already turning his body to face the attack of War Axe. My sword sliced down and slid off the mail and into flesh. I sawed the blade backwards and when a fountain of blood erupted then I knew that he was dead.

War Axe stood next to me and nodded, "I would have enjoyed killing him for Alerix was a friend. I cannot do that but I can do this." He raised his axe and took the head of the Gaul. He took a discarded Gallic spear and after ramming it into the ground impaled the head upon it.

Serpus and Bellerix joined us. Bellerix was distraught. He knelt by the headless body of his friend, "He was looking forward to becoming a father. He told me that he would ask Lord Bomilcar for permission to marry Aisha. Now that will not happen."

I wondered then about the wisdom of becoming a father. Had Alerix died because he was dreaming of a life with a wife and a child? Pucco came along, his eyes were wide and his hands were shaking. He had come close to death. I said, "You gave the alarm. Thank you."

He nodded, "I feared having my throat slit and as I needed to make water I rose. When I climbed over War Axe I heard a noise and as I emerged from the tent I saw Cai slicing through Alerix's neck."

"Your cry saved us."

"But not Alerix."

I kept my thoughts inside my head and did not give them air but I knew that it had been thoughts of a future that had doomed Alerix. While the camp was being cleared and the captain was at a council of war we buried Alerix. We dug a deep hole. War Axe was determined that animals would not disturb his body. We laid his cloak and brooch upon his chest and placed his head atop his shoulders. We put his sword in his hand and then covered his face, chest and hands with his shield. We laid flat rocks on the top and then covered the whole grave with earth. I doubted that we would ever return to this rocky place but we all had its location etched in our hearts and heads. The men looked at me. No one spoke. I think Bellerix was afraid to speak in case it unmanned him.

I was the leader and it was my duty to say farewell, "Alerix, you were a friend and a brother in arms. We will miss you. You were a gentle warrior and the bread you made honoured your mother and the tribe. Know that we will speak of you as though you were still here and when your child is born then there will be four fathers to ensure that Aisha has help. That we swear." I touched my brooch of Isis.

My men did the same and all intoned, "So I swear," as they touched their own brooches and amulets. It meant we would honour the oath. That done we went back to work. Work helped us to expunge the manner of his death. That his killer had been killed and his death avenged would never bring back Alerix. Another of the clan of the lone wolves was gone and there were just four of us left.

The men in our camp had, thanks to Pucco's warning, lost just five men and more than twenty Gauls, Cai included, had been killed. Hamilcar Barca was angry and he had ten of our prisoners executed and their heads joined Cai's on a spear. I thought it a petty act for it would not deter the enemy. I told Captain Bomilcar so.

"Those Gauls are led by Captain Autaritus. The men who were executed were Numidians. He will not lose sleep over their deaths."

The captain nodded his agreement but I knew he would not dare to question General Barca. "And the Gauls know how we fight. They may even guess at our passwords."

One effect was to make us move even more slowly. General Barca tried to lure down the enemy so that he could bring them to battle but each trick and trap was spotted by Spendius and his Gallic captain. There were more night attacks but we increased the number of men who were watching. That meant, of course, that we were all increasingly tired each day.

Eventually, we found ourselves in a narrow valley close to the village of Nepheris. We were all weary beyond words and the thought of a night of uninterrupted sleep was a dream. Perhaps General Barca was suffering too for his normally sharp mind failed him. As we rose, before dawn, and prepared to leave we found our path at the end of the valley blocked by rebel Libyan cavalry. When we tried to retrace our steps to the other end of the valley we found that our path that way was blocked by Numidian horsemen. The valley negated the use of our elephants and we were trapped. The two bands of horsemen who blocked our route needed to do nothing. They could simply wait for us to starve to death. We had water but not enough food. We were doomed. Men might be able to scale the mountainous walls that surrounded us but we would be outnumbered and our best weapons, our elephants, were useless.

While the general and his officers held a council of war we prepared for a battle. It was not in the general's nature to simply do nothing. He would attack even though such a move was doomed to failure.

Bellerix was particularly melancholic, "We shall all be joining Alerix soon."

War Axe shook his head, "I have no intention of dying in this valley. We will win and then when the rebels are routed I shall return to our home and see my child."

I admired his hope but felt it was misplaced. I also noted that he called it, 'home'. We had all changed.

I shrugged, "A man cannot foretell the future. He deals with the problems the gods place before him. We have endured situations as bad as this before. General Barca is a clever man but no matter what happens we do our duty. We protect Lord Bomilcar and Pucco for that is our job. If we fall, we fall."

Serpus had not said a word but now he did, "I do not regret, for one moment, our decision to leave our homeland and seek a life that is worthwhile. We are sad because nine of our friends are dead but think of the men we lost on the raid. There were more of them and they were better men than we. The village that nurtured us is no more and yet we survive. The gods gave us a second chance and, thanks to Bruneus, we have grasped it with two hands. So long as one of us lives to tell the tale of the Clan of the Lone Wolf then it will all have been worthwhile."

Serpus was, in many ways, the wisest of us and his words ended any more debate.

Chapter 13

When the captain returned he had a serious look on his face. "Things look bad and we have to find a way out of this trap. The general has asked me to use you and your men to find a way out of it. Bruneus, I want you and Serpus to see if there is a way past their sentries. You have both shown me that you have skills. Take no risks but find out as much as you can."

It was a hopeless task. It seemed to me that the only way to do what he wanted was to take risks but I nodded, "Yes, Captain."

We went to the fire and I told War Axe, Bellerix and Pucco what we were to do.

Bellerix was not happy. The death of his friend had made him morose and pessimistic. "We have lost Alerix and it seems to me that Bruneus and Serpus will soon be joining him."

I smiled and put my hand on his shoulder, "No, we will not. This will be like old times. Remember, Serpus, when we would sneak out of the hut and go hunting in the night?"

Serpus smiled, "Aye, sneaking past the sentries was an achievement, was it not!" His face became serious, "This will be different, Bruneus, then, if we were caught, we would have received a clip about the ears. This time, if we fail, we will die."

"Then we shall have to be careful. Come Serpus, put some of last night's charcoal on your face and hands." Not all the logs we had used had burnt out and the blackened wood might help to disguise us. I took off my cloak and then had War Axe pull my mail shirt from me. As I fastened the brooch to tie the cloak I said, "We will just need swords." I then smeared the charcoal on my face and the backs of my hands. I left the palms clear for

223

I needed to be able to touch and to feel. I clasped hands with War Axe. The scars from the oaths had healed but they touched. No words were needed. I did the same with Bellerix. "We will head up here and use these rocks for cover."

This was like being a youth again when Serpus and I had gone hunting in the woods near to Barcenis. Somehow that made me feel better. If I thought of this as a youthful adventure then the threat of danger would leave my head. We picked our way over the rocks and past bushes as we worked our way up the slope. We paused as often as we could so that I could sniff the air and look for shadows that moved. We had all night to do this. After almost an hour of tortuous movement we reached the edge of the valley and I stopped for I could smell horses. I moved behind a stunted tree that seemed to have managed to survive on this bare, rock filled hillside. I could see the dim glow of the fire of their sentries. They were far enough away for me to be confident that they could not see us. The light from the fire would make them night blind. Once I saw one I was able to identify more and I found the line of them. Two were slightly higher up the valley sides and that told me that there was no way out. This end of the valley was held by a tight line of men.

I was about to move when I smelled someone closer to me than the fires. The smell came from behind me and it was not Serpus. Even as I turned I felt the metal head of a spear prick my neck. I saw that Serpus was also held by two such spears. The Numidian smiled in the dark, "So you are spies?"

There was no point in denying it and so I said, "We were looking for a way out."

"You are deserters?"

I stood as straight as the spear in my neck would allow, "No, we are the bodyguard of Captain Bomilcar."

Surprisingly the man nodded and moved the spear away. He waved his hand and the spears were taken from Serpus' neck. My friend glared at the two Numidians as a tendril of blood trickled down his tunic. "I remember Captain Bomilcar and the wild warriors who guarded him in Sicily. My name is Lord Navaras and I command two thousand horsemen." He smiled in the dark and added, "They are the ones whose fires you were studying. I once served Carthage but they did not pay me. You are a mercenary and know the value of payment."

"I do." I wondered where this conversation was going.

"Spendius is a worse paymaster than Carthage." He paused and studied me, "We hear that Hamilcar Barca allowed men whom he had defeated to join his army."

"He did." I thought it prudent not to mention that he had executed some of them.

"My men and I would like to rejoin Hamilcar Barca for I admire him as a general."

My mouth dropped open and I said, quickly, "I am sure that he would like that."

"I will bring my men into your camp before first light. I wish you to go to your general so that we are not treated as enemies."

"Of course."

"As surety, we will hold your friend here as a hostage and when we arrive, he will be at the fore. If there is any treachery he will be the first to die."

I shook my head, "Unacceptable. I am the leader. Let Serpus go back and hold me as hostage."

It was his turn to be open mouthed, "You are a true leader. You put yourself in danger rather than your men." I nodded. "Nevertheless I give the orders and you will return alone. You are a leader and your words will persuade Hamilcar Barca that this is an offer he cannot refuse."

Was this an elaborate trick to gain entry to our camp?

Serpus said, "Bruneus, go back. I believe this man. If General Barca knows that they are coming then he can have defences prepared. I will be safe."

"And your men are brave too. Go now for I wish to be in your camp by dawn. The Gauls do not trust me."

I nodded, "I will pass on your message but if anything happens to my friend there is no rock under which you can hide."

"He will be safe."

I clasped hands with Serpus and then ran back the way I had come. I did not try to do so silently but I still surprised both sentries who had not heard my approach. I ran straight to the captain. War Axe and Bellerix were there. War Axe blurted out, "Where is Serpus? If he is dead..."

I said, "Peace, War Axe. General, Captain, Serpus is held hostage by a Numidian, Lord Navaras. He wishes to defect and will bring his men into our camp before dawn."

One of General Barca's lieutenants, Hannibal Paropos snapped, "It will be a trap! We should rouse the camp and prepare for battle."

The general shook his head, "I remember this Numidian, he was a good warrior." He turned to me, "What do you think?"

I was aware that every eye was upon me. For the first time someone was going to listen to what I suggested. If I gave the wrong answer then our whole army could be destroyed and Carthage herself placed in danger. I closed my eyes and heard my uncle's voice, *You have good instincts. Trust them.* I opened my eyes and nodded, "I believe him but even if he does lie we can be prepared. He has just two thousand men and we can line the sides of the valley with archers and slingers."

The general smiled, "Like you I trust him and believe this offer. Captain Bomilcar, have Drixus fetch ten elephants. The elephants will be surety against treachery and yet will not intimidate Navaras too much."

The general also sent for his bodyguards and when the elephants arrived we moved to the head of the valley. The sentries were told to stand down and we waited. We heard the horses of the Numidians as their hooves sent stones skittering from the road and the animals brushed the undergrowth. I saw that Navaras was riding next to Serpus and my friend's hands were unbound. He looked happy enough. Behind me I knew that War Axe was fingering his blade. I said, quietly, "All is well, War Axe, be calm."

"I will be calm, Bruneus, when Serpus is at my side."

Navaras looked at me and nodded. Serpus nudged his horse forward and rode towards us then the Numidian said, "We come to join you, General Barca. If you rouse your army then we can escape this trap."

It was as simple as that. I learned that Navaras was a man of his word. Hamilcar Barca was also a decisive man who knew the meaning of such gestures. "Welcome, Lord Navaras, if you lead we will follow."

The trap set by Spendius was, indeed, a good one. By placing his two large bands of horsemen at both ends of the valley, Spendius had effectively plugged the mouth of the amphora. He and his army were camped further away on the flatter plain. They had taken over a village and were well supplied. He had thought to starve us out but Navaras' defection had negated that strategy by taking away one of the bands of horsemen.

While the rest of the army broke camp we were reunited with Serpus. He sprang from the back of the horse. He embraced each of us and then jerked a thumb at the Numidian, "He is a good man. I am glad he is now on our side and he gave me the horse."

Pucco hurried over, "Captain Bomilcar needs the tent taken down, Bruneus."

I nodded. We would have to save our words for later. By the time the sun had risen we were a mile from the valley and, seeing the village and enemy camp ahead, General Barca now deployed our army for battle. Thus far the rebels had avoided battle but their occupation of the village meant that they could no longer do so.

Bellerix said, "What about the Libyans at the other end of the valley?"

Serpus said, "Lord Navaras said that as soon as we broke camp they would realise we had moved. There are too few of them to bring us to battle. They will rejoin the rest of the army."

He was right. A short while later the two thousand Libyans rode a mile to the left of us and headed for the village. Even if Spendius' sentries were asleep the rebels would soon be aware that an army was coming to fight them.

We now had a cavalry general and Hamilcar Barca and the Numidian joined with Hannibal Paropos to plan our strategy. When the council was over the orders were given and we took our allotted positions. The infantry and light infantry were spread out in a long line four men deep. This time there were no gaps for elephants. Twenty elephants were placed on the right and the rest, under the command of Captain Bomilcar on the left. The newly defected Lord Navaras was made a general and given command of all the cavalry. They were on the right. General Barca and General Properos were with the heavy infantry. We had a screen of light infantrymen, slingers and archers before us. The rebels poured from the village and formed their own lines. When the Libyans formed up opposite the Numidians I knew that Spendius intended to punish Navaras for his treachery. Serpus had told me that there was bad blood between the Numidians and Libyans and that had encouraged Navaras to defect. Allied to that was the fact that

Autaritus and his Gauls also distrusted Navaras. His
defection was now more understandable.

I could see that despite the Numidian cavalry we were
outnumbered. There looked to be almost thirty thousand
men, although numbers were hard to estimate. Unlike
our army the enemy fought in clans and warbands of
mercenaries. The numbers of each unit varied. Some
kept rigid lines like ours whilst others milled around.
This time Captain Bomilcar would be with Captain
Drixus and lead the elephants. I was keenly aware that
there were now just four of us left to protect Captain
Bomilcar and Drixus. Knowing that Autaritus was with
the army had changed things. This was almost personal.
The Gaul had reason to hate not only General Barca and
Captain Bomilcar but us. He had to have known that his
lieutenant, Cai, had died in the attack. Gauls like
Autaritus held grudges and swore oaths for vengeance.
He would seek our heads and we would be, if he was
able, the target of his ire. The problem we had was that
Captain Bomilcar had to be before the elephants to give
them the command. That, in turn, meant that we had to
flank him with Pucco behind. There was a gap behind us
between Drixus' elephant and the next one but that gap
was narrow. Once the elephants began to lumber they
stopped for neither friend nor foe. Drixus had told us,
when we had camped in the valley, that elephants when
panicked had been known to trample their own men. As
he had told us, the safest place in an elephant charge was
behind them! There were horsemen facing us but they
were few in number. The bulk of them were on the other
flank. What I saw facing us were the Gauls. I recognised
the distinctive helmet of Autaritus.

This time it was Hamilcar Barca who began the battle.
He had given precise orders and the line of infantry
moved towards the rebels. Navaras led the Numidians in
a threatening move towards the Libyan horsemen but our
elephants remained static. Hamilcar Barca had told his

leaders of the signals that would be used and we waited. We watched the battle unfold as our line bowed out. The flank phalanxes did not move as fast as the centre ones. The enemy reacted by charging the centre phalanxes and the clash as they struck echoed across our front. The whole weight of the enemy army hit the centre three phalanxes and they reeled. These were Carthaginian and loyal Libyan spearmen. Although they fell back they did so in good order for it was preplanned. The wisdom of keeping the flank phalanxes further back now became clear. The rebels funnelled towards the centre trampling over the dead of both sides. It was as the line became straight once more that I saw the cunning of Hamilcar Barca. The centre phalanxes kept retreating but the flank phalanxes held firm. We did not move and neither did the Numidians who had halted too. We were like a large sack and the enemy was obligingly putting his head into it. They thought that they were winning and driving the enemy back. They were heedless of their threatened flanks.

There was no horn but I saw Captain Bomilcar looking towards the general and when the flag was waved he said, "Drixus, forward." Our elephants began to move and when I looked to the other side I saw that Navaras was leading the horsemen too. The enemy would soon be surrounded.

I held a pilum but javelins hung from my pommels. I switched the pilum to my left hand and picked up a javelin as Captain Bomilcar led us to the rear of the rebels. Our three retreating phalanxes had now stopped and the battle was raging fiercely. The Carthaginian discipline held against the wild fury of what were, effectively, many warbands. I understood the fear on the faces of the men who realised their danger and turned to see the elephants as they charged towards them. We had elephants to our left and right and even mounted I felt intimidated. To the men on foot it must have been terrifying. The archers on the backs of the elephants sent their arrows at the rebels. They were few in number but they used their arrows judiciously. They aimed at the leaders. The screams of men and the crunch of their bones as the well trained elephants trampled them was heard by those in the centre of the enemy battle line and it made them look to the sides. On one side they saw elephants closing the neck of the sack and on the other a wall of horsemen. They halted their advance. Those who were at the rear of the line, the ones yet to be engaged, saw the trap closing upon them and they took to their heels. I had seen this before. When a man fights he might not see those behind him but he senses their presence and as men realised that their comrades were deserting they too began to run back. The enemy warbands were smaller than our units and they were like bubbles of air as they popped from the main army and fled.

We were now close enough to the enemy to use our weapons. I hurled my first javelin at a Gaul who wore no armour on his upper body but had a fine horned helmet. I had seen him at Drepanum. He was a leader of a band of Gauls who had lived far to the north of the mountains that were close to my home. He died far from his homeland. Serpus and Bellerix also hurled javelins. War Axe was able, thanks to his long arms and strength, to send his javelins further and men forty feet from the edge of the rebels began to die. We had almost closed the neck of the sack when the rout began. Men turned and fled. The elephants continued to trample and crush the warriors. My javelins expended, I took to my pilum. It was then that I saw Autaritus. He was mounted and he was leading his men away from the battle. He still had some control over them and they were in good order.

Captain Bomilcar saw them and shouted, "Drixus, those Gauls are escaping."

231

The Carthaginian shouted an order and ten elephants, including his own, began to move towards them. We went with the elephants. For the first time I would be fighting men alongside whom I had eaten and slept. I had to remember that they were my enemies and forget their kindnesses at Drepanum. Seeing the elephants charging them made Autaritus stop. He was a clever man. The conversations around the campfires at the siege lines had told me that. He halted his warband and they formed a shield wall. Other Gauls who were fleeing saw the wall and joined it. The ten elephants were charging a hundred and fifty men behind shields and spears. I saw that Autaritus was behind the wall and directing them. He had some men who were courageous warriors with him. He also had some who were so fond of fighting that they were happy to fight another when there were no enemy heads to hew. Two such men ran from the wall of spears and shields. I recognised them, they were Parcennus the Fierce and Gobannitio. Both men wielded axes. The weapons were like War Axe's and long ones. The two men ran and held the axes in two hands. It meant they had no shields and the archers on the backs of the elephants sent arrows at them. Even though both men were hit by arrows, it was though they had been merely bitten by mosquitoes. They came on. Parcennus hacked into the leg of an elephant which screamed in pain and reared. The two men on its back were hurled to the ground. The wounded man then ran towards Captain Bomilcar. The Gaul was bleeding from his wounds but he was determined to have a glorious death. I knew that men like Parcennus believed they would be reborn in a warrior heaven if they died in this fashion. The captain had no spear and the axe was swinging towards his unprotected leg when Bellerix rode between them and hurled his pilum into the neck of the Gaul. The axe slid to the ground from Parcennus' lifeless hands. The throwing axe that was hurled from behind the shield was well thrown. Gauls were handy with such weapons. When the axe struck his head Bellerix died instantly but his body was held in place by his saddle. His horse, maddened by blood and the noise, charged towards the shield wall. Gobannitio was in its path and he swung his axe at the horse's head. He smashed into the skull and as the horse stumbled to its death Bellerix's body was thrown from the saddle to fall before the shield wall. Even though our friend was dead it did not stop the Gauls from hacking into the body. It proved too much for War Axe who screamed a war cry and rode at Gobannitio. I think the Gaulish warrior had endured too many arrows already and was a dead man walking but War Axe's blade split his skull and as the nine remaining elephants and War Axe struck the shield wall, it disintegrated.

On the far side Navaras had closed the trap. The last ones to escape were Autaritus and one hundred survivors from our attack. The death of Bellerix and the elephant and its crew was too much for us and, Captain Bomilcar apart, we took no prisoners. By the time that General Hamilcar Barca sounded the end to the fighting and men surrendered in their thousands, we were bloodied, weary and, for the three of us, dispirited. Bellerix would be joining Alerix in the Otherworld but it was too soon for us.

Spendius and Autaritus had escaped along with many thousands of men but ten thousand rebels lay dead and four thousand had surrendered. With a wall of horses, elephants and spears around them the four thousand were given a choice by Hamilcar Barca, they could join our army as the other defectors had or be sold into slavery. It was an easy choice and they all joined our army. Our losses were lighter and so our numbers were swollen.

None of that helped us.

We headed for the enemy camp to take what we could. They had supplies and weapons that we confiscated. There was little treasure. Mercenaries carried their coins with them. The dead would yield gold as well as weapons but their camp was just somewhere to gain tents, food and wine. That night we returned to the battlefield, not for loot or treasure but to recover the body of Bellerix. He was not recognisable as a man. The wounds, the fall and the trampling of elephants had rendered his body a bloody and broken mass. The only way we knew him was by his brooch of Isis. We gathered his crushed remains in his cloak and took him to a place where he could be buried. The enemy dead were being burned and we found a grove that lay upwind of the pyre and the three of us, along with Pucco, buried Bellerix, friend of Alerix and yet another lone wolf who would never see his child. We buried him deep. It took longer than it had when we had interred Alerix. There were fewer of us and we did so in silence. I did not know the others' thoughts but mine were dark. I hardened my heart. For one brief moment in the battle I had remembered the Gauls as comrades. They were not. When you were a mercenary you fought your enemies as hard as you could. To do other was to let down your own dead.

After asking the gods to take him into their care we stood around the grave. There was no marker. If, in some future I could not imagine, someone dug up his bones they might wonder at this man from the land close to the mountains being buried in the desert with the sign of the goddess Isis. Then I realised that was true of all of us. I could not see any of us surviving for much longer. We were now three and War Axe's reckless courage told me that he might be the next one to fall. We were the last of the lone wolves and our pack would soon be but a memory.

It was Pucco who broke the silence. "I will miss all of those we have buried but Alerix and Bellerix, well, they were close to me. They were kind." We nodded for he spoke the truth. "And I fear for my life. When we were at Great Bomilcar I thought my life was perfect. I am scared, Bruneus, what if I am next and do not return to my new home?"

There was something in his words that made me ask, "Are you like the others? Did you leave a piece of you at Great Bomilcar?"

He nodded, "I left my heart there along with my hopes for the future. I have not yet lain with her but Sophonisba is the one who will bear my children. I have spoken with Daco and he has said that when she is a woman then she can bear my children."

I had not known that. I knew the girl who was on the cusp of womanhood. Pucco was just a year or two older and it made sense. I smiled, "Pucco, you will not die. Should the worst happen and the lone wolves fall in battle then you should flee. You have a good horse and you have wits. When we die then return to Great Bomilcar. We are warriors and you are not."

Serpus said, "Bruneus is right and when you do return then there are four children who will need you, Pucco, to tell them how their fathers were warriors who followed Bruneus, the leader of the lone wolves. They will be our shadows into the future."

Involuntarily I put my hand out and both of my friends did the same. With my other hand I touched my brooch of Isis. It was an unspoken confirmation of our blood oath.

For the next days we had nothing to do. The horsemen sought our enemies and others searched the desert for men who had fled and not surrendered. We were ready to fight again but our main task was to guard Carthage and to ensure that the enemy did not join Mathos in Tunis. We saw little of the captain. We escorted him to his meetings with the other generals but spent more time waiting in whatever shade we could find rather than speaking to him. When Navaras returned a week later we escorted the captain to the meeting. It went on until after dark.

As we headed back to the tent where Pucco was waiting with food, the captain said nothing for a while and seemed unwilling to eat. Eventually, I asked, "What is wrong, Captain?"

He seemed to see me for the first time, "Ah, Bruneus, I have been distracted. Lord Navaras found the enemy. They are at Hippo."

"Then we march there to meet them?"

He shook his head, "General Hanno went with his army to quell the rebellion in Sardinia and when he left the garrisons of Utica and Hippo were slain by their people. The rebel army has been swollen once more." I said nothing. That was depressing. Despite our victories we were still no closer to ending the rebellion and returning home. His voice became quiet, as though he was afraid of the words he spoke, "There is more. Spendius heeded the words and advice of Autaritus, who told him, so it is said, that men had deserted to the Carthaginians because he was not ruthless enough. My friend Gisco and the other seven hundred prisoners had their hands cut off, were castrated, their legs were broken, then they were thrown into a pit and then buried alive. General Barca will not offer surrender to any other men we defeat."

Serpus' face reflected his despair, "Then there is no end in sight to this war, Captain?"

The captain shook his head, "We will win, of that I am certain, but it may be that my son will be a man before that day arrives."

I saw the looks on them all as they took in the captain's words. Even the normally optimistic War Axe looked depressed. When Pucco had gone to undress the captain I said to the other two, "When we left Barcenis we had no family except for each other and we chose the way of the sword. That has not changed. We all made choices back at Great Bomilcar. You chose to enjoy the company of women and, in the process, become fathers. I did not do so. We are still warriors and as much as we all might want this war over that is not going to happen any time soon."

Serpus nodded as War Axe downed a beaker of wine taken from the rebel camp. Serpus looked at me, "You are right and now I can see that you are a leader. I thought I might be a leader as well as a warrior but Great Bomilcar has opened a door to a life I never thought I would have. We will not return to that life for some time but when we do I will embrace it and when I have enough gold and silver I shall leave the service of Lord Bomilcar and make a life for myself here in this land far from the land of my birth."

Serpus had changed too and I was suddenly aware that I was the last of the Clan of the Lone Wolf. Even War Axe now looked and sounded different. He was still a mighty warrior but that was not as important to him as the family he hoped to raise. Thanks to my meeting with Lady Dido, the touch of her hand, the pools that were her eyes, I was now tied to her family. I would guard her husband and train her son. That would be my lonely, solitary life. I had heard of hermits who lived alone. They were celibate thinkers who contemplated life and the world. I was a celibate warrior who was dedicated to the Bomilcar family. The gods had chosen my path for me.

Chapter 14

Mathos had not been idle in Tunis. More rebels had joined their cause and men had flooded across the border to join him from Libya in the east. When he eventually chose to leave Tunis to move towards us, General Barca knew that we would not have enough men to face him in battle. We moved north, back towards Carthage. Being close to Carthage meant that we could be reinforced. The Sacred Band with Mago Bomilcar came to swell our numbers. Lord Bomilcar visited their camp once but it was a brief visit. We did not go with him but Pucco did. He told us of the meeting. Mago, it seemed, had grown even more arrogant and Pucco said that he was scornful of his father. The attitude of Mago was highlighted when, at the same time, two of the sons of Hamilcar Barca arrived. One reason was that Navaras, as a reward for his defection, had been offered the hand of Hamilcar Barca's daughter, Salammbo, in marriage. The whole of Hamilcar's family came from Carthage so that the arrangements could be made and the couple meet. It was a harmonious meeting. When the rest of the family returned to their home, Hannibal and Hasdrubal remained. They would learn to be warriors by watching their father. To me they were more like Himilco than Mago and that was a good thing.

I knew that the sudden influx of enemy reinforcements worried Lord Bomilcar for he had left his home undefended. In addition, the arrival of Hannibal and Hasdrubal made him think about Himilco. Mago was lost to him. His son was at home as was his daughter as well as his wife. He needed to know if his home was safe. He asked the general's permission to visit Great Bomilcar and then return to our new camp which lay to the northwest of Carthage. It was a well chosen camp for it meant we could still watch Spendius in the west and react should Mathos launch an unlikely attack on Carthage. The general refused the request.

Lord Bomilcar had changed since I had first met him. He was now an older and wiser man. "Then can I send my bodyguards?" As usual we were within hearing distance.

The general looked over to us, "There are but three of them. Can you do without them?"

"Until either Spendius or Mathos sallies forth then it is unlikely that we will need to battle but if we do then I will take my chances. A warrior who worries about his family has only half his mind on his appointed task. Knowing that my family is safe will make me a better warrior and less likely to make mistakes."

The general, aware that his sons were listening, said, "The day you make a mistake, Lord Bomilcar, is the day you shall pay with your life." He was teaching his sons that a general had to be ruthless.

I saw a wry smile on our leader's face, "I know that so let me send my men."

"Very well but I think less of you for this. Carthage is more important than family."

I thought that was hypocrisy on the part of the general who had his family close to him and safe behind the mighty walls of Carthage. He had indulged himself and his family was being looked after but he would not allow a subordinate the same.

"Bruneus, take your men and travel back to my home. I would have you ensure that all is well. The journey will be a hard one for there are many enemies between here and my home. Mathos will have scouts out. If you think there is a danger then your duty is to protect my home. If you have to stay there to defend Great Bomilcar then that is more important than returning here. I will write a message for my wife to give you permission to do so but she thinks well of you. I am sure that the message is unnecessary. Take spare horses with supplies for the journey will be a long one."

I had come to see a different Captain Bomilcar since the war had started but that moment saw him rise in my estimation. For the first time he was more like my father and Barcas. "Yes, My Lord."

Pucco helped us to pack but he looked worried. "We will return, Pucco."

He nodded, "That is not what worries me. You are the best warriors that I know and I cannot see any of you failing. I fear that the rebels will raid and with no one to protect him then not only could he die but me too."

"That will not happen. Neither side is ready for a battle yet. General Barca awaits news from Sardinia and the rebels are still licking their wounds. While we have the elephants they will not risk a battle."

My words calmed him but I was not totally confident that I had spoken the truth.

The three of us left the next morning well before dawn. It was spring and while in our homeland it would still be cool, here the sun would soon be as hot as on a summer's day at Barcenis. We would rest during the heat of the day. We led two horses with the supplies. As leader I rode alone ahead of my dwindling pack. I smiled, thinking of Barcas' words about the wolf pack. We were a shadow of the pack that had left Barcenis but we were still a pack and if anyone sought to harm us then we were a dangerous one.

The route we should have taken, the shortest one, risked passing Mathos' army. We would give that a wide berth and instead we took the mountain paths. It would be longer and harder on the horses but we would be safer and have the advantage of height. We would be able to see our enemies below us. The mountains meant that it was colder at night and so, when we camped, I risked a fire. We did not stand a watch; there were too few of us for that but Stormbringer and Crow had shown that they were good watchdogs. They would neigh and stamp if danger approached. My two companions were in good humour for they would soon be seeing their sons or daughters. We had been away for almost a year. Their children would be months old by now. The deaths of Bellerix and Alerix had brought home to them how close they had been to miss seeing their offspring and the mothers of their children. They chattered away like magpies as they speculated on what their children would be. I was silent for I too was dreaming but it was of Lady Dido.

When we finally descended from the mountains we did so gingerly and with the utmost care. We had not feared an ambush in the mountains but we were now approaching land where Mathos' men might be seeking provisions and supplies. There were trees for there were forests to the east of us and with no people to fell them it was a verdant land. We used the trees for cover. We saw the road ahead. It was the one used by traders who passed through this land on their way to the smaller villages further south and west. Even though there was war such men still traded. Their goods brought higher prices in the remote places. War still brought profit to those with the courage to risk travelling. We saw no one and headed south and west along the road.

Being at the front meant it was my eyes that were alert to danger. Serpus and War Axe had relaxed a little for we were now just sixty miles from Great Bomilcar. If we rode hard we could be there in less than two days. It was me who spotted the dung left by horses. I could smell it and that meant it was recent. Whilst it could have been left by the horse of a merchant, I was suspicious. This section of road had little cover and it both twisted and turned. There were hidden bends. The stone surface also transmitted noise and whilst one horse might not make much noise five would. I stopped. Turning in my saddle I said, "There may be danger ahead. Prepare weapons and head down the road cautiously. I will try to get ahead of the potential danger."

Serpus said, "We should stay together."

"I will ride ahead." I donned my helmet. I next moved my cloak to free my sword arm and I hefted my shield to my left arm and held my pilum in the same hand. As I jerked Stormbringer's reins to take him to the right and over the rough ground I could not help but smile. The pilum I used had been taken on Sicily. Others had been taken, used or broken but this one seemed to bear a charmed life. It felt familiar and with my Roman shield I was as well armed and protected as any man.

The ground rose and then fell. The others would be moving slowly along the road and I urged Stormbringer to make haste when the ground fell. A few rocks skittered for this was not a man-made trail I was using. Animals had created it and it was narrow. It brought me around in a loop to cross the road further ahead. The animal trail was here long before man made his road.

I saw the four deserters almost at the same time that they saw Serpus and War Axe. I was behind them and I saw them point to my companions. That they were deserters was clear. They all wore the semblance of armour. They had a variety of helmets and weapons. One had a bow and the other three held long spears and carried swords. One rode the horse whose dung I had seen and the other three followed. They did not look like Gauls and their skin marked them as Libyans from the coast. I took all of this in with my first glance. I urged Stormbringer to gallop towards the four men who drew weapons at the sound of my horse's hooves. It was not a planned ambush but I knew that deserters would not pass up the opportunity to take four horses. As I transferred my spear to my right hand I speculated that these men were probably on their way home but that journey would take them close to Great Bomilcar. Serpus and War Axe had reined in and loosed the horses that they led so that they could prepare their weapons. Serpus hefted his shield and War Axe held his axe. The attention of the four men was on my companions but, as Stormbringer's hooves clattered on the rocks, heads turned.

I shouted, "Lay down your weapons and you shall live."

I had no need to make the offer but in any combat there was a chance that one of the three of us could be hurt or killed. I gave them the chance. The arrow sent at me told me that they had spurned the offer. I held the shield across my body and the arrow hit it. It was better that the arrow came at me and not at my men for the archer knew his business. I galloped at him as he nocked another arrow. It was a race. Who would win? The closer I came the greater was the chance that his next arrow would hit either my horse or me. To gain time and to put him off I jerked Stormbringer to the right and then back to the left. It bought me tiny moments but they were enough. I hurled the pilum as he drew back the bow. He was an archer and wore no mail, not even a breastplate. The spear cracked the bow and then slammed into his chest. I was drawing my sword as I passed his body. I turned Stormbringer to ride up the road where the three other deserters were attempting to slay Serpus and War Axe. I swung my sword across the back of the deserter mounted on the horse. I aimed above the pommels that held him in place. It was a calculated blow for if he wore a backplate, as Serpus and War Axe did, then the blade would find flesh below it. My blade grated against the backbone and I sawed it across. The arching arms told me that he was a dead man and in that moment Serpus slew his foe and War Axe split the helmet and skull of the last man.

Serpus smiled, "Your instincts were right."

I took off my helmet, "Barcas told me to trust them. He meant about leadership but the blood of my ancestors also helps. War Axe, fetch the horses. Come, Serpus, let us find kindling and burn these bodies. They were soldiers like us. Who knows we may have fought alongside them in Sicily. I would want my body respected in death."

He dismounted, "I heard your offer. You gave them a chance, Bruneus, and they chose to fight."

"Would we have done any differently?"

His silence told me that he agreed with me.

They had little food but we took it anyway along with their water skins. We found some dried and desiccated wood and used that for kindling. By the time War Axe had returned and secured the three pack horses we had made a small pyre. We laid the three bodies on it. The bow, arrows and broken spears were all made of wood and would burn too. We used my flint to start the fire and when it caught and the hair of the dead men began to sizzle and burn we mounted and headed down the road. I had recovered my pilum and was pleased that it was undamaged. Soldiers believe in luck and my spear was a lucky weapon.

The rest of the journey saw an increase in vigilance from all of us and the ride became more tiring as we scanned the land for danger. We were relieved when we finally saw the river and the farmed fields of Great Bomilcar. We reined in to take in the peaceful scene. That was the caution again. We peered at the fields and I was only content when we saw the familiar slaves tending to them. The sentries were still lounging by the gate and our home was safe. It had not been attacked or raided.

My two companions surprised me. They dismounted. I said, "What are you doing?"

Serpus unfastened his cloak and shook the dust from it. He laid it on the back of his horse and dusted his tunic. "I am returning to a child I have never seen. I would have the baby see a warrior whose hair is combed and does not give the child nightmares." He began to comb his hair. To my surprise War Axe did the same. My closest friends had changed since we had left my burning village.

When they were satisfied with their appearance we headed down. The time taken to lavish attention on their appearance had alerted the estate to our arrival. Men had seen us and both Craster and Daco greeted us when we passed through the gate. "Is Lord Bomilcar not with you?"

I shook my head as I dismounted, "No, Craster. He is with the general and they are trying to quell the rebellion. He feared for his home and we were sent to satisfy him that all was well and his family were safe."

Craster looked nervously around as though he feared an enemy was creeping up on him. "We are in danger?"

"Mathos has an army close to Tunis. Our army is between Tunis and Carthage. There may be danger."

He nodded, "I will take you to Lady Dido."

I left my two men with Daco. I knew that they would be reunited with Nefertiti and Charmion, the mothers of their children.

I wished that I had also attended to my appearance but it was too late for that now.

Lady Dido and her two children were in the courtyard with the fountain. I felt my breath catch as I saw her. She was like a marble statue, perfect in every way. Craster went and spoke to her. She waved a hand to dismiss him. I bowed and took out the lead scroll given to me by Lord Bomilcar. I handed it to her. As I did so our eyes met and her soft fingers brushed mine. No words were spoken but I felt my heart talking to her.

"Sit. Dido, pour Bruneus some wine while I read this missive from your father."

I sat and the girl who was rapidly becoming a woman poured me the wine and handed it to me. Himilco said, "Have you won the war, yet?"

I smiled, "We are winning but it is far from won."

"My father is well?"

"Yes, Mistress Dido."

"And the others are all well, Pucco, and your men?"

I glanced at Lady Dido, she had finished reading the message and she must have sensed that I had bad news to impart. She said, "If there is bad news then my son should hear it. It might help him to realise that war is not for the faint hearted."

"Alerix and Bellerix both died. The others are well and we saw your elder brother with the Sacred Band. He is also well but he has yet to fight in battle."

Lady Dido shook her head, "And now there are just three of you. What do you call yourselves? The lone wolves? You are less of a pack now and more a band of brothers." I nodded and drank some of the wine. She raised her goblet, "A libation to the dead. May Isis watch over their souls."

I drank and our eyes met.

"How long can you stay, Bruneus?"

"I will stay, Lady Dido, until I am satisfied that Great Bomilcar can be defended and then we must return to protect your husband."

She nodded and rose, "And now I must bear the news of Alerix's death to Aisha. She named their son Alerix and hoped that he would please his father. That is not meant to be."

"Alerix was my man and I will be as a stepfather to the boy as well as Bellerix's child."

Her face fell, "Bella and her daughter died in childbirth. They are now with Bellerix in the Otherworld." I could not help but touch the clasp of Isis. Lady Dido smiled, "Do not worry, Isis will find a way to reunite them in the afterlife." She said, "Come, daughter, you should learn how to bear bad news. Himilco, take Bruneus to the bath house. I had Craster ready it for him and his men to wash the road from their bodies when I heard they had been seen across the river."

"You are too gracious, my lady."

"You are worth it, Bruneus, you and your men, for you are oathsworn and as much a part of my family as my children."

The bath was wonderful but made more so by the unspoken words. Was I dreaming the looks she gave me? Did I read too much into the brush of her hand? As I lay there in the hot, perfumed water I decided that it did not matter. If she had made the gesture I would not act upon it so why not believe that she was attracted to me. It would hurt no one. I was a warrior. I was disciplined to endure pain and hurt. I would learn to live with the pain the empty future held for me. So long as Lady Dido lived then I had hope. I thought back to Barcenis; when the disease came they had no hope. I lived and the gods had not yet finished with me.

Serpus and War Axe joined me when I had almost dozed off. War Axe had the biggest smile I have ever seen on his tattooed face. "How is the child?"

He almost caused a tidal wave when he jumped into the pool. "Mardian is perfect. Charmion named him for her father. She did not think War Axe was suitable for a child."

I laughed, "And she is right. Are you happy with the name?"

"Of course, like my son, it is perfect."

"And you, Serpus, is Nefertiti well?"

He smiled, "She is. Her Egyptian blood has stood her in good stead. She has broad hips. My son, Serpus, is almost half the size of Mardian but that was to be expected."

I waited while they soaped themselves and sank below the water to cleanse the wildlife from their hair. "And Aisha?"

Serpus lost his smile, "She wept. Alerix and she were meant for one another. Her son is named Alerix."

"I told Lady Dido that I would ensure that he had a stepfather."

Serpus said, "He has three."

"Look after your own first. I have none."

"And will you have any? You would be a good father." I said nothing and Serpus smiled, "You are like the ocean. You are deep and who knows what currents lie beneath the waves or what monsters lurk there. Father a son for we need another Bruneus."

I waited a while and then rose to go to the colder pool, "Your sons are slaves. I would have my child a freeman."

"And we can buy our sons. I have spoken with Daco. Lady Dido has already said that we would not be robbed if we bought the freedom of our women and our sons."

"Have you enough now?"

He shook his head, "We either need a great victory and bodies to loot or more pay."

"Do not forget that the three of us are paid the same as when we were hired as bodyguards. Eight tetradrachm means you both have two a month coming to you and I will share out the pay of our dead friends, which I still have. There are ten tetradrachm between you."

War Axe frowned as he tried to calculate and Serpus said, "That means we can buy them at the end of the year. Thank you, Bruneus. A less honourable man would have kept it for himself."

"As Barcas told me, a good leader of a wolf pack thinks of the pack first and himself second."

When I was dressed I went to see Aisha and told her that I would be a stepfather to Alerix. I did not say that I would buy them both but that was my intention. That would need to wait until Serpus and War Axe had earned enough money to have a home. I had no family and Alerix and Aisha would have to have one with Serpus. I was confident that he would agree. Serpus had changed since we had left Barcenis but not that much.

Lady Dido insisted that we dine with her and her children. We did not refuse and, for the second time, we wore the rich garments that had been bought for us. Those of Bellerix and Alerix hung in our rooms, a sad reminder of their absence. Himilco sat opposite me and I was between the two Didos. Lady Dido sat at the head of the table and the opposite end was empty. The room felt as though there were ghosts in it. As we sat and answered Himilco's incessant questions I sensed the spirits of Alerix and Bellerix. I could not help but feel guilty that they were dead. Had I died then there would have been mourning but Aisha and young Alerix would have to live without a father and their mourning would last a lifetime.

Some of the questions could not be answered. That was not because we did not know the answer but Himilco wanted to know the details of the deaths of Alerix and Bellerix. Such words were not for this company. When we did not answer but looked down at the food before us, studying it as though it was the first time we had seen it, Lady Dido said, "Himilco, you are still a child but your sister recognises, as I do, the pain on the faces of these warriors. All you need to know is that Alerix and Bellerix died doing their duty, defending your father and for that we both thank and will honour them with an offering to Isis."

I smiled. Poor Himilco looked crestfallen. I do not think it was the rebuke but the reference to him as a child. To assuage him I said, "If it is any consolation I believe that General Barca and your father will defeat our enemies and the rebellion will be over. Then he will return home and we can continue your training as a warrior."

He brightened.

His sister said, "What of my brother, Mago? You said that you had seen him with the Sacred Band. Did he fight in a battle."

I looked at Lady Dido who was studying my face. She would know the lie if I told one. I shook my head, "The Sacred Band did not fight and, in any case, your brother is too young. He was a shield bearer." I hesitated and then gave the whole truth, "The Sacred Band are not the warriors that defended Carthage in the past. They are young nobles who parade with fine armour and arrogant attitudes. If they had to fight then I fear their end would be swift. General Barca showed no signs that he would use them."

Lady Dido smiled, "You are an honest man, Bruneus. Less honourable men would have given us the answer they thought we wanted."

I then told the tale of how their father had led the elephants in battle. Both the children seemed excited at the thought of such an act. I had to retell it three times and the food was all served by the time it ended. "Now it is time for you two to retire and I am sure that Serpus and War Axe are itching to be with their families."

The faces of Himilco and Dido fell but War Axe could not help the broad smile appearing on his face and he began to rise. Serpus shook his head, "Thank you, My Lady, with your permission my hasty friend and I will retire."

War Axe realised what he had done and tried to sit. I said, "You may leave, War Axe."

When the slaves had taken the children and my companions had gone, Lady Dido said, "Let us retire to the fountains. It is a pleasant night and the tinkling of the water is soothing. Craster, have a jug of wine brought out and then you may retire."

The butler looked at me, "Are you sure, My Lady?"

"Of course."

Once alone she reached over and touched the back of my hand, "Thank you for your diplomacy. As much as my son wanted to know the answer to his questions I know that the actual answer might have given him nightmares. Although I am a woman I am strong and I can handle the truth. Tell me all. I wish to know those parts you omitted." I hesitated and, after sipping the sweet wine, she smiled, "Come, Bruneus, you know as I do that there is a connection between us. We do not lie to one another for we both have honour. I may be a woman but my ancestors served Ptolemy and before him Alexander. There is Macedonian blood in my veins."

She was right and her admission about the connection between us made my heart soar. I told her all. I saw the pain as I described the death of Bellerix and saw the nod when I told how I had killed Alerix's killer, Cai.

When I had finished she said, "Thank you. You were right in your assessment of the Sacred Band. They were resurrected at the behest of Hanno. I agree with my husband that the Barca family is better suited to leading Carthage. My son will fit in well with the preening nobles who make up that empty shell." I could not hide my feelings and the disparagement of her son surprised me. She smiled, "As I said, Bruneus, you will always hear the truth from my lips. That is a promise I can make to you." I found myself reading much into her words. Her eyes flickered to the door. "There are eyes and ears everywhere. Fortunately the water hides our words and allows honesty. We made mistakes with Mago. His tutor, we dismissed him, was a man filled with bombast and arrogance. Lord Bomilcar and I were distracted for Dido was born and by the time we knew what had happened the boy was no longer rough clay, he was the spoiled youth you met."

I sipped the wine, "And you hoped that we might remedy the situation."

"We did but it was clear from the progress Himilco made and the attitude of Mago that it was not meant to be."

We drank the wine in silence for a while. Our eyes met occasionally and I read unspoken words in them.

Then she smiled and said, "Craster will not retire until I do." She lowered her voice and leaned over, "He does not like you."

I could not help but smile, "I know."

"Tell me now, while we are alone, do you think there is danger for us, here?"

I nodded and told her of the deserters. "I do not think that Mathos or Spendius will send an army here for if they did then they would be allowing General Barca to reclaim the lands around Hippo and Tunis. This war is fought between men who expect the other to blink. There will be a battle and when it is fought then the loser will die." I did not think it would be Carthage who lost. "The danger is deserters who might think to plunder. You need armed men watching the workers and animals in the fields. When we returned that was the first thing we saw. They are far from the protection of the walls. You and your family, Aisha, Nefertiti and Charmion are all safe for no deserter would risk breaching the walls."

She emptied her goblet and rose. I did so too. I took my cloak and placed it around my shoulders. My clumsy fingers struggled with the brooch. "Thank you, Bruneus. That was honest and informative. I will ensure that our workers are protected. We have men who do little in the villa. Perhaps a little exercise might make them realise that they have a good life." She faced me. Her head came to just above my chin. Her perfume filled my head and I feared that I would lose control and kiss her. I think that she realised that too. She reached up to ostensibly fasten my brooch and as she did her fingers accidentally touched my face. Her voice was husky as she said, "You would make a good father and a fine husband were a woman lucky enough to win your heart."

I looked down at her, "Perhaps it is already lost."

The eyes became sad, "Then it is fated to be broken." The moment seemed to last an age but, in truth it was but a heartbeat. "Enjoy your rest."

Despite the wine I had a restless night of sleep. I was alone for Serpus and War Axe were in the slave quarters with their families. No one noticed my tossing and turning. I felt totally alone for the first time in my life. I had lived in a home with my family and my uncle's. Since then I had shared a home with my brothers in arms. Even though there were now just three of us it still felt like a family but that night as I lay alone in my bed my head was filled with the bleak thought that this was my future. Serpus and War Axe would leave Lord Bomilcar at the end of the year for they would now actively seek treasure on the battlefield. When Lord Bomilcar returned home then I would just be the trainer of Himilco. Whilst that was something admirable I knew that my heart would ache for each day I would see the unattainable Lady Dido.

Chapter 15

The Battle of The Saw 238 BC

We stayed at Great Bomilcar for just two days and then I forced my two warriors to leave their families and depart before the sun had risen to ride back to the army. We left with supplies and more clothes. We also carried a written message for Lord Bomilcar. When Lady Dido handed it to me she kissed the leather that bound it and said, "That is for my husband. Take care, Bruneus, and keep safe until you return. There are many more reasons now for you and your men to come back to Great Bomilcar." Once more I read meaning into her words.

It was cool and dark when we left. My two companions were silent. Their minds were back with their families. Nights of passion all those long months ago had changed the two of them irrevocably. I had never thought that War Axe would wish for anything other than war. The birth of a son had changed that. We did not speak until late morning when we stopped at the watercourse close to the mountains. The water was fresh and bubbling and, thanks to the mountains, relatively cool. The giant had become gentler and it was reflected in his voice, "This feels different now, Bruneus." He waved a hand at the horses and the weapons.

I nodded, "You are both fathers now and that has made you different men."

War Axe shook his shaggy mane and headed to a rock to pass water, "Yet I am still the same man within."

"That changed the moment you lay with Charmion for the gods determined that you would be a father and when you become a father you ensure that your blood carries on into the future."

I smiled, "You have become a philosopher, Serpus."

"Perhaps, but I think of the others who died and with them the hopes of all the generations that went before them. Alerix has ensured that there will be someone who, perhaps, will be a baker or a warrior or, as in Alerix's case, both."

War Axe had finished and turned, "Bruneus, if Serpus is right, and I bow to him in all things to do with the mind, then you owe it to your ancestors to have a family."

I did not want to talk about this. "Time is wasting. We will ride until we find shade and then sleep until the day is cooler."

As we mounted Serpus said, "And that is the only answer you will get from our leader, War Axe, for even when he is not mailed he wears hidden armour around him so that none can get close to him. I thought I was close but now I see that Bruneus is truly the lone wolf."

The journey back to the army was uneventful. Perhaps we were all wrapt in our own thoughts and were able to be more vigilant without the distraction of the chatter and banter that normally accompanied such rides. When we reached the camp I saw that it had grown. More men had arrived and it was clear that the campaign to rid the land of the rebels was gaining momentum. Pucco was delighted to see us. He told us that the captain was in a daily meeting with the general.

"Your arrival is timely, Bruneus. Spendius and Mathos have been blockading Carthage. Because they have no ships it is not harming the city but they have grown bolder of late and have tried to raid the walls. The citizens of Carthage and the senate are not happy. General Barca has decided to take the war to the rebels rather than squatting here like a toad."

"What about Hanno the Great?"

"The men sent with him to retake Sardinia rebelled and killed their officers. Hanno the Great was lucky to escape with his life. He is now returned and Sardinia is lost. General Barca invited him to join forces but Hanno is his own man and refused to share the leadership. He used the ships that brought him here to take the Sacred Band back to Carthage. He would be the saviour of Carthage. It is why General Barca has taken steps to save Carthage."

I could not believe the arrogance and pride of such men. Had this been my village there would have been no dissension. Everyone in the village would have banded together to fight the common enemy but here politics ruled. In my heart I knew it would be its downfall.

I put it from my mind. I could do nothing about such politics. Instead I spent time with Pucco. Lady Dido had sent presents for her husband's body slave. He had, like us, new tunics and sandals. She was a kind lady.

When the captain returned I saw the relief on his face. He insisted upon a detailed report of our visit. We told him all. I saw his face when I mentioned the deserters. I hurriedly added, "Lady Dido was determined that the workers would be protected in the fields, My Lord, and your walls would deter such deserters. She has armed men watching the fields. The only danger would come from the whole army of Mathos and Spendius. I do not think that your estate would merit such an attack."

He nodded and looked relieved, "You are right and I thank you."

"Lady Dido sent this." I handed him the leather-bound lead package. "She kissed it."

He smiled and he kissed it too. He went off to read it and we sorted out the old clothes in our tents. Pucco had watched over them while we had been away. When Captain Bomilcar returned he said, "We are leaving this camp in the next two days. The general wishes to draw the rebels away from Carthage. If we can make them hungry they may choose to either fight us or leave the city alone. The plan is for the Numidian and Libyan horsemen to raid the enemy supplies lines. We will be with the elephants and infantry. We shall be the safe haven for the horsemen. They are mobile and we will be like a slow moving citadel. We will move just twenty miles a day so as not to exhaust the elephants and we will stay close to water. The general wishes to draw them away from Carthage and then, when they have done so, trap them and bring them to battle."

For the first time since we had gone to war, War Axe did not show any displeasure at the lack of a battle. We would be guards for the camp but that pleased War Axe. The four warbands of horsemen left before dawn and we headed south. We were just twenty miles from our camp when we made a defensive camp by the small river that hurried to the sea. The horsemen rode in at dusk and the heads of the men they had slain hung from their horses. They had also taken supplies. That first day saw all four warbands enjoy success. It tailed off after that as the enemy used more men to protect the men bringing supplies raided from the farms around Tunis. However, so successful were the horsemen that we slowed their supplies to a trickle. After a month the siege was lifted. It was not a cause for celebration for our horsemen told us that the enemy had been reinforced by an army of Libyans under the command of a warlord called Zarzas. The enemy now had fifty thousand men and outnumbered our army by almost two to one. Suddenly the war changed and it was we who were hunted. They were not trying to starve Carthage but weaken the army of Hamilcar Barca. The enemy used the same tactics that had worked before the battle with Autaritus and Spendius. They kept to the high ground where we could not use our elephants and our horses were less effective. They raided at night and we were in a constant state of vigilance.

The general had become more ruthless following the killing of Gisco and his seven hundred men. Whenever we captured the enemy they were executed by being trampled to death by elephants. It was a horrible end and, in my view counterproductive. It resulted in fewer desertions from the enemy.

However, that mistake apart, General Barca showed that he was a clever man and he knew his homeland well. While some of his officers complained about the raids on our camp Hamilcar Barca planned and plotted. I noticed that his two sons, Hannibal and Hasdrubal were his constant companions. It was a way to train young warriors and I admired him for it. It was Drixus who spotted the strategy and one night, as we sat around a fire and ate the wild ducks Serpus and I had brought down with our slings, he told us what the general was doing.

"He is a cunning man and what we are doing is manoeuvring the enemy to a place where they cannot escape battle."

"Is there such a place?"

"Aye, Bruneus. There are many such sites. He seeks somewhere that does not allow the enemy to evade battle and cannot flee. Remember the valley where he had us trapped?" I nodded. "He seeks such a place. The general wants the land of Carthage to be his ally. Spendius is Roman, Mathos is Libyan as is Zarzas. They do not know the land."

When we learned that Mathos had left the army, taking ten thousand men to Tunis, we wondered if we would follow him but the general knew that Mathos could do little with ten thousand men and the odds were now in our favour. However, I worried that taking a city so close to Carthage might come back to haunt us. The general used his Libyan horsemen to prod and poke the rebels. One day they returned to tell the general that they had lost Spendius, Autaritus and Zarzas. The enemy was mobile and had moved during the night. The general was not angry but he did send Navaras and his men out the next day and we moved not towards the place the enemy had been lost but in the opposite direction towards the mountains. Captain Bomilcar and Drixus were in a good mood as we headed to a place that would not suit our elephants. We would not be needed to fight.

When he and his men came back, Navaras brought good news. He had found the rebel army and they were in a bowl close to the mountains. There was water for them and the mountains protected their backs. The place was known as The Saw for it resembled that tool. We moved quickly and reached the enemy camp by the afternoon. That the general knew the place became clear. We, the elephants and the horsemen, had been given our orders and we advanced towards the enemy camp as though we intended to make a sudden attack. The archers had nocked arrows and we held shields before us. The enemy formed ranks and presented spears. Thanks to the shield wall of Autaritus they knew how to hold off elephants. I recognised Autaritus and his Gauls. I knew, from Drixus, that we were not there to attack but to pin them, while the infantry dug ditches and planted stakes in ramparts. We were making a line of siegeworks to pen them close to the mountains. The general intended to starve them into submission. It took the rest of the day and we were wilting in the heat as we waited but there was no fighting and when we were called back to our new lines the enemy realised that they were trapped. They had water but no food. They had no means of raiding to get supplies and they could not attack us. We, on the other hand, were well supplied with food and we also had the same access to water. We waited.

Those weeks while we waited for their surrender were long ones. We had to be vigilant. We kept a strong line of sentries day and night. The raid that had cost us Alerix was a stark reminder of the danger of a lack of vigilance. On the odd occasion when the rebels looked to sortie, the elephants were brought out and they forced a retreat. There were just seventy of the animals but they were a formidable weapon. We had men who spied upon the enemy camp. It was they who reported that the rebels were reduced to eating their horses. That helped us as it limited how they could fight us when the battle eventually came. I thought it would be a matter of days before they were starved into submission. I knew that they would fight rather than submit. The treatment of prisoners determined that. However, a week later they had not surrendered and we learned that they had begun to eat their prisoners. It made me horrified. I could never eat a human being. We continued to be supplied and our sentries were vigilant. They grew desperate and one night thirty hungry rebels left their camp and slit the throats of some of our sentries. Stormbringer's ears alerted him and his neigh awoke me. I was up in an instant and with sword and dagger in hand ran outside. Serpus and War Axe were with me. I shouted, "Awake! Danger! Pucco, guard Lord Bomilcar."

We stood outside our tents as the men ran at us. Stormbringer had stopped them from having a free rein but they were men without hope who needed food. Such men are dangerous. Heedless of the alarm I had sounded and the men who were now arming themselves and looking for the danger, they raced at us. They came without mail and wore no helmets. They had been weakened by hunger and the carrying of mail would have been too much for them. They wore breeks only and carried just swords. War Axe took the first two with one mighty sweep of his axe. I blocked a sword with my blade and ripped my dagger across the rebel's middle. Serpus was fighting not just for his life but his family's and I had never seen such ferocity from my friend. The three of us were beleaguered but we stood close together and, with War Axe's long weapon making them try to get around the side, Serpus and I were able to deal with them. Captain Bomilcar emerged with Pucco. Even the slave was armed and when they joined in the fray it soon ended. Indeed by the time others arrived the last of the would-be attackers lay dead.

A half-naked Hamilcar Barca, sword in hand, arrived. One of the men with him had a burning brand and he held it so that the bodies could be examined. One of his bodyguards turned over a body and the dead rebel gave evidence of their hunger. His ribs could be seen.

Hamilcar Barca nodded, "We are winning but I want the night guards doubling. Better a night without sleep than we lose men unnecessarily. They cannot hang on much longer."

"Yes General."

He turned to me, "Once more you have shown your worth. Hang on to these men Mago, they are like gold."

When the rebels started to eat their slaves then we knew the end was in sight and messengers were sent to parley with Hamilcar. The three leaders, Spendius, Autaritus and Zarzas came with their lieutenants and bodyguards. I suspected that before Gisco had been killed there might have been some sort of negotiation but as soon as they were brought into our defences the men were disarmed and bound. They were not even given the opportunity to state their terms of surrender. There was no honour in it but how could there be honour when speaking to cannibals? General Barca then ordered us to attack. I had fought in many one-sided battles but none were as one-sided as the Battle of The Saw. The enemy were starving and leaderless. We charged demoralised men. The elephants trampled and the horsemen speared. The infantry simply hacked and slashed their way through the camp. No prisoners were taken and the battle, if it could be called one, lasted less than two hours. We lost barely a man and we had taken all of their leaders. Only Mathos and his ten thousand men remained in Tunis. I did not celebrate the victory for the men had been half starved and leaderless. This was all down to the execution of Gisco and that had been on the orders of Spendius and the advice of Autaritus.

Serpus and War Axe combed the battlefield, ostensibly to see if any had survived and to give them a warrior's death but the reality was that they were looking for the treasure that would buy them a home. That was now their priority. Every coin that they took brought them closer to buying their families' freedom. The rebels might have been hungry but they had all accumulated treasure and my two friends returned to the camp laden.

When we reached it we saw the leaders, the ones betrayed at the parley, were now in chains. When Autaritus saw me he tried to struggle to his feet shouting, "Let me have a warrior's death. Let me fight Bruneus. I do not wish to be trampled by one of these monsters."

Hamilcar Barca had two of his men force the Gaul back to a seated position. The general smiled but it was a cruel smile, "You will not be trampled. I have a better and slower death than that. You will not be castrated as was my friend Gisco, nor buried alive but your death will be painful. You will be crucified outside Tunis so that Mathos can see his fate when we bring him to justice. Your rebellion is over and your rotting bodies will be a reminder to other rebels not to repeat it."

It was almost as though he had not heard the Carthaginian. He shouted to me, "Are you afraid, Bruneus? They say you are a great warrior now. Prove it and fight me."

I turned to Captain Bomilcar, "I will fight him, Lord Bomilcar."

Hamilcar Barca snapped, "You will not and any further words from you, mercenary will result in your joining them on the cross."

Lord Bomilcar led me away, "It would be a foolish gesture and while I know you could beat him that would cheat the general of his vengeance. If Autaritus won the general could not allow him to live. Whatever noble thoughts lurk in your head rid it of them. This is not an honourable war." He put his arm around me to lead me away from the captives. He shook his head, "It is hard to see a war that is honourable. Since I boarded the ship with you at Gades my eyes have been opened. When this war is over I think I will retire to my estate."

I thought it a perfect time to speak up for my friends. "Serpus and War Axe wish to buy the women who bore them sons and their two children. They want to buy land and have families."

He stopped and smiled, "Lady Dido said as much in her message to me. When my wife decides something then I go along with her for the sake of a peaceful life, but in this case I agree."

"Thank you."

"Would you not wish the same? Alerix's woman and son need a father."

"And I will be their stepfather. I would happily buy their freedom too but I do not wish to be a farmer. I swore an oath to you and I would keep it."

"If I retired and left the army then I could release you from the oath. If I lived on my estate I would not need a bodyguard."

If that happened then I would be leaving Great Bomilcar and never see Lady Dido again. I could never attain her, that I knew, but just seeing her would be enough. "Himilco needs to be trained and even if I was released I would still wish to serve you and your son."

"Good, for I would be loath to lose you. I said that war is not honourable but you give it some dignity, Bruneus."

We headed for Tunis. In full sight of the walls but out of range of their weapons, the ten rebel leaders were all crucified. I had seen the results of crucifixion before but this was the first time I had seen it carried out. The Carthaginians seemed to like this form of execution. I did not. Hamilcar Barca wanted his leaders to witness the punishment and so, along with Serpus, War Axe and Pucco we watched. Holes were dug and the crosses laid on the ground. The prisoners were held against the crosses and an iron nail, almost as long as my hand, was driven through the palms of their right hands. Care was taken with the left hand so that the arms were not stretched too tight for that might result in a quicker death. It was not an act of kindness. The general wanted the men to suffer a long and slow death. With the two hands secured the ankles were crossed over and a nail driven through both of them. Some of the prisoners cried out but Autaritus was determined to remain stoically silent. He was a tough man. His eyes bored into me as his cross was raised. Earth was packed around the base and trampled hard by slaves.

Hamilcar Barca then rode before them and shouted to the walls of Tunis, "Thus die all enemies of Carthage."

We did not wait for their deaths. That might take more than a week. Men were left to watch both them and the rebels.

The army was then split in two. Hannibal Paropos had one half and they guarded the north, the side closer to Carthage. We had the south. Senators came from Carthage to view the crucified rebels and they stayed, first with us and then with Hannibal. It was while they stayed with us that I learned about Carthaginian politics. As these senators were influential people the bodyguards of Hamilcar Barca were joined by the rest of the bodyguards to ensure their safety. I was stood close enough to hear the conversations. I knew none of the names of the senators but I could tell, from their clothes and the deference shown by Hamilcar Barca, that they were important men.

One who seemed to enjoy his food and had a body which reflected that love sat close to Hamilcar Barca and it was his voice which dominated the conversation. He clearly liked the sound of it.

"Hanno the Great wishes for peace with Rome, General Barca. You should know that the Romans have helped to put down the rebellions in the provinces we held."

"But as we gave up those provinces it is in their interest."

"The Carthaginians who live there appreciated the gesture. They are still our people." He drank some wine and shook his head, "Have you no better wine?"

I did not see the general's reaction but I heard the sarcasm in his voice, "Our supplier has let us down I fear." The food that they were eating was a feast. While we ate our diet was bland in comparison. The general had been away from Carthage but he obviously had spies there who told him what went on in the Senate. "The mercantile party is not happy about the peace. I hear that Hasdrubal the Fair opposes the terms of the treaty of Lutatius."

"Hanno the Great is the one with power." The senator lowered his voice slightly but I was still close enough to hear, "You are blamed for this rebellion, General. They say that your offer to pay more than the going rate to the Celts caused resentment. This war might be over but it has cost us dear. It is not just your men who have suffered. Farms have been raided and our economy suffers. We need a period of peace to give us some stability."

When the senators left Lord Bomilcar spent the next day in conference with General Barca. The general's sons were there too. The meeting told me much about the relationship between the two men as well as Hamilcar Barca as a father. Pucco waited on them and he told us all when the meeting was over.

"The visit of the senators was no accident, Bruneus. It is not just Hamilcar Barca who is blamed for the treaty, Lord Bomilcar is also seen as culpable."

"What could happen?"

"If the senate decided then they could be crucified."

I was shocked, "But the general did not lose a battle."

"The Carthaginians, as I have learned since Gades, have little mercy in them. The general hopes that a victory here will ensure that he does not suffer a major punishment. He might just be banished or exiled."

Hopes of a victory ended when a rider galloped in from the camp of Hannibal Paropos. He had been entertaining the senators but his men had been lax. Mathos had sortied from Tunis and attacked the camp. The senators and Hannibal Paropos were taken along with all the baggage. Half the army of Hannibal Paropos was destroyed and the rest fled. It was a disaster. Hamilcar Barca took the only decision he could. We broke camp and headed for the Bagradas River where we had enjoyed our first victory. Now it felt like we had been defeated. We were with the elephants once more and as we headed north I spoke with Drixus who had become a friend.

"This war has changed, Bruneus. Most of the mercenaries who began this rebellion are dead. Mathos is Libyan and he now leads an army made up of the men from this land. The mercenaries wanted gold. These people seek freedom and their land. You can buy off mercenaries but not so those who wish freedom. We will have to fight hard to win."

Serpus and particularly War Axe, were disheartened by the news. The treasure that had been taken at the Battle of The Saw meant that they were in touching distance of attaining their dreams. Those hopes had been shattered thanks to the incompetence of Hannibal Paropos.

Navaras and his horsemen still scouted for us and it was they who brought the news that the same crosses used for Spendius, Autaritus and the other rebels were now occupied by Hannibal Paropos and the senators. I wondered how long it would take the fat senator to die.

Mathos was sending a message to us. He would inflict the same punishments on us as we did on the rebels. We made our defensive camp by the bridge which had been so pivotal in the Battle of the Bagradas River. Hamilcar Barca placed a phalanx of spearmen to guard the sand bank we had used and we waited for Mathos to bring his army and fight us.

This time Captain Bomilcar was worried about his home. He confided in me one night when he had returned from a meeting with the general. "The land of Byzacium is a rich land and lies not far from Great Bomilcar. What if Mathos chooses not to come here and fight a battle with a general he knows can defeat him but, instead, heads for Byzacium? If my family was destroyed then my life would be over. I would have to take my own life."

I was shocked. Such a thought would never have entered my father's head. These Carthaginians had a different attitude to life. If our family had been destroyed then my father would have done all in his power to wreak vengeance upon them. Had Barcenis been destroyed by an enemy then we would not have become mercenaries but hunted down the killers of our families. We had not done so for you cannot hunt the pestilence.

"My Lord, you are speculating on things that might never happen. In my view you take each day as it comes and deal with the problems that arise, one by one. At the moment the danger lies here. We have a good position and we know this area. If Mathos comes here then the general will defeat him. We know that they cannot take Carthage and his men are deserting him."

"How do you know that, Bruneus?"

"I have spoken with Drixus. He is a wise man and he told me that the men who fight us now are not mercenaries but men like Mathos, Libyans and disgruntled Numidians."

He reflected and smiled, "You are right and I was blind not to have seen it. I will still worry about my family though. When Mathos is defeated I will return home. We have lost many of our provinces and I tire of a cruel war with no gain for anyone. When we defeat Mathos all that we shall have will be our own land. The general knows my views and he has asked me to see this to the end and then I can leave with honour."

When I told Serpus and War Axe their spirits soared. We now had a good reason to fight and to win. For them the end was in sight.

The news of the enemy strategy, when it came, made all of us take a breath. Mathos had decided to head south. He was moving towards Byzacium and Lord Bomilcar's worst fears had been realised. He would be closer to Great Bomilcar and his raiding parties might choose to take the juicy plum that was the estate of Lord Bomilcar. More bad news came when it was announced, as we headed south and east, that Hanno the Great had been reinstated and he and Hamilcar Barca would be joint leaders. We were all Hamilcar Barca's men and we had serious doubts about Hanno the Great. He had failed to hold on to Utica and Hippo and he had lost in Sardinia. Our defeats had not been the fault of our general. We could end up losing because of a bad general. There was, however, some good news. Every man of military age had been conscripted. Just the Sacred Band would remain to hold on to Carthage. We had twenty five thousand men but the best of them were the core of infantry, cavalry and elephants that had followed Hamilcar Barca for the last couple of years. The enemy numbers were uncertain. All we knew was that they were heading for Byzacium and the rich city of Leptis Parva.

When Hanno the Great joined us with the militia there was tension in our camp. We all knew that the two men did not get on and wondered at the tone and mood of the meeting. Lord Bomilcar's father had served with Hanno the Great and so our leader was invited to the meeting. Pucco went to serve the three of them wine. The newly arrived militia kept to themselves, perhaps intimidated by the tough looking veterans who looked at them with open contempt.

When the two leaders emerged, they were arm in arm. Even the veterans cheered. We learned, from Pucco, what had gone on at the meeting. "Hanno the Great wanted sole command but General Barca pointed out that the senate had asked for joint leadership. He also reminded Hanno that our army had not lost a battle nor had they lost a camp. Hanno conceded the point and said that, while the rebel army remained, they would work together. He also pointed out that perhaps General Barca's recent refusal to take prisoners might have cost us."

Serpus nodded, "He is right. That was a mistake."

War Axe was sharpening his axe. He did it whenever he could. "So what do we do?"

Pucco looked around to see if anyone was listening and spoke in a quieter voice, "The generals are going to keep harassing Mathos and try to bring him to battle."

That pleased War Axe who beamed like a happy child, "Then within the year I shall be with Charmion and my son. I will hew heads as though they were trees."

I shook my head, "We guard Lord Bomilcar. Unless the enemy choose to attack him there will be little opportunity."

He looked crestfallen.

We left the next day and we were still with the elephants. We now had a hundred for some had been procured in Carthage. Drixus still commanded them and Lord Bomilcar commanded Drixus. The problem that created was that we moved at the speed of the elephants. It was clear that both generals were worried that the elephants might become a target for the enemy when fifty Numidians were assigned to guard them on the march. The elephants had proved crucial in every battle and we knew that they would do so in the battle we all hoped would end the war.

For War Axe and Serpus it meant that they were both within touching distance of a life with their families. Their lives as mercenaries had been dangerous but now they would reap the reward. With coins in their purses and the promise of land, both of their lives would be idyllic.

Chapter 16

We were close to the city of Xama when Mathos
attempted to hurt the elephants. We had erected a brush
fence on a rampart with a ditch and the Numidians stood
guard on the far side of the ditch. Our horses were
tethered close to the elephants. They were now fully
familiar with each other and seemed happy. It was, once
more, Stormbringer who raised the alarm. His whinny
woke me and I rose, rousing the other two as I grabbed
my sword. Remembering the last night attack I also
picked up my shield and padded out of the tent. I saw
shadows moving and they were inside the brush fence.
They were enemies. I shouted, "Alarm! Alarm! Alarm!"

The shadows rose and became dark skinned, half-
naked men wielding axes and the vicious curved swords
favoured by Egyptians. They were the perfect weapons
to hurt elephants. The Numidian sentries had been slain
and there were just three of us to face an unknown
number of men. I heard Drixus' voice behind me,
"Awake you worthless dogs! They are trying to take our
animals."

We three ran to get between the enemy and the
elephants. Serpus had also picked up a shield but War
Axe, half-naked, simply held his axe in two hands. We
recklessly threw ourselves at the enemy. As War Axe
had his axe and needed the room to swing we allowed
him to lead and Serpus and I guarded his sides. War Axe
screamed his war cry. It was terrifying to hear. The two
men who turned to try to get at War Axe made the
mistake of discounting me. I slashed at the side of one
and punched the boss of my shield at the other. War Axe
took the head from a warrior with a curved sword and
that distracted them from the elephants. The rest of the

271

attackers switched their attention to us for they knew that they would have to take out the three of us first.

Behind us I heard Drixus as he organised his men. We would have support but until help arrived we needed to hold off what might prove to be a vicious fight. My problem was that while my shield protected War Axe, it did not help me. I had to turn to face the two men I had stopped from attacking War Axe. The bear like warrior carried on with his reckless charge. That was his way. The man I had slashed with my shield raised his sword to hack at me but the act worsened the wound I had made and he fell to the ground. I lunged with my sword and as the rebel had no shield my sword drove through his upper arms, scraping the bone and penetrating his shoulder. Blood spurted and I hurried to get back to the side of War Axe. Although two men lay dead close to him and Serpus was fighting two more men on the other side I saw that War Axe's leg had been cut to the bone. Blood was oozing from the wound. He had been struck by a bladed pole weapon. He was a tough man but it would only be a matter of time before the loss of blood weakened him. I rushed to get to him and the warrior who triumphantly raised his own axe to strike at War Axe's unprotected side suddenly felt pain as I stabbed under his raised arm. My blade slid between ribs and into his heart. He crumpled to the ground. Serpus shouted as he was stabbed in the leg and even as I took another step closer to War Axe a curved sword slashed across my friend's arm. The wielder of the sword died but War Axe now had two wounds.

I shouted, "Drixus, we need help!"

Four men ran to end the life of War Axe and I threw myself at them. There was no subtlety in the move. I merely held my sword above my shield and ran at the four of them with my shield held horizontally. I managed to hit three of them with my shield, body and sword, and they fell but in doing so I stumbled. My sword impaled one of them and my shield covered another. Those two tried to push me up. I saw War Axe's blade take the head from the fourth man but another three took his place and he turned to face them. I had to get to my feet for two warriors, seeing my plight, ran at me. I put my sword, not in the ground but into the shoulder of one of the felled men and as I pushed myself up drove the blade through it. As I rose I lifted my shield and brought the edge down the neck of the other man. It drove through his windpipe. I was barely in time to deflect not a sword but a spear. I was not totally successful in doing so and the edge ripped along my thigh. Ignoring the pain I hacked at the spearman's neck.

Serpus shouted, "Bruneus!"

Where were the other guards?

I turned and saw that Serpus was struggling. He was no longer mobile and two men were attacking on opposite sides. Worse, War Axe was now bleeding from another wound. I had to make a choice and I ran to hit one of the men fighting War Axe. I knocked him to the ground just as an axe struck Serpus' shield. It was a well struck blow and Serpus' arm drooped. Hoping that the wide swinging axe of my friend would keep him safe I lunged at one of the men fighting Serpus. They had neither shields nor armour and my blade found flesh. Serpus slew the other but I saw that not only was blood pouring from his leg he had been cut in the upper right arm. It was then that Drixus and the elephant drivers and archers reached us. I turned, just in time to see War Axe sink to his knees. His left arm was cut through to the bone. The Nubian with the axe raised it to take my friend's head.

I screamed, "No!" and, using a dead Nubian's body to help me, leapt into the air. My blade had been well used but it was still sharp enough to hack through his neck and when blood fountained in the air I knew he was dead. The three of us had slain more than half of those who came to harm the animals and when Drixus and his men fell upon them then it was over.

I rammed my sword in the ground and, after dropping my shield, knelt by War Axe. Blood was oozing from so many wounds that there was no way that the torrent could be stemmed. I put my hand under his head and he opened his eyes. He gave a sad smile and the great bear's voice was so quiet and gentle that I thought it belonged to another, "Bruneus, I go to join our brothers in arms. Swear to me that Mardian and Charmion will be free and have a home."

I nodded, "I so swear."

"And you will watch over them?" I nodded. He smiled, "It has been a good life, Lone Wolf." His eyes closed and, with a soft sigh, he died.

I turned and saw that Serpus was kneeling too. I could not lose two friends in so short a time. I ran to his side and he opened his eyes. I said, "War Axe is dead. Stay with me, Brother!"

He sighed, "I am sorely hurt, Bruneus. I fear I will be a warrior no more."

Just then Captain Bomilcar and Pucco ran up. Pucco had honey, vinegar and bandages as well as needles and gut. Captain Bomilcar said, "You two see to Serpus. I will secure the elephants." I heard the concern in his voice. We were no longer just his bodyguards; we were his friends.

Serpus had passed out but his chest still moved. He was alive. He had a number of wounds. I knew his left arm was hurt but it was not bleeding. His leg was bleeding and I saw that he had a wound to his left shoulder. The leg was clearly the worst injury. I took a leather thong and tied it above the wound. "Pucco, wash the wound on his leg with vinegar. I will stitch it. Pour vinegar on my hands." I found it hard to thread the gut as my hands were shaking. To help me concentrate I gave instructions to focus my mind as I fought to save the life of my best friend, "Smear honey on the wound and then clean his shoulder." I could see the bone, showing white. This was a bad injury. Somehow I managed to thread the bone needle and I began to stitch. Some of the other dead lone wolves had been better with a needle but, as the only one who was whole, it was up to me to save the last of my tiny pack. I made the stitches as neat as I could and then said, "Loosen the thong."

I waited to see if any blood came from the wound and when it did not, I smeared more honey on the stiches. It was then that I looked at the wound to his shoulder. As Serpus was unconscious, now was the time to stitch. It needed just four stitches. By the time Captain Bomilcar and Captain Drixus returned we had finished and Pucco had bandaged the wounds.

Pucco said, "And now, Bruneus I will tend to your wound."

I looked down at my thigh. I had forgotten it. "It is nothing."

Pucco sighed, "It may not be as deep as Serpus' but it needs stitching. Sit on that rock." I obeyed. My mind was on the dead and the wounded. I did not feel the bone needle as Pucco sewed my wound.

Drixus looked at the body of War Axe and shook his head, "I thought he was immortal."

I stood and shook my head, "No man is immortal and the three of us fought thirty men."

Drixus said, "I am sorry we were so tardy." I said nothing. Had he and his men been ready to fight as we were then War Axe might still be alive.

Captain Bomilcar said, quietly, "It is small comfort but I will give Charmion and Mardian their freedom."

I nodded, "And I now have another stepson."

Captain Bomilcar looked at Serpus, "Will he live?"

I nodded, "He will live."

I said to Pucco, "Help me to carry him to our tent."

I had just emerged when General Barca arrived. Dawn was breaking and he saw the carnage of the battle. He shook his head, "And three men held these?"

Drixus nodded his head and said, "Three mighty warriors held them, Lord Barca, and they have saved your elephants."

He nodded and then looked to the southeast, "Enough of this chasing. I will take the cavalry and hurt the rebels." He turned back to Captain Bomilcar. "The army will follow us but I want the elephants to rest. It is now clear to me that they hold the key to victory. We will cosset them. Men will be left to guard them and you can follow tomorrow. The baggage train can accompany them and that way both will be safe. I will leave infantry to guard them."

Drixus helped Pucco and I to dig the grave to bury War Axe. Serpus slept and as Drixus said, that was the best medicine. The grave was the largest I had ever dug for my friend had been a huge man. I made sure that the brooch of Isis lay in the centre of his chest and then placed the war axe he loved so much to run down the length of his body. We covered his remains with his blanket and then laid rocks upon it. We were in the kind of place that carrion scavengers haunted. After we had covered it with soil Drixus brought Layla to trample it. Only we would know where the body lay and none would disturb it. The animal stood silently as I spoke the words to send War Axe to the Otherworld.

"I never thought that I would bury you, War Axe. I thought that you would be the last lone wolf and you would bury me. I am struggling to find the words to say to my most loyal of warriors. You were always at the fore and I knew that so long as you lived we would not lose. I pray that your spirit will find the others and that the clan will be waiting for me. Know that I will, so long as I am able, watch over your son and Charmion. I have never broken an oath and I do not intend to begin now.

Farewell." I had more to say but emotion rose in my throat and I feared to unman myself.

Drixus said, "Go now and watch Serpus. Others will watch the herd tonight. I know that the loss is a hard one to bear but know that it is not only the general who is grateful. My men and I thank you and we will find a way to honour War Axe."

Serpus had not woken and I sent Pucco back to Captain Bomilcar. "I will watch Serpus. Thank you for what you did."

"It was little enough, Bruneus. If I could have done more then I would have. I am sorry that we could not save War Axe. He was a special man."

"That he was."

It was the rising of the sun that caused Serpus to open his eyes. He looked up at the tent and it was almost as though he did not know we had fought a battle. Then his eyes widened and he tried to rise. I put my hand upon him, "Peace, Serpus, do not undo my needlework."

"Then it was not a nightmare. It was real." I nodded. "War Axe?"

"He fell and he is buried. His spirit is in the Otherworld."

Serpus closed his eyes, "He was so desperate to get back to Charmion and Mardian. Now his son shall never see that giant of a man."

"Lord Bomilcar has said that Charmion and Mardian are free and I have said that I will be as a stepfather."

He opened his eyes, "War Axe had the money to buy them but what will they do? We both dreamed of a farm." A sigh slipped from his mouth. "And that was the dream of Alerix and Bellerix. Perhaps it is wrong to have such dreams. The gods toy with us. They give us hope and snatch it away."

I stood, "Then we must make hope. I have coins enough. With the money War Axe had and mine then you can buy some land and farm. That is your hope,

Serpus, and mine too. I fear I am fated to be a lone warrior for my whole life but you have a chance of a good life and I will do everything in my power to see you achieve it. Whatever I earn will go to the heirs of the lone wolves." He smiled and looked relieved.

When we moved I knew it was too soon for Serpus but it could not be helped. General Barca had given us two extra days in the camp as he and Hanno the Great sought the enemy. Just mounting his horse proved almost too hard for Serpus. I had to ask some of Drixus' men to help me. Captain Bomilcar's face showed that he knew he now had just one bodyguard. I realised that the position was cursed. Bodoster and the others had all died and now my lone wolves had perished, one by one. As we were following the trail of the army then we were relatively safe and, while Pucco rode next to the captain, I was able to stay close to Serpus. He still winced each time Crow slipped a little on rough ground but he bore the pain like a warrior. My wound was merely uncomfortable. Pucco had only needed to use five stitches.

Our small herd of horses were now tethered to the rear of the wagon. As we rode I smiled and said to Serpus, "Perhaps we should have a horse farm. We have animals now and we know that they are good ones. With Stormbringer and Crow as sires the mares would breed good horses."

He nodded and brightened. "As much as I would like to continue to be a warrior I fear that my days of fighting are done." His left arm was in a sling and his right arm was heavily bandaged. Even if he tried to fight mounted, for his wounded leg would not support his body, he could not hold a shield nor a sword. "For my part that does not worry me. War Axe and I had planned on this being our last campaign but I feel guilty that I will be deserting you."

"Put that thought from your head. It is I who is leaving you. I brought all of you to this place and it has proved a disaster. So many young men have had their hopes dashed. I should leave Lord Bomilcar and watch you, your family, War Axe's and Alerix's but I cannot."

He nodded, "You swore an oath and you are an honourable man, Bruneus, you have no reason to reproach yourself. We all knew the choices that we had and none of them would have chosen anything different."

We rode in silence and that silence showed me the pain that Serpus endured. When we stopped I went to Captain Bomilcar, "My Lord, Serpus cannot ride. I would have him put in a wagon."

He nodded, "Pucco has told me how severe the wounds are that he suffered. You may do so and tell Serpus that I release him from his obligations. As with War Axe, I grant freedom to Nefertiti and his son."

"Thank you, My Lord, that will put his mind at rest."

"And you, Bruneus, do you wish to be released? The gods know that you deserve it."

I shook my head, "I swore an oath and besides Himilco needs a teacher if he is to be a great warrior. General Barca's sons, Hannibal and Hasdrubal will need good captains if they are to fight alongside their father."

He looked relieved and he smiled, "Good, Lady Dido is fond of you and I know it will make her happy to know that you will continue to live in Great Bomilcar and to watch over our son."

Both Lord Bomilcar's words and the relative comfort of the wagon brought a change in Serpus. Lying on the sacks of grain he was not jolted as much and knowing that his family was now free allowed him to plan.

It meant that I was able to ride with Captain Bomilcar and Drixus. Riders brought us daily news when they came to fetch supplies for the two main columns. We learned that the new tactics were working. There had been skirmishes between the rebels and our scouts. We had emerged victorious in each one. The huge enemy numbers were being whittled down. Some of it was in combat but others simply deserted. The two generals, despite their differences, were working well together and inexorably driving the rebels back. The land of Byzacium was a rich one and each part we reclaimed made Carthage stronger and the rebels weaker. It took ten weeks to reach Leptis Parva and when we did we finally rejoined the main army.

Serpus had recovered well but he continued to ride in the wagon. He no longer rested on the sacks of grain but sat next to the driver. He was healing but it would take time for him to be the man he once was. The more I watched him the clearer it became. Serpus could never be the warrior he had been. In battle any weakness could prove fatal and Serpus had a weak leg and two weak arms. My wound had long since ceased to be itchy and I had removed the stitches just four weeks after the fight. I was still a warrior. I was the last lone wolf and I no longer led a pack.

We heard that Mathos had stopped and made a camp. He intended to fight and there would be a battle. Drixus commented that the rebels might have hoped for ships so that they could be taken to Sardinia. The Carthaginian fleet was still a force to be reckoned with and they were anchored off Leptis Parva. Hopes of escape by sea were dashed and that left the gamble of a battle; one last throw of the dice.

I accompanied Captain Bomilcar to the council of war. Drixus was there too. We now had a large number of war elephants and I knew that they would prove crucial in the battle. We met, not in a tent but the courtyard of an abandoned villa. The owners may have died or fled, we knew not, but the courtyard with the fountain was a cooler place to meet. It made me think back to my last night at Great Bomilcar and the wine I shared with Lady Dido. I noticed that it was Hamilcar Barca who spoke. That he and Hanno the Great had discussed the matter was clear for when Hamilcar spoke Hanno nodded his agreement.

"This Mathos is not a general. He has squatted behind walls and avoided battle. Spendius and Autaritus, they knew how to fight. This man has decided to fight us here. Perhaps he thinks his superior numbers will bring him victory. As we showed these rebels at the Bagradas River, superior numbers are no guarantee of victory." The two men might now get on better but Hamilcar Barca was still reminding the older general that it was he who had enjoyed the victories. "We will form a solid line of infantry. They have phalanxes too but they are not Carthaginian. The cavalry will be in two equal groups on the flanks and they will be behind the elephants. The elephants will crush their flanks and drive the infantry into the centre. The horsemen will finish off the work of the elephants. When we charge then we move as one." He paused, "I want this over and I want to lose as few men as we can. If they surrender then we will accept it. When Mathos and his men are defeated and Byzacium is saved then we can recover Utica and Hippo. This war has cost Carthage dear and we need a time of peace to help our people and our land to recover."

He had said all that he needed to and we knew our business. When we reached our tent Captain Bomilcar said, "And Pucco, I will not need you tomorrow. Stay and watch Serpus."

"I am no longer afraid of battle, My Lord. I can come. I may be of help."

I said, more sternly than I intended, "You should be afraid of battle, Pucco. I know for I have buried eleven of my friends and my closest friend can no longer fight. Besides, Lord Bomilcar and I will fight all the better knowing that you are safe and we do not need to worry about you."

I could see that I had hurt his feelings but better that than either a bad wound or death.

Serpus could not move well but he could watch and as I prepared my weapons and armour he commented. "You will find it hard to protect the captain alone."

"These are not the same men we fought before. All the ones who fought us in Sicily are dead. They were men to be feared. These are not."

"The driver of the wagon told me that there are Seleucid warriors who have joined the rebels."

The Seleucids fought with a long spear, a sarissa. They could hurt elephants. "I do not fear them. For while it might be true that they are good warriors, they cannot be in enough numbers to trouble us. Besides, the two of us will fight with the elephants and you and I know that the enemy fear them. All will be well." I was not lying to my friend. A man does not do that, but neither was I telling him my true feelings. I feared that I would die on the battlefield. I took my precious bag of coins, "Here, Serpus, watch over my gold. Each time we have fought I feared that I might lose it. You can watch over it."

He took it and then said, quietly, "Bruneus, I know you as well as I know myself. You are giving me this for you think you will not return from the battle."

I chose not to answer. I began to sharpen my swords. I would have one hung from my pommel and have the shorter one on my baldric. I felt Serpus' eyes on me and eventually said, "If it is my time to die, and that will mean that the captain is dead, then take my money and use it for your family and my other two dead friends. Be there to teach Himilco how to be a warrior and watch over Lady Dido. She is a strong lady but..." I found I had to stop for if I continued I might either reveal my true feelings for Captain Bomilcar's wife or I might unman myself.

I was not sure how much Serpus understood but he said, quietly, "Of course."

When all was prepared I prayed to my gods, Isis and Baal Hammon, the horse god. Despite the words of Hamilcar Barca I knew that I would need all the help I could get if I was to survive the battle the next day. We rose early. The elephants had been cosseted as much as possible since the night attack which had cost War Axe his life and denied Serpus a life as a warrior. The beasts had been well fed and were eager for war. Stormbringer, too was keen. I went before I breakfasted to prepare him and Aeneas, the captain's war horse. Crow was with them. He did not know that he would be staying behind and all three seemed keen. After feeding and watering them I gave them a good grooming. They fought better if they had been well cared for. I did Crow, too, even though he would be staying behind. When I saddled Aeneas and Stormbringer he waited patiently but when I led the two horses away from the horse lines he snorted and stamped the ground. He wanted to come. I tethered them near to our tent. Serpus limped and with two wounds to his arms struggled but he had helped Pucco to prepare our food.

When we had eaten Pucco waited on the captain. Serpus stood by as I donned my padded undergarment and mail shirt. It seemed a long time since I had first donned the mail that was already old. It was comforting to wear it. There were a couple of links which needed to be repaired but it would still do. I put on my head protector to cover my hair but left the helmet hanging, like my shield, from one of my pommels. The last thing I did was to fasten my cloak around my shoulders. I made sure that the brooch of Isis was in the centre and then threw the cloak over my back. I did not wear a backplate as most of my men had done but the oiled cloak added to the protection of the mail. However it was Isis, touched by Lady Dido, that would give me even more protection. I felt the connection to that lady as I touched the brooch to adjust it. I was ready to face my fate.

When the captain emerged Pucco had groomed him too. His cuirass gleamed and his greaves had been polished. He smiled when he saw Aeneas, "He looks like Bucephalus. You have done well, Bruneus. Perhaps the enemy will see Alexander come amongst them. Let us mount." He turned to Pucco, "You have the message for Lady Dido secure?"

"Yes, My Lord."

It told me that he was prepared for his death. We helped him to mount. "Today I will use a spear, Pucco."

Serpus said, "You should take a shield too, my lord."

He shook his head. We asked him each time we went into battle to carry a shield but he always refused, "I ride better with just a sword or a spear. A shield always seems to get in the way."

Serpus said, "I think that is the point, My Lord, it gets in the way of enemy spears."

"This will suffice. Come Bruneus, Drixus is waiting."

I just nodded to Serpus. We knew each other's minds and no words were necessary.

The elephants were in a column of fours. Drixus had metal coverings for Layla's tusks. Her head was protected by mail. The archer on her back, behind Drixus, had two bags of arrows. I knew that he was a powerful warrior but if he used every arrow then he would be exhausted along with his supply of arrows.

"A good day for battle, Captain."

"It is, Captain Drixus, and are Layla and the other elephants ready?"

"They are eager to crush rebels and destroy any hopes of victory."

"Then let us take our positions."

Our army, despite the militia from Carthage, was largely mercenary. I saw Balearic slingers and Cretan archers along with Celtiberian spearmen. They might have been worried about fighting other mercenaries but this hotch potch rebel alliance did not daunt them. There was a confident atmosphere. The weeks of marching and hunting the rebels was wearying. Battle was not.

The two generals had not yet arrived but the infantry were forming up. As the elephants were marshalled into a long line, one thing that I noticed was that their general seemed to be just copying our formation. His light infantry were a screen and his few horses were on the flanks. The bulk of his men were armed with spears. Some of them were armed with the Macedonian sarissa. There were Seleucid warriors present.

When Hanno and Hamilcar rode to take their place the whole army cheered. It would intimidate the enemy and it showed the confidence our men felt. I knew that was because this was a Hamilcar Barca led army. Hanno the Great's presence merely gave it the backing and authority of the senate. The two generals showed their new solidarity by placing themselves behind the central phalanx of infantry. We were ready and could have begun the battle immediately but Hamilcar Barca knew how to intimidate the enemy. We waited. The elephants and horses were all keen to battle and when they began to stamp their hooves and feet and the elephants trumpeted, I could see the men facing us turn to look at their neighbours. When some of the elephants reared a little, more faces turned. The general waited a few more moments and then our horns were all sounded. It was not just one horn but a veritable chorus of them. The whole line lurched forward.

No matter how fast the infantry moved, elephants and horses would always move more quickly. The slingers and archers ran to duel with their opposite numbers. As ours were professionals there would be just one outcome, we would win that particular encounter. It meant we would not have to endure the irritation of arrows, javelins and stones. When the survivors fled back, the enemy cavalry charged but the slingers and archers were ready and they ran back through the corridors left between the horses and elephants. Once they had passed through, the lines closed and there was a clash as our cavalry smashed into theirs. As with the light infantry there was only one outcome and their horsemen fled. Our cavalry should have then continued to charge the infantry but the hot blood coursed through their bodies and most of them raced after the fleeing horsemen.

I saw Drixus shake his head. Captain Bomilcar was close enough to speak to me, "General Barca will not like that. His plan was to hit their line as one."

I saw that ahead of us was a phalanx of sarissa armed warriors. They were too far to my right for me to worry about but I wondered how the Libyan and Carthaginian spearmen who would face them would fare. Drixus had told us that the Romans had managed to defeat the long spears by using their gladii and getting in closer to them. We collided with the infantry first. The heavier armed infantry smashed into them a heartbeat later. The rebels had no chance. Archers loosed arrow after arrow from the back of the elephants and with cohesion gone the elephants trampled the few brave souls who tried to stand in their way. I had javelins and I hurled my three at the leaders who tried to rally their men. I was a leader and knew the value of leadership. I just had my pilum left when disaster struck. The sarissa armed phalanx had moved obliquely to attack the elephants in the flank. It was a bold move. We did not see it for our view was obscured by the war elephants to our right. The first we knew was the trumpet of a dying elephant as it was speared by four men. Even as Drixus shouted a command to turn and face the new threat and as the phalanx was damaged by archers, three men broke through and speared Aeneas. The captain was hurled from the back of his falling horse. Even the four pommels could not prevent that. He crashed to the ground and the spearmen, seeing their opportunity, seized it. They ran to skewer the Carthaginian captain who lay not moving near his dead war horse. I hurled my pilum and speared one. I leapt from Stormbringer's back. I was Captain Bomilcar's last bodyguard. He might be dead already but my duty was to guard his body.

I swung my shield around and screaming, "Clan of the Lone Wolf!" ran at them. I heeded Drixus' words. The elephants could not help me. If I was to survive and recover the body of the captain and take it back to Lady Dido I had to fight as a Roman. It aided me that I had a Roman shield and a shorter sword. Four other warriors were racing to join the two who were running to spear the captain. I was faster and the sarissa's five pace length made the end harder to control. It was easier if there was a line of them. I blocked one with my shield and deflected the other with my sword. I was between them and I ran at the two men who both wore breastplates. Their faces changed from exultation to horror as I neared them. I did not hesitate for time was not on my side. If the advancing four spears were all thrust at the same time then even my mail would not prevent my death. I slashed across the throat of one of them and as the other tried to swing his unwieldy weapon around I stabbed him under his arm.

As they fell I ran back to stand before the body of Captain Bomilcar. I saw no blood but that meant nothing. The collision with the ground could have killed him. I was shouting and I did so in my language. If I was doomed to die then it would be with the language of my homeland on my lips. "Come and face the last of the lone wolves. Come and taste death for I am not afraid to die!" Somehow my hopeless position gave me the courage of War Axe. I was going to die but I was prepared and I would die well.

I do not know what they thought I had said but it seemed to enrage them. Perhaps it was the fact that a single warrior had slain three of their friends that angered them. They sought revenge and came at me, their spears held above their shoulders, the tips pointing threateningly at me. I would struggle to get inside all of them. I lifted my shield and turned it so that it was horizontal. It gave me more protection for the four spears were all together. Realising that the spears were aimed at my head, as the spears neared me, I dropped to one knee. It was a technique I had practised as a boy when we were learning the shield wall. If the four spears had hit the shield square on I would have been bowled over. As it was they scraped over me and as I rose the scutum lifted the spears into the air and I charged into them. They had breastplates but there was a gap at the bottom and I tore my sword across the middle of one of them. I raised my right hand and as the spears were lifted stabbed a second in the throat. The other two knew that their weapons were useless and they discarded them. They drew their short swords. They now had the advantage for they separated and came at me from two sides. I ran at the nearest one and punched him with my scutum. His sword rang against the boss and I drove my sword into his unprotected middle. I began to turn but I expected a sword to take me. As I turned I saw the raised sword and then the look of joy on the spearman's face turned to horror as Drixus' archer's arrow slammed into his back. The rest of the Macedonians were dead, slain by arrows and the battle line had moved on.

Drixus shouted, "The battle is done and you have done your duty. Men will talk of this tale long into the future. You guarded the body of the captain against seven men. It was heroic."

"And I thank you, Drixus!"

He smiled and patted his elephant's head, "Layla would never forgive me if I let the last lone wolf die."

I sheathed my sword and took off my shield. I had saved the body of Captain Bomilcar but failed to save his life. I was a failure, despite all my efforts.

I went to him and as I took off his helmet, I heard him murmur. He was alive. I shouted, "Drixus, he lives, fetch a healer!"

I would not have to return to Lady Dido with the body of her husband, I could take his injured body home.

Epilogue

We did not leave for Great Bomilcar immediately. The captain had suffered a bad break to his right shoulder. Until the bones began to knit movement would be impossible. The wound meant that he would never be able to wield a sword again. His days as a warrior were over but, as he had already made that decision, he was not unhappy. It took more than four days before the doctor said that he could be moved. General Barca himself came to praise my efforts. He bade farewell to Captain Bomilcar knowing that he would never serve Carthage again. His next service would be as a senator where he could back the Barca family and their ambitions. He had sent word to his wife of his wound for he did not want to give her a shock when she saw him.

Drixus and the other elephant men came to say goodbye to us and they brought with them coins and treasure. Drixus smiled, "You were doing what a good bodyguard does, Bruneus, and you tended to your master. We took from the dead that you slew. It is right that you have the reward."

When they had left there were just four of us remaining at the battlefield. Of course the carrion crows were there. The bodies had been burned but there were still enough body parts and rotting flesh to satisfy the creatures who lived here. We had twelve horses and a tent. Our journey back to Great Bomilcar would take just two or three days. The danger would be any who had escaped the battle and saw four travellers as easy prey. Pucco had both grown and changed since we had met the scrawny youth in Gades. He was now a good rider and it was he who would lead the string of horses. Although Serpus could ride, he was still recovering from his wounds and I did not wish to risk a fall by his leading the horses. Captain Bomilcar was in an even more fragile state. Every step of his horse sent jolts of pain through his shoulder. He rode War Axe's old horse for he was big and moved more slowly than the others. We hoped to minimise the pain the captain had to endure. We went at a slower pace than normal to help the captain.

We left before dawn and headed south and west. There was a good road and even villages and farms along the way. Whenever we stopped there was water and we had enough coins to pay for food. The captain had said little since the battle. Part of that was the result of the draughts the physicians gave to ease the pain. Pucco had a flask with more of it and instructions on its use.

It was when we had left the battlefield behind and the screeching of the carrion birds had ceased that Captain Bomilcar finally spoke about the battle. Perhaps the proximity of the battlefield reminded him of how close he had come to death. "I have yet to thank you properly for saving my life, Bruneus. I knew nothing about it but others have told me of your courage."

"My Lord, I am a bodyguard and I was merely doing my duty."

I heard Serpus snort behind me and it evoked a smile from Lord Bomilcar. He chuckled, "Serpus knows, as I do, that you could have saved your own life and no one would have thought badly of you." I said nothing for I knew that he was right. "I no longer need a bodyguard, Bruneus, but I would have you as the mentor for Himilco. I want you to live in my home and I will pay you well to make him as much like you as you can."

"My Lord, that is generous beyond words for I think well of Himilco, but Charmion and Aisha need me as a stepfather for their sons and until he is well Serpus will need help if he is to be a trainer of horses as we planned."

"I have spoken with Serpus for the doctor visited us both. There is a place I would give Serpus as a home for him, his family and the others. It is by the river and has good grazing. It would be a perfect site for a horse farm and it is just a mile from Great Bomilcar. Your duties with Himilco would leave your evenings free. You could spend evenings at the horse farm. What say you? I know that Lady Dido, not to mention my son, would like you to be his mentor."

Pucco was just behind and he piped up, "It is the sensible thing to do, Bruneus. Serpus can raise horses but you are a warrior."

"I will think about it." Our route brought us to the road from Carthage and it crossed the river from the west. It added hours to the journey. We rode faster for the last two miles. We were helped by the eagerness of the horses to get to the river water, which they could smell.

My decision was almost made by the time we rode through the gates. There were men watching from the walls and we had been spied in the distance. Craster and Daco were there to greet us and as we passed beneath the gatehouse I saw, appearing in the door of the villa, Lady Dido and her two children. I could see that Himilco had grown in our absence. I suddenly wanted to be the man who would mould the young Carthaginian and make him something his brother would never be, a good warrior. The sun was setting behind us in the west and I waited on my horse until Lord Bomilcar had dismounted. Pucco then helped Serpus down and it was only at that moment that I dismounted. It was the setting sun that cast my shadow and as I dismounted, the shadow of my body and Stormbringer was cast on the wall. Himilco said, "Look, it is the shadow of the wolf!" I looked up and saw that the shadow my horse and I made did indeed resemble a wolf.

Lady Dido smiled and her eyes locked with mine, "Yes, my son, Bruneus the lone wolf casts a long shadow but now that he is here, in our home where, I hope, he will live, we are all safer."

Lord Bomilcar said, "He has not made that decision yet. Will you stay, Bruneus?"

There was but one answer I could give. I had already decided that I would stay but it was the look in the eyes of Lady Dido that sealed the bargain. I knew that I would have the pain of unrequited love but that mattered not. Fate had determined that this was my future and I would now become the warrior they all thought me to be. "Yes, My Lord, I would be honoured to serve this family."

Young Dido clapped her hands together. Himilco ran to me and hugged me while I looked into the eyes of Lady Dido and she searched my soul. When Stormbringer neighed and stamped his foreleg everyone laughed for my horse gave approval too. It also broke the spell and Lady Dido said, "Come, it is too hot to be outside. Daco, have slaves see to the horses and help Serpus to his family. The war is over and the warriors have returned."

Himilco took my hand and led me into the cool atrium. My old life was ended and my new one begun.

The End

Glossary

Baal Hammon - Chief God of the Carthaginians; one of his symbols was a horse

Exomis - a Spartan tunic with short sleeves

Cothon - Harbour

Gades - Cadiz

Iberos - River Ebro in the Iberian Peninsula. It was what the Greeks called Spain and Portugal

Maleth (Melite) - Malta- the first in Carthaginian and the second in Latin

Moloch - Carthaginian god

Pentēkónteros - Carthaginian warship

Pugio (pl pugiones) - Roman dagger

Tetradrachm - a large silver coin worth 4 drachmae

Xama - Zama (Tunisia)

Historical Background

I have used, largely, the modern names for places like Sardinia, Sicily, Corsica, Rome and Carthage. I hope it makes it easier for a modern reader to get a sense of the geography.

Ancient cavalry saddle notice the four

The Isis brooch

The battles are all faithful to the ancient sources wherever possible. On Sicily Hamilcar Barca kept large numbers of Roman soldiers occupied in trying to defeat him and thereby extended the war. His taking of Eryx was accomplished through speed of movement. Hamilcar Barca was blamed for the rebellion. The Gauls did threaten to defect while in Sicily and he paid them more than the going rate. Gisco sent them back piecemeal in the hope that they would not make demands but it was in vain.

Hamilcar practised moving horses and elephants through his lines and he routed a superior force at the battle of the Bagradas River. The story of Navaras' defection may sound like the invention of a writer's mind but it is true. Trapped in a valley Barca was going to have to either surrender or negotiate when the Numidian came to defect. He later married one of Hamilcar's daughters.

The Romans did help the Carthaginians put down the rebellions in Sardinia and Corsica. They even repatriated the Carthaginian troops there but they had their own motives and they took over those islands.

Pulley hoists, as used on the ships, go back to the ancient Egyptians. To send an enemy under the yoke was a practice in ancient Italy whereby defeated enemies were made to pass beneath a yoke constructed of spears either to humiliate them or to remove blood guilt. I used the term phalanx to describe all the infantry formations. The days of the Macedonian phalanx were a memory but men still fought with shield and spear.

The elephants were crucial to Hamilcar Barca. The Romans learned how to deal with them but the rebel forces had no answer to the tank of the time. North Africa had indigenous African forest elephants during this period. These were typically about 2.5-metre-high (8 ft) at the shoulder and should not be confused with the larger African bush elephant. It is unclear if the Carthaginians used structures on the backs of the elephants and there is much debate about this. Bearing in mind the size of the elephant, I chose to believe that they had a driver and an archer sitting on the backs of the animals.

This part of North Africa was not a desert. There were forests and rivers. The climate began to change once the forests were hewn down. I made up Great Bomilcar but its site was a later Roman settlement. When Rome finally defeated Carthage they tried to expunge every trace of the rival empire.

The executions of Gisco and the Carthaginians are well documented as are the crucifixions of Spendius and the others who came to parley. The cannibalism at the Battle of The Saw did happen and might explain why the rebels thought they had to negotiate. The attacks on the camps happened. The one with Hanno was a disaster. The one where Hannibal Paropos and the senators died was also a major setback. That Hamilcar Barca did not suffer such a devastating defeat shows his skill as a general.

The rebel leaders are all real. I did not make them up.

The site and numbers for the battle of Leptis Parva are largely unknown. The figures I use are collated from as many references to the battle as I could find. The outcome was recorded. The Carthaginian losses were light and the rebels were either killed or taken prisoner. Mathos was taken to Carthage where he was dragged through the streets and tortured to death by the citizens.

Griff Hosker
November 2025

Books used in the research

Celtic Warrior - Allen and Reynolds

Carthaginian Warrior 264-146 BC - Fields and Noon

The Carthaginians 6th -2nd Century BC - Salimbeti, D'Amato and Rava

Other books by Griff Hosker

If you enjoyed reading this book, then why not read another one by the author?

Ancient History

Carthaginian
(The Punic Wars 247 BC-200 BC)
Shadow of the Lone Wolf

Roman Rebellion
(The Roman Republic 100 BC-60 BC)
Legionary*
Sacrifice

The Sword of Cartimandua Series
(Germania and Britannia 50 A.D. – 128 A.D.)
Ulpius Felix- Roman Warrior (prequel)
The Sword of Cartimandua
The Horse Warriors
Invasion Caledonia
Roman Retreat
Revolt of the Red Witch
Druid's Gold
Trajan's Hunters
The Last Frontier
Hero of Rome
Roman Hawk
Roman Treachery
Roman Wall
Roman Courage

The Wolf Brethren series

(Britain in the late 6th Century)
Saxon Dawn*
Saxon Revenge
Saxon England
Saxon Blood
Saxon Slayer
Saxon Slaughter
Saxon Bane
Saxon Fall: Rise of the Warlord
Saxon Throne
Saxon Sword

Medieval History

The Dragon Heart Series
Viking Slave *
Viking Warrior *
Viking Jarl *
Viking Kingdom *
Viking Wolf *
Viking War*
Viking Sword*
Viking Wrath*
Viking Raid
Viking Legend
Viking Vengeance
Viking Dragon
Viking Treasure
Viking Enemy
Viking Witch
Viking Blood
Viking Weregeld
Viking Storm
Viking Warband
Viking Shadow
Viking Legacy

Viking Clan
Viking Bravery

Norseman
Norse Warrior*
Dragon Rock*

The Norman Genesis Series
Hrolf the Viking *
Horseman *
The Battle for a Home *
Revenge of the Franks *
The Land of the Northmen
Ragnvald Hrolfsson
Brothers in Blood
Lord of Rouen
Drekar in the Seine
Duke of Normandy
The Duke and the King

Danelaw
(England and Denmark in the 11th Century)
Dragon Sword *
Oathsword *
Bloodsword *
Danish Sword*
The Sword of Cnut*

New World Series
Blood on the Blade *
Across the Seas *
The Savage Wilderness *
The Bear and the Wolf *
Erik The Navigator *
Erik's Clan *
The Last Viking*
The Vengeance Trail *

The Conquest Series
(Normandy and England 1050-1100)
Hastings*
Conquest*
Rebellion*
Treachery

The Aelfraed Series
(Britain and Byzantium 1050 A.D. - 1085 A.D.)
Housecarl *
Outlaw *
Varangian *

The Reconquista Chronicles
(Spain in the 11th Century)
Castilian Knight *
El Campeador *
The Lord of Valencia *

The Anarchy Series
(England 1120-1180)
English Knight *
Knight of the Empress *
Northern Knight *
Baron of the North *
Earl *
King Henry's Champion *
The King is Dead *
Warlord of the North*
Enemy at the Gate*
The Fallen Crown*
Warlord's War*
Kingmaker*
Henry II*
Crusader
The Welsh Marches

Shadow of the Lone Wolf

Irish War
Poisonous Plots
The Princes' Revolt
Earl Marshal
The Perfect Knight

Border Knight
(1182-1300)
Sword for Hire *
Return of the Knight *
Baron's War *
Magna Carta *
Welsh Wars *
Henry III *
The Bloody Border *
Baron's Crusade*
Sentinel of the North*
War in the West*
Debt of Honour*
The Blood of the Warlord*
The Fettered King*
de Montfort's Crown*
The Ripples of Rebellion

Sir John Hawkwood Series
(France and Italy 1339- 1387)
Crécy: The Age of the Archer *
Man At Arms *
The White Company *
Leader of Men *
Tuscan Warlord *
Condottiere*
Legacy*

Lord Edward's Archer
Lord Edward's Archer *
King in Waiting *

An Archer's Crusade *
Targets of Treachery *
The Great Cause *
Wallace's War *
The Hunt*
The Prince and the Archer*
Warbow

Struggle for a Crown
(1360- 1485)
Blood on the Crown *
To Murder a King *
The Throne *
King Henry IV *
The Road to Agincourt *
St Crispin's Day *
The Battle for France *
The Last Knight *
Queen's Knight *
The Knight's Tale *

Tales from the Sword I
(Short stories from the Medieval period)

Tudor Warrior series
(England and Scotland in the late 15th and early 16th century)
Tudor Warrior *
Tudor Spy *
Flodden*

Conquistador
(England and America in the 16th Century)
Conquistador *
The English Adventurer *

English Mercenary

Shadow of the Lone Wolf

(The 30 Years War and the English Civil War)
Horse and Pistol*
Captain of Horse*
The Lion of the North*

Modern History

East Indiaman Saga
East Indiaman*
The Tiger and the Thief
Bloody Assaye

The Napoleonic Horseman Series
Chasseur à Cheval*
Napoleon's Guard
British Light Dragoon
Soldier Spy
1808: The Road to Coruña
Talavera
The Lines of Torres Vedras
Bloody Badajoz
The Road to France
Waterloo

The Lucky Jack American Civil War series
Rebel Raiders
Confederate Rangers
The Road to Gettysburg

Soldier of the Queen series
Soldier of the Queen*
Redcoat's Rifle*
Omdurman*
Desert War*
An Officer and a Gentleman*
For King and Country

The British Ace Series
(World War 1)
1914*
1915 Fokker Scourge
1916 Angels over the Somme
1917 Eagles Fall
1918 We will remember them
From Arctic Snow to Desert Sand
Wings over Persia

Combined Operations series
(1940-1951)
Commando *
Raider *
Behind Enemy Lines*
Dieppe*
Toehold in Europe
Sword Beach
Breakout
The Battle for Antwerp
King Tiger
Beyond the Rhine
Korea
Korean Winter

Rifleman Series
(WW2 1940-45)
Conscript's Call*
Soldier's Stand

Tales from the Sword II
(Short stories from the Modern period)

Books marked thus *, are also available in the audio
format.

For more information on all of the books then please visit the author's website at www.griffhosker.com where there is a link to contact him or visit his Facebook page: Griff Hosker at Sword Books or follow him on Twitter: @HoskerGriff or follow Sword Books (@swordbooksltd)
If you wish to be on the mailing list then contact the author through his website.

Printed in Dunstable, United Kingdom

77292580R00178